LESS THAN A WIDOW

Kathleen Evenhouse

LESS THAN A WIDOW

Kathleen S. Evenhouse

PRINCIPIA
MEDIA

Less Than a Widow
@2014 Kathleen S. Evenhouse
Published by Principia Media, LLC, Grand Rapids, MI
www.principiamedia.com

ISBN 978-1-61485-321-3

All rights reserved. No part of this book may be reproduced or transmitted in any form by any means, electronic or mechanical, including photocopying and recording or by any information storage and retrieval system, except as may be expressly permitted by the 1976 Copyright Act or by the publisher.

Requests for permission should be made in writing to:
Principia Media, LLC
678 Front Avenue NW
Suite 256
Grand Rapids, MI 49504

Scripture quotations in this publication are from THE MESSAGE. Copyright © by Eugene H. Peterson 1993, 1994, 1995, 1996, 2000, 2001, 2002. Used by permission of Tyndale House Publishers, Inc.

Printed in the United States of America

21 20 19 18 17 16 15   7 6 5 4 3 2 1

Cover Design: Joe Hoksbergen
Interior Design: Kathleen S. Evenhouse

DEDICATION

to
God, who wrote the whole story

to
John, my strong support

to
so many others who
inspired,
read,
critiqued,
and
encouraged

TABLE OF CONTENTS

PREFACE 9

NOW | RUTH & BOAZ | BETHLEHEM | AROUND 1320 B.C.

    Chapter 1 15

THEN | BOAZ | BETHLEHEM | 23 YEARS EARLIER

    Chapter 2 23

    Chapter 3..27

    Chapter 4 31

RUTH | MOAB | 3 YEARS LATER

    Chapter 5..37

    Chapter 6 41

    Chapter 7...49

    Chapter 8 53

    Chapter 9 57

INTERLUDE | TAMAR | CANAAN | ABOUT 450 YEARS EARLIER 65

    Chapter 9 (Continued)... 81

BOAZ | BETHLEHEM | 2 YEARS EARLIER

    Chapter 10 85

    Chapter 11 91

INTERLUDE | RAHAB | JERICHO | 1 GENERATION EARLIER 105

    Chapter 11 (Continued) 119

RUTH | MOAB TO BETHLEHEM | 2 YEARS LATER

    Chapter 12 123

    Chapter 13 129

    Chapter 14 135

    Chapter 15 141

    Chapter 16 147

    Chapter 17 155

    Chapter 18 163

RUTH & BOAZ | BETHLEHEM | 2 YEARS LATER

    Chapter 19 175

    Chapter 20 179

    Chapter 21 185

    Chapter 22 191

    Chapter 23 197

    Chapter 24 207

    Chapter 25 217

    Chapter 26 223

    Chapter 27 235

    Chapter 28 239

ADDENDA

    Cast of Characters 247

    Map 250

PREFACE

If establishing precise timelines is important to you, I would gently suggest that researching ancient history might not be your best career choice. The wide gaps that exist between dates and data result in disagreement and discussion between historians (both secular and religious), archaeologists, and scholars.

After extensive study and careful thought, I chose to forego specific dates. Instead, I strove to be as accurate as I could in telling the stories of the lives of these characters in the culture, times, and places where they lived. When faced with conflicting timelines, I based my choices on the biblical narrative, the flow of the story, and the characters.

The basis of the stories in *Less Than a Widow* did not come out of my imagination, but from the Old Testament in the Bible. Using biblical chronology and details, I built the characters' personalities and actions. Research of their culture, religions, lifestyles, and the world at the times they lived gave me the setting for their stories.

Although the story of Ruth and Boaz took place around 1320 B.C., in many ways it is our own story today.

N·OW

RUTH & BOAZ
רוּת / בֹּעַז

BETHLEHEM
ABOUT 1320 B.C.

ONE

It is time to put the plan into action.

The flat hill above Bethlehem is a lonely place visited only by incessant breezes. These few weeks following the completion of the wheat and barley harvests are the exception—it looks like the whole city is there. There are canopies and booths where people can eat and drink. The rich have their own private tents off to one side—upwind, of course.

It's late, but sleeping is the furthest thing from Ruth's mind as she settles down in her hiding place to wait for the night's festivities to finally end. The torches and fires throw eerie lights and shadows on the scene below, but Ruth knows the layout—having watched from this same spot during the daylight hours a day ago. To pass the time, she visualizes the activities that have been taking place on this usually abandoned spot in the hills above Bethlehem.

Oxen plod in endless circles pulling a heavy sledge over the harvested stalks to separate the grain from the chaff. Men throw everything into the air with pitchforks, and dry plant material blows away in the obliging wind while the heavier grain falls back to the ground. Women sieve the remains and pile the grain in ever-growing mounds around the edges of the work area, in separate heaps per farmer. It's hot, thirsty work—labor made lighter by community effort and the anticipation of celebrating when the job is complete. This harvest is the largest in years, and some make an early start on the festivities even as the work is ongoing.

Concealed behind a rocky outcrop, but still part of the festivities, a small group of tents is visited by men and soon-to-be men who furtively travel the windy path. Because of the plentiful yield, the women working in these tents will earn enough to feed themselves for months. A violent shiver twitches through Ruth's body as she watches a man step through the door-flap and make his way back to the threshing floor.

"That may be the only option left if our plan doesn't..." Ruth rejects her thought and focuses instead on the business at hand. "This is not the time to get cold feet," she chides herself.

To pass the time, Ruth removes her sandals and massages her feet with perfumed oil from a small flask. She rubs more of the oil into the remaining calluses on her hands. Her hands, roughened and scratched from the hard work of gleaning during the barley and wheat harvest, have responded to Naomi's ministrations of the past week. Her skin is soft and smooth, her clean hair combed and perfumed.

Down on the plateau this morning, rabbis had led prayers of thanks for this year's bountiful harvest. The celebration was in full frenzy by early afternoon with singing, dancing, eating, laughing, and drinking, and the merrymaking didn't slow down with the setting sun. People are still dancing in the flickering firelight. Tomorrow will come soon enough, when everyone has to go back to work carting the grain to storage barns.

Watching from her hiding place on the upwind hill, Ruth hugs her knees to her chest and lays her cheek on the smooth surface of her overdress, so silky compared to the widow's garb she has worn for the last year. Wrapping a shawl around her shoulders, she rubs her fingers over the embroidered section that Naomi added to disguise a mended rip. Ruth is wearing the best of both of their wardrobes and all their remaining jewelry.

"I'm dressed as a bride—surely Boaz will respond in the way that Naomi is so positive he will," Ruth worries. As rising fear threatens to squeeze her heart in its tight grip again, Ruth forces herself to look at the tents of the prostitutes to help her regain control of her thoughts, "That's where I don't want to be. Breathe in—deep breaths. Fill my lungs; expand my ribs. Blow the air out slowly. Focus on breathing. Be calm. Be quiet."

The night is half over before quiet engulfs the plain below. The last of the revelers have finally returned to Bethlehem or fallen asleep where the week's hard work and the night's drink caught up with them. Even the trail to the prostitutes' tents is empty.

Ruth stands slowly and picks out the best path to the encampment below. She feels a rush of adrenaline churn in her stomach and spread through her body. Hands on her face, she takes one last deep breath.

"Don't rush. Is there anyone still awake and watching? Where are the guards?" she whispers to herself.

Ruth stretches her arms and legs to ease their stiffness after hours of cramped waiting. Tucking the edges of the overdress into her belt, she begins to descend toward the flat plain below. The slight crunch of her sandals and the echo of dislodged pebbles rolling downhill shout out her progress, but no one appears to be listening—at least there are no sounds of stirring in the sleeping tents of the upper classes as she weaves her way through them toward the threshing floor and the mounds of grain on its opposite side.

Pausing in the shadows at the edge of the open ground of the threshing floor, Ruth sits on her heels and scans the open flat circle in the faint light of the crescent moon and stars. Going directly across the open area would make her visible to anyone still awake, but the shadows along the edges hide only sleeping bodies which are practically invisible in the dim glow of the banked embers in the fire pits.

Naomi had warned her about the guards, but she said they would be stationed on the far side of the grain piles to watch the surrounding desert for thieves. "It's so late—please let them be asleep, too," Ruth pleas silently. Naomi was confident about where she would find Boaz: "He never hires a guard for his grain, but takes pride in doing the job himself." Ruth locates the food merchant's booth, counts the mounds of grain, and notes the direction of the valley where Bethlehem lies sleeping. "Those must be Boaz's grain piles," she decides.

Mentally replaying Naomi's confident instructions, Ruth creeps across the open ground bathed in the faint moon's glow. "Boaz will be on the edge of the plain between his piles of barley and wheat. Be very quiet, and don't let anyone see you. He might not be asleep, but if he is..." Ruth holds up her hand as if her mother-in-law were actually beside her instead of in her head. "Enough. I'll take it from here, hamot."

Ruth tiptoes around a pile of wheat, straining to see any signs of danger, but the shadows are dark at the base of the grain piles. She is almost upon a guard before she knows he is there—the sound of liquid gurgling down his throat and a loud belch alerts her just in time. Hoping that drink has dulled his senses, she backs up the way she came and makes her way around the inner edge of the mound, and around another.

"Just one more...This should be it," she thinks.

Worried that the night is passing too quickly, Ruth extends her hands and feels with her toes before each step, groping for something besides sand and gravel. Her breathing comes in shallow gasps, as fear takes over her thoughts again, "Could Naomi have been wrong? Where is Boaz?" As she reaches the desert's edge and follows the grain pile curving back toward the threshing floor, Ruth almost sobs in tension. "Did I make a mistake? Am I in the wrong place?" she worries. A sound freezes her in place—until it repeats itself—the slight whistle of exhaled breath. Again it sounds and again, and Ruth allows her lungs to suck in some much-needed air.

On hands and knees now, Ruth follows the sound until her fingers touch the edge of a rug. Her heart thumps so hard it rattles her ribs. "Surely, he can hear it!" she thinks as she tries to see the face of the man snoring in the gloom, then skips a beat when he stirs and turns toward her. She freezes in place until his breathing settles back into the pattern of a man deep in sleep. Only then does Ruth slowly stand, remove her outer garment, fold her shawl, and finger brush her freshly washed and perfumed hair.

Clad only in her shift and wedding jewelry, Ruth carefully lowers herself to the rug, carefully lifts the edges of the cloak spread over Boaz, and slips underneath it to lie at his feet.

Naomi's confident voice chants its instructions in Ruth's mind: "Boaz will be in good spirits having feasted and drank his fill, content and satisfied over the work accomplished—the harvest was a good one this year. He will understand why you are there—a beautiful young widow who is done with mourning, and lies—perfumed—at his feet in petition. Listen to him, and do what he tells you..."

But Ruth doesn't share Naomi's confidence as she tries to keep herself still as she waits, and waits, for him to wake up.

One second he is asleep, and the next Boaz is crouched above her, knife in hand.

"Who are you?!" It sounds more like a threat than a question.

Ruth opens her mouth to speak, but her voice deserts her.

Boaz moves astride her, pinning her arms at her sides with his knees, and puts his knife to her throat.

"Who are you?" he growls again as he strains to make out her features in the gloom.

THEN

BOAZ
בֹּעַז

BETHLEHEM
23 YEARS EARLIER

TWO·

The market just inside Bethlehem's gates has always been Boaz's favorite place—full of people bartering, fantastic smells, excitement, and life. Although Bethlehem is barely large enough to qualify as a town rather than a village, it is in a strategic location on a caravan route—nothing so important as the King's Highway, but a principal stop on a trade route that continues north of Bethlehem. Boaz loves how the marketplace combines the familiar and the strange—both things and people.

As a young boy, whenever he could escape from studies, duties, and his mother Rahab's discerning eye, Boaz and his friends romped around the market—it was the best playground ever.

Boaz always suspected his mother knew about his escapades, because she loved to tell him, "A mother understands what a child does not say."

In no big hurry to deliver a report on crop conditions to his father today, fourteen-year-old Boaz's plan to cheer himself up with a detour into the market has the opposite effect. Outside of Bethlehem's protective walls, the blowing wind made the sand come alive—showing more life than is evident in the marketplace today. Boaz pulls the scarf from his head, shakes it out, and swishes the last swig of water from his waterskin to get rid of the grit between his teeth.

A few hopeful vendors are open, but the only ones who are seeing any action are those who are selling foodstuff. "At least what we call food now," Boaz mutters to himself as he walks past a man with meager piles of shriveled figs spread on a cloth. The few young boys he sees are not weaving their way through crowds at a run, dodging in between people in a rough-and-tumble game of tag until the merchants shake their fists—a sport he had enjoyed at their age. Instead they are slumped in the shade; only their eyes are vigilantly making the rounds of the marketplace.

But as he walks toward his cousin Elimelech's booth, Boaz notices the street children moving alongside him. "What do they see that I don't?" he wonders. Boaz steps into an alley and looks around.

Elimelech is not on his usual perch among his pottery, but Boaz spots him arguing with the food vendor in the adjoining stall. Behind the potter stands a thin woman with a toddler clutching her skirts, both inhaling the stew's

LESS THAN A WIDOW

aroma as if it had nutritional value. The vendor thrusts an empty basket back into Elimelech's hands and points at a pile of pots, baskets, and cloth lying at his feet.

"The last thing I need is another useless basket," the vendor bellows. "Unless she has something of value to trade, no food."

When Elimelech holds up a coin, the vendor grabs a round flatbread and ladles a small portion of mess from the pot into it. As the woman grabs it and sinks to the ground to share it with her son, Elimelech pulls the coin back from the vendor's groping hand and points at his pile of flatbread. Only when two loaves are grudgingly presented does he let the proffered coin change hands.

Spreading his legs wide, Elimelech positions himself between the woman and the approaching street children. "One piece for each of you—none of you will get even a taste if you so much as touch this woman's skirt." He talks quietly and looks into the faces of the gathering children, "You know I speak the truth."

As dirty hands reach out, Elimelech tears pieces off of the circles of flatbread and passes them out to eager children. "Stop pushing—there's enough for everybody." When one enterprising youngster palms his piece of bread and tries for another, Elimelech slaps his hand away.

Watching from the alley, Boaz fights off guilt for the ample meal that began his day and the fact that there will be more to fill his stomach as the sun sets tonight, thanks to his mother Rachel. If it were up to his father, everything they have would have gone to feed all the hungry people in Bethlehem by now, and his family would have already joined their ranks. Wanting to hear what his cousin Elimelech thinks about this, Boaz is about to step out of the shadows when he spots Uncle Imlah making his usual grand entrance into the marketplace with his son Balak tagging at his heels.

Sitting on his stool, eyes staring at nothing, hands pulling at his beard, Elimelech doesn't see them coming.

"Feeding those wretched beggars only encourages their laziness and thievery." Uncle Imlah's pompous tones of a long-suffering elder statesman carry across the open yard.

Elimelech rearranges the pots on display before responding, "Your insights, as usual my dear Uncle Imlah, come from the depths of your heart."

Balak kicks the table on which the pots are displayed. They rock dangerously, and Imlah places a pudgy hand on his son's shoulder. "There is no need for anger, son. The day will come when my sister's son recognizes the wisdom of my words and wishes he had paid more attention."

Slapping his cane on the table top causing an expensive goblet to topple over, Imlah turns back to Elimelech. "What you call compassion is really weakness. It takes strength to remember that in times like these your first priority is to care for your family as I do. A prudent man would follow my example and seize any opportunities for gain that come his way." With an imperious wave of his hand, Imlah ignores Elimelech's response and continues, "It is for love of my sister that I am speaking to you, my boy. If you go on feeding the rabble, you and your family will soon join the ranks of the destitute. When you come to me for help, we will remember this talk."

Elimelech picks up the fallen goblet and packs it carefully in his cart. "I hear what you are saying, Uncle, and I assure you that I will never forget your words."

Imlah leans on his cane with both hands and pushes his face just inches from Elimelech's to get the last word. "Remember, my *dear* nephew, I am your go'el. It is to me that you must come when you have need for a loan, for which I will gladly hold your fields as collateral. If my wisdom falls on deaf ears, you will have only yourself to blame for the consequences."

Boaz tries to melt into the stone wall he is leaning on, but Uncle Imlah stops at the end of the alley and beckons to him. "Young Boaz, is your father well? He was looking rather worn out at the last council meeting."

Boaz nods, but at his uncle's unflagging stare finally answers aloud. "He is fine, thanks."

When Uncle Imlah turns away, Balak smirks as he shoulders Boaz before mimicking his father's imperial manner as they sweep out of the market.

As Boaz approaches, Elimelech chuckles. "You're not going to hit me, are you?"

Boaz looks down at his clenched fists, straightens his fingers, and wiggles them in the air. "You're safe." Then he sees that all of Elimelech's pottery is packed into his cart. "You're leaving?"

"Look around," Elimelech sweeps his arm to encompass the empty marketplace. "You see any reason for me to stay?"

"You're just going home, right?" Boaz is worried now. "You're not going to listen to Uncle Imlah, are you? Father says that we all just have to help each other and wait for Yahweh…"

"In the middle of all his greed and two-faced talk, our dear uncle managed to speak some truth."

"But where will you go? The whole country is dry with this drought."

"It's raining across the river in Kir-Hareseth."

"Where?"

"Kir-Hareseth, in Moab. The caravan master who buys my pottery has his home there—it's right on the King's Highway. The city is like a fortress, high on a cliff surrounded by fruitful valleys."

"Kir-Haraseth…That's the kind of place my mother escaped from."

"It's a heathen place, yes, but they have food and money to buy my pottery. And as Uncle Imlah so politely reminded me, I have to take care of my family."

"But…" Elimelech's glare stops Boaz mid-sentence.

"Be a good lad and help me take down the canopy—and no more questions! I have to save up all my arguments for Naomi."

When everything is packed up, Elimelech puts both hands on Boaz's shoulder. "Today these children had a nibble of bread, and it may very well be their last. I can't feed everyone—ncither can your parents—no matter how much we would like to. Uncle Imlah was right about that. But I won't stay around until I'm so desperate that I have to make a deal with that old snake. One day you will have a wife and children; maybe then you will understand. I have to feed my family—so I'm going to Moab."

Boaz watches Elimelech throw his weight into his shoulder harness to get his cart moving and wonders if he will ever see his cousin again. There's nothing left for him to do, but go home and tell his father Salma about the stunted crops even in the protected fields with the deep well that still provides a trickle for irrigation.

His father's words echo in his mind: "Famine strips people to the bone and lets you see what they are made of. When the growl in people's stomachs becomes a constant bellow, their bones are visible for all to see—even the bones of the lucky ones who still have enough to eat."

THREE

THREE YEARS LATER

Bent at the waist, men grab handfuls of grain and hack them off at the base with a scythe, dropping the stalks in piles as they go. Dust kicked up by their feet mixes with sweat—they are gray with salty sand and chaff. Grab, chop, toss aside, step.

Boaz settles into a steady rhythm under the early morning sun, looking up only to make sure he's still ahead of the other men. Most of them are older than he is at seventeen and have served as harvest laborers for his family for years. They were the ones who had lifted Boaz's father Salma onto a cart when he had collapsed in this very field during last year's harvest and brought him home. It was days before Salma opened his eyes and weeks before he could speak intelligibly. Walking has remained difficult—a persistent weakness in his left side still makes it hard for him to leave the family's home.

Last year Boaz had been one of the farm laborers, bantering with his coworkers, showing off for the women who stack the sheaves, and laughing in the sparse shade during breaks with his friends. His carefree days ended the day his father collapsed. Today, Boaz pushes himself hard to reach the end of the row of barley steps ahead of anyone else.

"No complaints," Boaz thinks with a groan as he straightens his back. "At least the rains came often enough this year to give us more to harvest!"

"You'll have to learn to pace yourself, boy. It'll be a long day."

"I am pacing myself," Boaz tells the older man waiting for him at the edge of the field. Elon, his father's retainer and his mother's brother, has been a part of his family as long as he can remember. "I'm just this fast." Boaz grins at Elon's pursed lips of fake disapproval. "How's the pavilion coming?"

"See for yourself." Elon points to the unwalled tent next to the field.

"And the water jars?"

"Full—in spite of these young pups' disgust at doing women's work."

Boaz grins at Elon's gruff tone. "They'll learn to appreciate it when they are old enough to work the harvest. And I remember very well your powers of persuasion when someone resists a job that needs to be done."

"And now you're the man in charge." The habitual frown doesn't hide his pride as Elon claps Boaz on the shoulder. After a nod to the men finishing up their rows and a signal to the boys to bring the donkey, Elon and his youthful workers head back to Bethlehem.

"What's all this?" A suspicious crew member points to the pavilion.

"Shade and water—a token of appreciation from my father to the hard-working people harvesting his fields." Boaz hopes that using his father's influence will ease their suspicions at this break from tradition.

"You won't dock it from our wages?"

"It's a gift," Boaz raises his voice so that all the men can hear him. "What is good for those who reap the grain also benefits their employers. What could be better for all of us than shade and water?"

Women's voices are audible before they come into view. They're here to stack and tie off the grain into sheaves.

"You can always hear them coming..." Boaz says with a grin and gestures toward the pavilion. "Men, why don't you have a drink and enjoy a break in the shade while I get them started." The married men head for the water jars in the shade, but the young men loiter a few minutes posturing in hopes of being noticed by the girls.

Boaz proves to still be one of the young men as his eyes dart from face to face trying to find Sarai in the approaching crowd of women. Teasingly she hides behind others until they are almost on top of Boaz before stepping to the side with a smile just for him.

Waiting for Boaz to acknowledge her, Aviva, the women's taskmaster, finally clears her throat a little louder than is really necessary. Boaz's face reddens as he realizes he's been gawking while she has been standing right in front of him waiting for orders. "Your betrothed is beautiful," she says in her hoarse voice. "But, as you can see, we are all here now and ready to get started."

Boaz tries, but fails to come up with an answer that would recover his dignity. With a flourish, Sarai covers her face with her scarf.

Boaz gives up all hope of propriety and bows in Sarai's direction. "That's better—now I can concentrate."

"Harvest...sheaves...barley," Aviva prompts him with a knowing smile.

"Oh, right. I remember now. You're here for the harvest." After acknowledging their laughter, Boaz turns a solemn face to Aviva, who takes her role as leader of the women workers seriously.

"Would you remind the women to not stack any of the cut stalks in the corners of the fields. As I think about it, the grain is a little thin at the top of the field this year, so leave larger corner areas untouched. The rain is returning, but there are still many gleaners depending on our generosity."

Aviva nods and turns toward those in her charge, but Boaz has more to tell her.

"When anyone needs a drink or it's time for a break—there are water jars and plenty of shade under the pavilion."

Aviva looks at the men relaxing in the tent's shadow and frowns. "What about the men?"

"They will use it, too."

"This is not how it is done."

Boaz nods in agreement. "It is unusual, I agree. However, my father and I are concerned about all those who need to work in this heat, especially with the strong winds of the last few years. Only Yahweh can change the weather—and we praise him for the long-awaited rain we received this year—but we are also created with the knack to find a better way to live with the weather we receive. Is this not true?"

Boaz pauses until Aviva reluctantly murmurs her concurrence before presenting the rest of his argument. "Shade and water are essential for both men and women, and so we—my father and I—thought to provide these comforts for everyone who participates with us in the harvest. This is a good thing, yes?"

When Aviva couldn't disagree, Boaz went on. "We have only one pavilion for shade. However, if you would prefer, we can arrange to have the men and women take breaks at separate times. Will that satisfy all the rules?"

"And your father approves this arrangement?"

"We have discussed it, but the decision was mine."

Hands on hips, Aviva considers.

"It is for you—for all of us—that we provide these necessary things," Boaz tries to mimic his father's patient but firm voice that means it is time for discussion to end and action to begin. "If we have shade to rest in and enough water to drink, we will be better able to do the hard work of harvesting."

"People will talk." Aviva shook her head.

"And I will explain."

Aviva throws up her hands in defeat. "It is on your head, young Boaz, son of Salma."

"So be it." Boaz pats his head and can't resist pretending to stagger under a heavy weight as he heads to the pavilion for a much-needed drink. The first and second gourd-fulls dipped from the water jar go down Boaz's throat. The third he pours over his head.

"Break time is over. Let's give those women more barley to stack."

The men pick up their scythes and step back into the bright sunshine.

FOUR

TWO YEARS LATER

Spending a few days with Yared and his sons tending flocks of sheep and goats was as much pleasure as it was duty for Boaz. He was six the first time his father sent him out with the shepherds to learn how to tend the flock—Yared's family had tended the family's sheep and goats since his grandparents settled in Bethlehem. During each of the following thirteen years, Boaz has spent time in the fields with them.

Nights have always been his favorite time—when the sheep are contained, and the shepherds pass the night in the opening to form a living, sleeping gate. Fascinated by the stars and moon, Boaz often lies awake imagining shapes in the sky, unwilling to close his eyes. Of course, that means the sunrise comes far too early.

"How is the water level in this cistern? Did the winter rains replenish it?" Boaz's main reason for this trip was to confirm the location of the springs and cisterns that had recovered from the years of drought. He didn't have to visit them all—he only had to ask the shepherds who knew these hills better than anyone else—this is where they spent their days and nights.

As the day drew to a close, they gather the flock—grabbing the horn of one obstinate goat that has other plans and dragging him along—and herd them into the evening's enclosure. The animals will spend the night safely confined in a small meadow backing up to a shallow, wide-mouthed cave dug into the side of a stony hill. The shepherds had built—and regularly reinforce—a stone wall that circles the meadow, leaving only a small opening wide enough for one animal to walk through at a time. Yared's sons prepare the evening meal over a cooking fire, Boaz refills his waterskin from the cistern, and Yared tends to a ewe whose leg is torn and bleeding.

That's when the boy spots them and yells from the neighboring hill, "News for Boaz."

Boaz corked his waterskin and hurried to meet the exhausted messenger. "The midwife sent me to find you. Your wife's labor began last night, and I have been searching for you all day."

LESS THAN A WIDOW

Despite the setting sun and the shepherds' warnings against hiking the treacherous trails in the dark, Boaz paused only long enough to grab his carrying sack and waterskin before hurrying toward Bethlehem. His fastest pace was a brisk walk over occasional flat but rocky terrain, but he often slowed to a groping shuffle as he climbed paths cut into steep hillsides.

Although this was Sarai's first pregnancy, Boaz was familiar with childbirth. Even as a boy he had been banished to the courtyard at night with the other men and boys in the household and had heard women crying out at the pain of childbirth. During the day the men busied themselves elsewhere as the sisters, mothers, cousins, aunts, serving women, and midwives bustled about with warm water, oils, salt, and cloths—supporting, soothing, and helping the mother give birth. He knew the torment of listening to the moans of pain, waiting for the lusty cry of a newborn baby.

But the woman crying out in childbirth had never been his Sarai. "It's too soon."

Boaz shakes his head and struggles to keep his mind on navigating the dangerous trail. Remembered moans echo through his head—this time with overtones of Sarai's voice. And he strains his ears to hear a baby's cry, even though he knows he is too far away.

"It's too soon." Fear won't leave him alone.

Boaz chants out loud as he walks: "Yahweh, grant..." on the right step, "your mercy," as the left foot falls. Finally, after a steep climb—sometimes on hands and knees, feeling his way in the shadow of the cliff—Boaz stops to catch his breath. Lungs heaving, he pulls his prayer shawl from his pack, drapes it over his head, and lifts his arms to the heavens. "Almighty God... help her. Help my child."

With legs still shaking from weariness, Boaz carefully stows his shawl into his carry sack and pushes himself to start moving again. The final approach to Bethlehem is slightly uphill, the track broad and well-worn. Boaz increases his pace to a ground-covering trot, focusing on praying with each step, "Yahweh... grant...your...mercy."

יהוה

The midwife wipes her blood-covered hands on a towel, then dips a cloth in a bowl of warm water and wipes Sarai's face, crooning softly to her as she does so. "Sleep, my dear one, sleep. May Yahweh grant you healing in your body and healing in your heart. Sleep, my dear one, sleep."

As her helper cleans up the aftermath of the birthing process, and the midwife cares for Sarai, Rahab picks up the dead infant and cradles him in her arms before gently washing the tiny body. Her salty tears mingle with the warm water and the spiced oil she rubs on the blue-tinted skin.

A maidservant steps to her side. "Boaz has arrived. I told him Sarai's sleeping. He wants to see his child."

Rahab wipes the tears from her eyes, wraps the tiny body of her grandson in swaths of linen, and holds it close as she enters the courtyard. Boaz reaches out his arms for the child, but she shakes her head.

"I'm sorry, Boaz, but your son never took a breath in this world. If you hold him, lifeless as he is, you will be unclean for seven days."

The news, although expected, feels like a physical blow to Boaz. He can hardly force the question—the so-important question—out of his mouth, the words unwilling to make their way between his clenched teeth and into the early morning air. His mother waits patiently, tears making their way down their cheeks as she shares his pain.

"And Sarai?"

"She is sleeping. She lost a lot of blood, and I thought we might lose her too, but Yahweh is merciful. The bleeding stopped; your lovely wife will heal."

Boaz starts to push past Rahab to enter the room, but she blocks the doorway. "Please, wait a little longer while the women care for your wife. Then you may come in, but sleep is very important right now. Sarai will need all her strength, and yours, when she wakes up to face her sorrow again."

Boaz reaches out and lifts the cloth from the baby's too-still face, and orders, "Mother, I would hold my son."

Rahab places the tiny form gently in the arms of his father and retreats into the room to let Boaz grieve in private.

יהוה

The morning sun creeps its way overhead and its glow gradually fills the walled courtyard, illuminating Boaz sitting on a rug, staring as if he is memorizing the face of his tiny son. Rahab's bare feet whisper on the hardened dirt as she makes her way to his side.

"Boaz." He doesn't move. "Boaz, my dear son." She kneels down beside him and puts her hand on his shoulder.

"Let me take him now, Boaz."

He tries to speak, coughs, and finally manages a growl. "I sent for Elon. He will go with you to lay my son in the family tomb."

"Then let me prepare his body, now." As Rahab gently lifts the baby from his arms, she adds, "Go and wash away the dust from the trail. You will want to be at Sarai's side when she wakes up."

יהוה

Boaz hesitates outside the door, finding it hard to step over the threshold, and argues with himself. "What are you afraid of? Standing out here won't change anything." But he still hesitates to enter. "How can I comfort her when I can't comfort myself? What if she doesn't recover?" He bows his head in a silent prayer, "Help me, Yahweh," and steps through the doorway.

At first he can't see much in the gloom of the room lit only by a few oil lamps, but as his eyes adjust, Boaz moves to Sarai's side and kneels on the mat next to his still-sleeping wife. He lifts a stray lock of hair from her face and thinks, "How can she have suffered so much pain and still be so beautiful?"

As if she heard his thoughts, Sarai's eyes flicker open and she mouths his name. Boaz takes her hand, puts it against his lips, and gently kisses it. Her eyes close again, but not before a tear overflows and slips down her cheek.

Boaz lies down beside her and molds his body around hers, and Sarai leans into his embrace as they fall asleep.

RUTH
רוּת

MOAB
3 YEARS LATER

FIVE

Nobody else is at the well. Ruth has already filled her vessel with water, but is not in a hurry to get home. The ribbons of light and shadow chase each other through the streets, find her hand, and dance up the dark skin of her arm. Dust motes in the sunbeams look more alive than the early risers yawning and shuffling their feet.

"Orpah won't be here until much later, but Mother said I had to go now—Father must be in one of his moods," Ruth puckers her forehead in worry at the thought. Orpah is Ruth's only friend, and their meeting place is the well. Two six-year-olds doing a woman's job because Orpah's mother is always pregnant or nursing, and Ruth's mother tries to keep Ruth away from her father. So, the youngsters meet at the well twice every day with jars small enough for them to carry even when they are heavy with water.

Orpah loves to talk—when her eyes are open, so is her mouth, at least that's what her brothers tell her. Ruth loves to listen to Orpah's chatter and laugh with her—a sound that is seldom heard at home. Going to the well is not a chore for Ruth—it's a gift of free time that her mother gives her.

Ruth lingers, watching the sunbeams slowly establish their claim on the open area around the well, and wonders what made her mother so nervous this morning. She woke Ruth early, quietly with a hand over her mouth and a whisper in her ear. "I have to go back and see what's going on. Surely Father has left for the market by now." With that thought, Ruth balances the jar on her head and sets off for home taking the long way through the alleys to avoid the temple square. Her father's stall is there, and this is his busiest time of year.

When Ruth steps into the courtyard, her mother jumps and drops the shuttle. By the time she pours water from her vessel into the large standing pot, Mother has dropped it two more times. Ruth frowns in concern and looks around warily as she thinks. "This is our peaceful time of the day, when Father's gone selling cloth in the temple square. What is going on?" Usually her mother's fingers are flying at top speed across her loom as Ruth sits beside her carding wool and spinning thread. It's the only time of day that her mother smiles and her little sister sings.

But Mother isn't smiling today, and her hands are shaking as she tries to untangle the knot created by the last fumble of the shuttle.

LESS THAN A WIDOW

"Where's Durha?" Ruth drags the basket of fiber close and settles herself on the mat. Mother doesn't answer, doesn't even seem to hear her.

"Durha, come here, silly girl," Ruth calls, trying to match her tone to the late winter sunlight rather than her mother's gloom. "I need my best helper."

"Let her be," Mother voice is shrill. "I told her to stay inside."

"Is she sick?" "Maybe that's why Mother is acting so strangely," Ruth muses.

"Want Ruthie." From the doorway two-year-old Durha talks around a mouth full of thumb.

"Durha! I told you to stay put until I came to get you." Mother stands quickly.

"Want Ruthie. Don't like dark." Durha puts her chubby arms around Ruth's neck and leans on her back.

Mother doesn't answer; she is focused on the street and pulls Ruth to her feet at the sound of approaching footsteps. Pushing her daughters, she hisses at Ruth. "Hide her."

Knowing that tone demands instant action, Ruth grabs Durha and wriggles into a narrow opening between the round oven mound and a wall, pulling her sister along with her. Pushing back as far as she can, Ruth collapses into the corner and pulls Durha close, covering both of them with her head scarf. "Shh, baby, don't talk," she whispers.

"Woman, fetch your daughter." Father is using his run-and-hide voice, and Durha tries to bury her head in Ruth's stomach. Survival tactics are learned early in this family.

"I, um, she's not here. Ruth took her along when she went to fetch water this morning."

Ruth feels guilty about leaving Mother to face him alone. "Maybe if I distract him, he'll hit me, but I can run away and hide," she thinks guiltily. Durha pants her fear, and Ruth realizes she has to stay with her, hide her, protect her—it's what Mother wants.

Father's rings flash in the sun as he gestures to the slave behind him. The slave dips his hand into the water jar and lets the water trickle through his fingers.

Father throws back his head and laughs. "You really think I would fall for your puny lies?" With Father, laughter is bad.

"Where is she?"

"I don't know," Mother gasps. "I don't know where they are."

"Don't lie to me or I'll sell you back to the Egyptian slave traders where I found you!"

Mother cries out as Father shoves her.

"Please, don't let them sacrifice my baby."

"The fault is yours—you only give me daughters, so I must find some use for them. If I give Durha to the priests for sacrifice, she will fill my purse instead of emptying it."

Pulling her scarf from her head, Mother shakes her long dark hair loose, approaches Father, and puts her arms around his neck. "Then, let's couple and make a son," she whispers in his ear. For a moment as he pulls her to him and caresses her hair, she thinks her plan will work. But Durha moves suddenly, and the sound of her foot hitting the hollow oven echoes through the courtyard.

Grabbing Mother by the hair, Father flings her to the ground, and she cries out in pain.

"Om'ee!" Ruth claps her hand over Durha's mouth, but it's too late. Father reaches behind the domed oven and pulls the little girl from Ruth's arms.

"Leave her alone!" But his foot hits Ruth's stomach, and she can't breathe. Gasping and pinned in an impossible position, Ruth tries to wriggle out of the narrow opening.

"Chemosh will smile on us now." Father rubs his hands together. "The priests are waiting." He turns on his heel and struts out of the courtyard. "Bring her."

The slave slings the little girl over his shoulder, head dangling at his back and follows Father. "Want my om'ee!" Durha's crying fades as the men make their way toward the temple square.

Ruth manages to crawl out from behind the oven, but has to lean on the wall to stop her head from spinning and get her eyes to focus. Durha wails again, "Om'ee!" and Ruth runs after her, bumping into people, still too dizzy to run in a straight line. They curse and push back, but Ruth knows where the men are going, and runs, walks, crawls toward the temple square. Beyond the market stalls, Father ascends the steps of the temple of Chemosh; his slave follows with a now-limp child-shaped bundle slung over his back.

"Come back!" Ruth picks up a rock and throws it, screaming, "Bring her back!" But the men disappear into the gloom of cruel Chemosh's bloody temple. "I hate you," Ruth's screams echo unheard, and the rock she hurls falls far short of the mark, bouncing harmlessly down the stairs. She throws another stone and another until merchants come out of their stalls brandishing clubs.

Dodging and twisting, Ruth escapes through the tangle of booths and shoppers, ducks down an alley and into a shadow in the courtyard of Father's house.

Mother is still on the ground rocking and moaning, blood oozing from a cut by her eye. Ruth dips a corner of her scarf into the water jar and gently wipes away the blood from her mother's face. When she doesn't respond, Ruth hugs her close, but her mother still doesn't react or open her eyes.

"I'm sorry, Mother," Ruth sobs. "I couldn't stop them."

SIX

For days Ruth's mother's mind seems to have left her body. She eats what is put in her mouth and moves only with urging and direction. When she finally utters a word, it is only one—Ruth's name—spoken hoarsely with a quick caress of her cheek. Overjoyed, Ruth hugs her hard and pulls a special treat out of her pocket—a fig she'd slipped from Father's plate when she'd served him supper the night before.

"Look at what I have for you," Ruth holds it out to her. When she doesn't respond, Ruth puts it in her mother's hand and helps her lift it to her lips. "It's a fig—your favorite."

Mother takes tiny bites, making it last, and as Ruth watches her mind screams questions: "Why wouldn't you look at me or talk to me for all this time? Are you going to die? Don't you love me anymore?"

But she really doesn't want to know the answers in case they're bad, so the only words she says are, "I love you."

The next day Ruth's mother gets up from her bed, walks to the courtyard, and sits by her loom, hands reaching out to the partially finished cloth before returning limply to her lap. Ruth brings small bowlfuls of Cook's delicious soup to her mother throughout the day, urging her to eat, to get stronger.

Ever since *that day*—Ruth can't bear to think about what had happened to Durha; it's just *that day*—her trips to the well are the only time she leaves her mother's side, coaxing her to eat, braiding her hair, and singing to her while she rubs oils into her dry skin. Ruth brings wool to card and flax to spin into thread while she sits next to her mother.

Father insists that Ruth serve him at dinner, but the rest of the time she manages to stay out of his sight, out of mind, she hopes. That becomes easier after he orders that she and her mother be moved to the slave quarters, sleeping in the same room as Cook and her assistant. Cook grumbles at having to make space for four in that small room, but she loves her former mistress. The tiny room is large enough for two to sleep in, but when all four mats are spread out for sleeping, they have to crawl over each other to get out.

As Mother improves, she begins weaving again, but progress is slow and some days it seems as if the cloth doesn't grow at all. Things never return to normal after *that day*, but they don't talk about it until Cook joins them in the shady pavilion, sits down next to them, and offers Mother a cup of tea, then looks at Ruth.

"Ruth, your father wants his quarters cleaned top to bottom by the time he comes home this evening." It's obvious that she wants to speak to Mother alone. When Ruth doesn't move, Cook tries again, more firmly this time. "It's a big job, Ruth. I'll sit with your mother. You go help the others clean this afternoon."

"Now?" Ruth wants to stay and hear what Cook has to say to her mother, so she loiters, winds the thread around the spindle, drops it so it unwinds, and begins the process again.

Cook clears her throat, and her voice has a no-nonsense edge. "Ruth! Do what I tell you."

Ruth pouts out her lips and flounces away, but stops as soon as she rounds the corner, crouches down, and strains her ears to listen.

"The master...new wife..." It's hard to hear their quiet conversation—just a few words come through clearly. "...have to start weaving again...no more food."

Ruth forgets that she is not supposed to hear this conversation, that she's supposed to be busy working. She scrambles around the corner and yells at Cook. "She's sick. How is she supposed to work?"

Cook looks around in alarm to see if anyone else is within earshot.

Ruth's mother reaches out and takes Ruth's hand, pulls her down to the mat beside her, and strokes her hair. "Shh, dear one. Don't worry. I can weave. It will be okay." But her slurred words and trembling fingers aren't reassuring.

"What is going on?" Ruth puts her arm protectively around her mother and glares at her. "You have to tell me."

"Oh, Ruth. I didn't want to upset you," Cook sighs. "But I can see that unless I do, there will be more trouble, not less." Cook looks down at her folded hands in her lap, then looks Ruth full in the face. "You father has renounced his marriage to your mother, which means that now you are both slaves. This is how it will be from now on," Cook shrugs her shoulders. "The best thing you can do for your mother and yourself is to keep quiet, work hard, and do what you're told."

Ruth hates to be afraid—so she chooses anger. Pulling away from her mother, she glares at Cook.

"You will only make things worse for your mother if you keep on like this," Cook heaves her bulk from the mat and lays a firm hand on Ruth's shoulder. "The new wife will be here soon, and she will be watching you. Any sign of trouble, and she will make sure you are beaten or sold." Cook sighs when Ruth's face remains screwed into a scowl. "Do you want your mother to get a beating because you cause trouble?"

Fear returns, and Ruth fights back tears thinking, "They wouldn't do that, would they? Father and his new wife wouldn't punish Mother if I do something

RUTH : MOAB

wrong, would they?" But she knows the answer and all the fight drains from her body.

"I didn't think so." Cook's voice softens, and she gives Ruth a little hug before pushing her toward the door. "Now, go. Do as you're told."

Ruth looks at her mother for support, but her mind is off to some other place again. Without any other options, Ruth joins the other slaves in the major cleaning project.

יהו׳ה

The next few years as a slave make Ruth look back at her early childhood differently. She'd thought life had been difficult then, but it's a lot harder now. Mother—reduced to the status of slave—can no longer give her a few minutes here and there of free time, time that is hers alone to explore the city and meet up with Orpah. Nine-year-old Ruth is kept running all day long and into the night as long as Father—her *master* now—or either of his new wives are awake and want anything.

Mother sits in front of her loom weaving all day long. That's what she's always done, even before they were slaves, but then Mother's loom had been located under a shaded pavilion. Father's new wife has taken mother's position as First Wife, and her loom sits in that spot now. From her cushioned seat in the shade, she asserts her power as often and as cruelly as she can.

Mother's loom is in an airless corner of the courtyard that is shaded only in the afternoon, and the hot sun is taking a toll on her health and energy. When Ruth asks First Wife, very politely at first, if she could use some ripped, old clothing to make an awning for her mother, First Wife laughs. Ruth loses her temper and says things she should never say out loud, and she is lucky to be able to walk after that caning. Plus, her mother was made to work at her loom from sunrise to sunset for a week.

Ruth learns to keep her thoughts to herself with no hint of them on her face. And she pretends that going to the well to retrieve the household's daily water supply is something she hates. Ruth even manages to get the job assigned to someone else for a while—an eternity of days—to prove to First Wife how much she "hates" the task. So, it's now her permanent chore, and since the growing household uses more water, it needs to be done multiple times daily. Ruth is careful to always look unhappy and drag her feet as she leaves the courtyard. However, it's harder to put that discontented face back on when she returns from her reprieve from the oppressing house.

The desire for revenge keeps Ruth going, gives her life a focus. She can't do anything to Father or his wives without harm falling on her mother, but her thoughts spin until they settle on a scapegoat: "None of this would have happened if Chemosh didn't demand child sacrifices. The god's priests—how evil they must be to do something so awful!" Gradually, Ruth's revengeful

LESS THAN A WIDOW

planning shifts from her father and his wives to the priests and priestesses of Chemosh, and she declares a secret war.

יהוה

The sweat stings her eyes as Ruth tosses a rock into the air and catches it. Toss. Catch. Toss.

"Ouch!" Stinking flies. They also like hiding in the flax drying on the roof of this house, judging by the bites on her arms and legs. "If the priests don't come soon, I'll have to go home. It wouldn't be good if Father's second wife wonders why it took me so long to fetch water today." At the worried thought, Ruth stirs restlessly in her hiding place.

The slap of feet and the tinny clang of finger cymbals sound from the road below, and Ruth drops to her knees. She lines up five stones on the ledge, peeks over the edge of the roof, and reminds herself, "Wait for it." Ruth's sweaty hand grips a rock; with arm already flexed she crouches down in the flax watching priests and guards parade by on the road below. As the last of them pass by, she steps to the edge and throws the first stone. The second leaves her hand before the first grazes the back of the head of a robed priest. As she throws the third, a guard turns and catches sight of her on the roof, points, and shouts.

Pushing through the hanging flax, Ruth stumbles down the outdoor stairway into the shadow of an alley. Guards round the corner and give chase. "How did they find me so quickly?" she wonders as her sleeve catches and rips as she squeezes through a narrow crack into a decaying building. Glancing over her shoulder, Ruth sees a guard trying to push his large frame through the same small opening. A cramp in her side makes it hard to breathe, but she squeezes it with her hand and urges her feet to keep moving. One more turn and she quickly slows to a walk, evens out her breathing, and matches her pace to that of the others walking on this busy city street.

A group of women chat as they herd their young children through the streets. Ruth follows a few steps behind, close enough to look like part of the group, but far enough behind to not attract their attention. When they turn into a courtyard, Ruth walks alongside a heavily-laden donkey train making its way to the merchants' booths at the city center. She keeps her head down, careful not to catch anyone's eye—a master at the art of invisibility in a crowd.

"Here's the spot."

Glancing casually around to make sure no one is looking her way, Ruth slips into the hiding place where she had stashed the water jar earlier and checks out her ripped sleeve. "That was too close," she mutters to herself. Heaving the full jar up to her head she realizes they were expecting another attack.

"They were watching the rooftops. I'm going to have to think of another way," she thought.

Back out on the streets, Ruth heads for home from the direction of the well. When she reaches the courtyard, she sets the water jar in its place by the wall—she has grown enough to carry the large jar—and sidesteps around the loom of Father's new wife which now occupies the prominent spot in the courtyard. Ruth avoids looking this hateful woman in the face as her shuttle stops and her kohl-painted eyes, big and black against her pale skin, travel from Ruth's scuffed toes to her sweaty brow.

"There you are." Mother's quiet voice floats from the corner that gets the afternoon sun—part of Father's new wife's campaign to make mother's life miserable. Her warning glance speaks volumes. As Ruth moves toward the pile of wool waiting for her to card and spin, she notices the widening bruise on her mother's arm and touches it softly. Wincing, her mother grabs her hand and pleads with her eyes for Ruth to swallow her anger.

"I just want to make a matching bruise on that pale witch's arm," Ruth thinks as she struggles to keep her thoughts from showing on her face.

Mother gives her hand a pat and forces a smile. "Your father needs some cloth brought to him right away. Be quick."

"I'll go right now." Ruth lifts the basket, and her shawl falls from her head revealing light-colored stalks of flax in her dark braids. She quickly readjusts her shawl, but not before the quick eyes of Father's now-favorite wife spot them.

Ruth ducks her head to hide her angry glare, but it's too late, so Ruth looks her full in the face and lets her face show what she is thinking, "I'll get you back—you can't do that to my mother!"

First Wife looks at Ruth, shifts her gaze to her mother and back to Ruth with lifted eyebrows and a cruel smile. She doesn't have to speak the message out loud for Ruth to understand her implication, and Ruth's shoulders slump in defeat as she realizes the woman's intended meaning. "I get it, you old witch. Whatever I do to you, you will do to my mother." Ruth stomps out, fuming with helplessness.

יהוה

The next morning Ruth searches for a way to help her mother as she dallies on her way to the well, and a crowd already fills the square by the time she gets there. Orpah waves impatiently from her spot at the end of the line. Ruth doesn't hurry to stand next to her as she usually does, but greets each woman individually as they wait their turn for water.

"Do they know what is happening to my mother? Do they care?" Ruth wonders.

"Good morning, Baba. Mother said to ask how your new grandson is doing." A smile creases the old woman's face in return as she murmurs, "He cries loudly to be fed. He is a strong one."

LESS THAN A WIDOW

Ruth continues down the line with a nod and a smile for each woman waiting at the neighborhood well. "Hello, Auntie. My mother sends her greetings." Most of the women acknowledge her with a smile or a nod, but some turn their backs to Ruth—deliberately. She pretends not to notice.

"Did you even do your hair this morning?" When Ruth finally makes her way to the end of the line, Orpah tries futilely to tuck curly black hairs into Ruth's nest of braids. "Missed you yesterday."

"I came early—had to do errands for Father." Ruth says it loud enough for the women to hear. Even though Orpah is her best friend, she can't tell her about her acts of revenge on the priests.

Orpah chatters on. Ruth smiles and nods her head, still watching the women waiting in line. Their heads are close together as they whisper, and once in a while they look back at her. Her faint hope that someone will help fades, and she thinks, "They know—they know what's happening to Mother, but they won't do anything about it."

"Ruth, you're not listening." Orpah's elbow digs into her friend's ribs. "What's got into you this morning?"

"Sorry." Ruth clears the worried frown from her face and turns to her friend. "What did you say?"

"There she is again—that Israelite woman. Her name is Naomi. See her? No! Don't turn around."

"How am I supposed to see her if I don't turn around?"

Orpah rolls her eyes. "Go move our jars closer to the well and look in the shadow of the alley across the way. I'll keep our place in line."

Ruth does as Orpah has instructed and can just make out a woman's shape in the gloom. When she returns to her place in line, Orpah pulls her closer and whispers, "Did you see her?"

"I saw someone. How do you know she's an Israelite?"

"They moved into that old dump next to us." Orpah makes a face. "You know, where old Salmanu kept his goats."

Orpah's family is crammed into a few rooms on the edge of a nasty part of town, and Salmanu's goat shed reeks. But Orpah's tongue is off and running, and Ruth realizes she has missed a lot of details already.

"...the roof, and now they're building an oven in the courtyard. I think the man makes pottery. They have two boys. The older one—I don't know his name—works all the time, and he doesn't even look at me. But Killion—he's our age—he sneaks out to play with my brother and asks him all about me..."

Orpah tosses her hair and flashes her eyes as she repeats his name, "Killion."

"Of course, there has to be a boy and, of course, he notices Orpah. When you're with Orpah, if you stop listening for a second, you can miss vital information," Ruth almost smiles at the thought.

"...their donkey was so skinny, and Salmanu thinks he got the best of the bargain."

"What are they doing in Moab?" Ruth asks her friend.

"Mother says there's a famine in Israel so they came here..."

Ruth and Orpah finally reach the well, fill their jars, and say their goodbyes. The Israelite woman waits until the area is empty before leaving the shadows and stepping up to the well.

SEVEN

FOUR YEARS LATER

The courtyard is full of men dressed in their finest, chatting in groups, eating, drinking wine—it's Ruth's job to see that each and every uplifted goblet is filled quickly. As the days and the flow of wine continues, it becomes harder and harder for her to avoid the groping hands and pinching fingers of her father's guests.

After being pulled onto the lap of one drunk man and enduring his putrid breath and scratchy beard, Ruth makes sure to approach from behind to fill his goblet so he doesn't see her coming.

Serving these guests is like a dangerous and delicate dance—a quick sway and sidestep here, a hip swing and dodge there—while always looking demurely down, never spilling a drop, and certainly never seeming to be deliberately avoiding the men's attentions. Most importantly, she keeps any trace of sorrow from her face.

Only the hired mourners ululating their purchased sorrow reveal that this is not a festive celebration, but a funeral. Ruth, hiding in the storage room after refilling her pitcher with wine, wipes tears from her cheeks as she watches the crowd. Father's grand funeral clothes—made from fine linen woven by Ruth's mother—are all for show as he soaks up the extra attention her death brings. At her death, Mother was returned to the status of wife to give her father the opportunity to increase his customer base. For him, the days of mourning are a chance to impress the visitors, strengthen his ties with current customers, and fish for more.

"The only one who ever really loved Mother is me," and a picture of Durha on her mother's lap rises in her mind, but Ruth blocks it out quickly. She can taste the stomach bile as it threatens to spew out of her mouth again, so she rubs her bruised cheek—courtesy of Father's Second Wife who accused her of feigning illness to avoid her duties—and the pain brings her back to the present. Crying opens the door to disaster.

Ruth hides behind a pillar watching her father play the role of a generous host in spite of his make-believe grief. "Father pretends to be sad, but he got rich on Mother's skills. He doesn't miss her—he only misses the money he made at the expense of his best weaver's bleeding fingers," she thinks. "Mother told me he originally bought her for her beauty—and life with him soured quickly–but he kept her because of her weaving abilities."

Thirsty men begin to grow impatient for more wine, and Ruth sees her father's eyes searching for her.

"Oh, no—I'm in trouble now!" Ruth thinks and she steps out of the shadowed doorway bearing a full pitcher and hurries to refill empty goblets. She glances up from her task, meets her father's eyes, and reads the promise of what her lapse will cost her this evening when the guests go home.

During the four years since *that day*, Ruth's mother just faded into a shadow of herself—a slave shadow. Her life was one of endurance, not living. When Father brought home a new wife and then another, they added their vitriol to his.

Ruth works to keep her angry thoughts from showing on her face. "I hate him—he killed her, he and Chemosh's wicked priests."

Wives two and three—all pale skin and painted eyes, bellies full with child—receive visitors in the women's court. They're wearing jewelry that had been Ruth's mothers along with their own bangles as they pretend to dab fake tears from their eyes.

"But do they let me sit with them in mourning for my own mother, receiving condolences and tokens of sympathy? No! I am the daughter who no longer exists, my identity was stolen and replaced with that of an annoying slave," Ruth thinks as she serves the women.

They look down at Ruth, who resembles her beautiful mother with clear brown skin, large dark eyes, and curly hair. They wanted her mother to disappear, to die, and they didn't have to wait very long.

"They don't appreciate being reminded of her—and every time I walk by, they can't help but remember that she was First Wife," Ruth almost smiles at this thought. "I am the only one who loved my mother."

Ruth fights down her bitterness, adjusts her features to keep it from showing on her face. "I am now a slave who serves food, pours wine, and tries to follow orders quickly enough not to get slapped. But it doesn't matter how quickly I respond, I'll get slapped anyway."

The wives watch Ruth all the time, plotting ways to get rid of her, but so far, Father has refused purely for the sake of his pocketbook—it would cost good temple coin to replace a slave, especially one skilled at spinning even, strong thread. If they had any suspicions that Ruth may have something to do with the attacks on Chemosh's priests, they would confine her to the courtyard. So they continue to send her to the well for water twice a day—viewing this heavy work as punishment.

"If they only knew." Ruth stops the smile before it reaches her face. "Mother and Durha are both dead—the only ones who ever loved me were sacrificed to Chemosh—one on the altar and the other by her grief. If they catch me attacking the priests, they will kill me, too. No, I won't stop, but I will have to be very careful."

EIGHT

ONE YEAR LATER

Ruth curls in a ball and protects her head with her arms, but he kicks her back. She tries to roll away, but his stick finds her legs, her arms, her stomach. Her timing was wretched—accidentally knocking a roll of cloth from the table just after Father had unsuccessfully tried to placate an unhappy customer. As hardened to beatings as she is, Ruth realizes that her father's rage is so intense today that he won't stop until she is senseless—or dead.

She thinks, "I am going to die right here in the temple square, one more sacrifice to that bloody god Chemosh."

Something gold clinks as it lands in the dust next to her, and Father's stick misses a beat. Another coin. Another whistle of the stick as it whips her legs. Two more coins.

"It's a fair price."

Father glances at the coins lying on the ground next to her and then raises his stick for another blow.

"A dead slave is worth nothing. I will have to withdraw my offer." The quiet words are spoken in a peculiar accent. Ruth tries to catch a glimpse of the speaker, but her eyes won't focus.

"Your offer insults me. She is healthy and strong." Father takes pride in his ability to get the most coin for anything he sells, no matter how worthless he thinks it is.

"Your actions tell me a different story about her value."

"Does he want to buy me?" Ruth is so busy thinking she just might live through the day, that she doesn't notice Father's stick swing her way again. She screams when it lands on her leg.

The Israelite bends down next to her and picks up the four gold coins. He looks into her eyes for just a moment before he straightens up, turns his back to her, and faces the cloth seller.

"I am a fellow merchant, not a fool. Obviously, she is not trainable, a waste of good temple coin." The Israelite gestures toward Father's stick. "No, I'll save my gold for a donkey." He opens a bag and drops the coins in one by one.

"A donkey?" Father throws back his head and brays his cruel laugh. "That's just what I have here—a beast of burden—but so much cheaper to keep."

"No, I don't think I am interested after all." The potter tucks his coin purse into his robe.

"My dear Elimelech, a donkey would be a continual waste of coin. They eat you out of house and home and require daily mucking." Father aims a kick at Ruth, which she manages to avoid. "This one, she only eats your scraps and cleans up after herself."

The Israelite looks at the filthy girl lying in the dirt. "Can you stand?"

Ruth's struggle to get up on her hands and knees brings on dry heaves.

Elimelech turns his back in disgust. "It appears that your beating has greatly reduced her value. I can only offer two gold coins for such damaged goods."

Father molds his face into outrage. "Your insults are not to be suffered. Two coins won't begin to pay for a strong slave to work your clay. Besides she is young and will serve you well for many years."

"But she will be worthless for weeks—if she recovers—and it will take more valuable coin to feed her and mend her wounds. It appears you may have done lasting damage."

"My friend, you are overlooking the great service I have done for you with this beating." Father places his arm around the Israelite's shoulders. "She has merely been taught the follies of disobedience." He turns to Ruth and bellows, "Stand up!"

Ruth tries to stand and walk, but not because of her father's command. She tries because of the unexpected hope she feels—hope that she will live through the day, hope that she will escape her father's house. That is enough. So she stands; she walks.

"For this well-trained beast of burden, I can take no less than five temple gold." Father's false friendliness is replaced by a shrewd bargaining tone.

"Five coins?" Elimelech shakes his head and turns to go. "You forget her condition. I doubt that she would be any good to me at all."

"No, don't leave here without me," Ruth's mind screams silently. Ruth stumbles over to the heavy bundle of cloth she was carrying before the beating started and heaves it to her shoulder. That starts her head spinning again, and she drops to her knees.

"Perhaps she will heal enough in time. I'll give you three."

"You are taking food out of the mouths of my sons," Father whines. "You know how it is—you have two sons of your own to feed. I appeal to you as a father. I can give you this slave for no less than four temple gold—that's a much better price than you would be able to find anywhere else in this city."

"Your appeal—father to father—leaves me no choice." Elimelech pulls out his purse and counts four coins into Father's outstretched hand. He spins on his heel and walks away.

Ruth stumbles after him, thinking, "You lose, Chemosh. I'm still alive."

Despite her swollen eyes and injuries, Ruth manages to follow the blur of her new master's robe and sound of his soft padding sandals. She wills her feet to keep moving, step after step, until she bumps into Elimelech who' had stopped without her noticing.

"Oh, the poor child. What happened?" Surprised to hear a woman speaking, Ruth painfully lifts her head to squint at the speaker.

"It's Orpah's Hebrew woman, Naomi," she thinks as she lets her head sink back down.

"She made her father angry," Elimelech tells his wife.

"Her father did this?" Ruth doesn't need to see clearly to sense the woman's anger. "Who is she? Why did you bring her here?"

The woman's voice turns shrill with fear at a new thought. "What trouble are you bringing on us, Elimelech? Why was her father beating her?"

"Quiet, woman!" That's when they notice the unusual absence of noise—the usual neighborhood sounds are missing. Passers-by aren't passing by, but are clumped in small groups in the street peering into the courtyard. Neighbors stare from their rooftops.

Naomi moves closer to Elimelech and asks in a hoarse whisper, "Whose daughter is she?"

"You know the cloth merchant whose booth is right by the temple stairs? This is...was his oldest daughter."

"But she's so dark—she doesn't look like him at all." As she studies Ruth, her husband's words sink in. "What do you mean, *was*?"

"I bought her." Elimelech sounds quite proud of himself. "It doesn't matter who her father is any more. She belongs to us; she is our slave."

"What am I supposed to do with a slave girl?"

"Asks the woman who complains about not having any other women around to help her."

"But she's a Moabite..."

"And we are followers of Yahweh."

"But, I don't think..."

"Naomi," Elimelech cajoles. "Ruth's father sold her as a slave—a terrible thing! But remember, Judah, Reuben, and the others sold their own brother Joseph as a slave, and look what a wonderful plan Yahweh had in mind for him. His brothers committed an evil deed, but Yahweh had good things in store for Joseph, for his chosen people, and for Egypt. Who knows what Yahweh has in mind for Ruth?"

Naomi's reservations are clear, but she nods her head to show that she has heard his argument. "Surely you don't think..."

"Yahweh's hand is in this, and it's done. Take her inside." Elimelech's patience evaporates. He claps his hands and raises his voice. "Boys, come on. We have work to do."

LESS THAN A WIDOW

"A Moabite slave in a Hebrew home—what good could possibly come from this?" But Naomi's hands were gentle on Ruth's arm as she guides her into the house.

NINE

THREE YEARS LATER

In spite of Naomi's misgivings, good did come from Elimelech's purchase—for Ruth in this Hebrew oasis situated in a large city deep in the Moabite desert. Her first eleven years had been a fight for survival in that gritty landscape, but safe in this family's home she finds nourishment for both her body and her soul.

She still misses her mother. When she closes her eyes, Ruth can still see her mother's hands speeding across the loom and her tired, satisfied smile at the beautiful patterns in the cloth she is weaving. It makes Ruth's heart ache, but it's the only warm picture Ruth has from her first life, so she paints this mind picture daily.

Ruth tries not to remember Durha—that picture brings intense heat, not warmth, as flames fill her mind when she thinks about her little sister. It burns away Durha's face, and the feeling of her chubby little arms around Ruth's neck is replaced by choking smoke. Ruth doesn't let herself think about Durha during the day, but has found no way to banish her from the dreams that plague her nights.

"Ruth, the bread!" Naomi flattens kneaded balls of dough as Ruth cooks the resulting dough wheels on overturned bowls placed over hot coals in the fire pit. At least, she is supposed to be cooking—not burning—them. In a hurry to flip a circle of blackening bread, Ruth scorches her fingers and sticks them in her mouth.

"What were you thinking about? It certainly wasn't what you were doing..." Naomi's accompanying chuckle takes away the sting from her words, but not from Ruth's fingers.

Ruth examines her burnt fingers carefully, and thinks, "I still don't know how to answer that kind of question. Nobody cares what slaves think about." Except Naomi, who wants to know all about the eleven years of Ruth's life before Elimelech bought her, but Ruth's memories are the only things that belong to her alone, so she changes the subject.

"Naomi, will you tell me the story of how Yahweh made everything?"

LESS THAN A WIDOW

"Again?" Naomi rolls her eyes, but she really loves it when Ruth asks about her people and their God, Yahweh. She clears her throat and chants in the sing-song cadence of a storyteller:

"Earth was a soup of nothingness, empty, bottomless, inky black.

Yahweh's spirit hovered over it like a bird above a watery chasm.

Yahweh spoke, 'Light.' And light appeared.

Yahweh saw that the light was good,

and he separated light from the dark.

Yahweh named the light Day, and the dark was called Night.

It was evening; it was morning; it was the first day.

יהוה

Sometimes Ruth can forget that she's a slave. In the last three years since Elimelech brought her home, she is expected to work hard, but so is everyone else in this household. Instead of being locked in an airless cubbyhole at night, Ruth sleeps in the main room with the family, in spite of the fact that she sometimes wakes them with her nightmares. She has clean clothes to wear, plenty of food to eat, and nobody beats her.

"I am less a slave now than I was in my own father's house." But Ruth doesn't say her thoughts out loud—experience has taught her to keep silent.

Most amazing to Ruth, she eats with the family. Of course, meals involve a lot of Hebrew ceremonies which she's had to learn: they don't eat until everyone's hands are washed—three times each—and a blessing is spoken. After that, no other word can be uttered until after the recitation of the blessing on the bread:

"Blessed are You, HaShem, our God, King of the Universe,

who brings forth bread from the earth."

The blessing ends with everyone taking a bite of bread together, and then they get to eat the other food. This pattern is set in stone—it never changes. When the meal is over, Elimelech prays, and everyone responds with the proper words that have become second nature to Ruth by now.

The courtyard and the rooms that open onto it no longer smell like goat after all the hard work and major repairs made by this Hebrew family. Elimelech's potter's wheel—his pride and joy—sits in the shade of a bower. Made up of two flat circular stones, the top one is separated from the other by a wooden shaft. The bottom of the double-wheeled shaft is set on a rock in a shallow recess in the ground, and it extends up through a hole in a table, with the top wheel balanced only an inch above its surface. Elimelech usually turns the bottom wheel with his feet to spin the top wheel as he throws the clay, except when he is teaching his sons from the Torah, then Mahlon or Killion spin the wheel for him—something they've done for their father since they were small children. Blocks of earth wrapped in damp cloths are stored in a pit dug in an arched recess in the wall. Watered clay soil, waiting to be kneaded until it is ready for forming, sits in a large covered pot next to the pit.

A second awning shades the women's work area, with a fire pit for cooking and a large grinding stone. An upright loom is strung between the two side beams holding up the awning. An L-shaped wall of mud and stones blocks direct access to the courtyard from the street, with a small opening that can be closed off when desired.

Their sleeping room, the largest of the whole structure, also doubles as the space for food storage. A kiln is in the farthest corner of the yard next to the old goat shelter that now has shelves for curing and finished pots. Elimelech's cart sits off to the side, waiting to be loaded with pottery for the next market day. A stairway leads up to the roof—it's there the family says morning prayers. But the courtyard is in the center—it's where life happens.

Naomi insists that Ruth be a part of everything. "This is a Hebrew household," she says. "It's true for everyone in it."

Elimelech pretends this is all his wife's idea, but he is the one who insists that Ruth be in earshot while he teaches his sons. "Listen well," he tells the boys with a glance at Ruth to extend the command to her as well. "We are Hebrews even though we live in a foreign land. It is important to know our laws and our stories. They tell us who we are."

"Today we will learn about the law of yibum or levirite marriage—a law we were given and have obeyed since Yahweh chose us to be his people."

Elimelech works at his wheel building a large jar from the bottom up as he talks. Killion sits opposite his father, turning the wheel with his feet. Mahlon sharpens the pointed sticks used to carve designs into the pottery before it is put in the kiln.

Ruth puts a handful of barley into a depression in the large flat grinding stone. Leaning into her hands to push and pull, she rolls a smooth oval stone over the grain to grind it into a smooth flour.

LESS THAN A WIDOW

Elimelech begins with a review of previous lessons—his favorite teaching tool.

"Jacob, also called Israel, was the son of Isaac, the son of Abraham. We have been speaking of his twelve sons who were jealous of their father's love for their younger brother Joseph and hated him because he dared to dream that he would rule over them.

"With no outlet over the years, bitterness grew and blew up when an unforeseen opportunity came their way. Isaac sent Joseph to bring back a report on his older brothers who were out in the wilderness tending their flocks of sheep. If you remember, two of the brothers, managed to stop the others from killing the unfortunate boy immediately. Reuben convinced them to throw Joseph into a pit, thinking to secretly pull him out and send him running home that night while his brothers were sleeping. However, the brothers continued to work themselves into a rage to do the vile deed, until Judah spotted a slave caravan and managed to persuade them to sell Joseph instead.

"When the slave drivers reached the market in Egypt, Joseph was purchased by Potiphar, Pharoah's chief executioner..."

Killion coughs loudly and temporarily stops kick-turning the wheel. Elimelech looks up at him with a frown. "So, you think you know all this already?"

Killion shrugs. "I haven't forgotten it since yesterday, Abi."

Mahlon chokes back a laugh, and Ruth covers her mouth with her hand. Elimelech gives up on his feigned disapproval, and reaches out a wet-clay-covered hand and leaves a streak on Killion's cheek. "That quick tongue of yours will bring you trouble some day." His smile softens the reproof as Elimelech pretends to think hard to recapture his thoughts.

"Now, where were we? Oh yes, the law of yibum...We'll leave Joseph in Egypt and see what's happening back home.

"With Joseph out of the way and coins in their pockets, the brothers slowly made their way home to their father. They showed him the blood-smeared colorful coat, told their lies, and brought great sorrow and pain to their father. They continued to live the lie day after day, month after month, until Judah could not stand it any longer.

"Unwilling to betray his brothers by telling their father the truth, Judah moved away from his family and lived with a man named Hirah. He married a Canaanite woman, the daughter of Shua. She gave birth to a son, and Judah named him Er. His wife named their second son Onan. The family was living at Kezib when she gave birth to a third son whom she named Shelah.

"As his eldest son Er came of age, Judah arranged for him to marry a young woman named Tamar..."

INTERLUDE

TAMAR

CANAAN

ABOUT 450 YEARS EARLIER

TAMAR'S STORY

My father arrives home full of himself, boasting about his shrewd bargaining skills. He and my brothers drink themselves into a stupor celebrating.

Always the obedient daughter, I wait in my tent imagining what life will be with my handsome Pigat. Ever since our mothers introduced us at the festival, I've been praying to our gods fervently, pleading that my father will enter into a marriage agreement with his father Hurriya. I've gone hungry, offering them a daily share of my cooked grains in an effort to win their favor.

My mother brings the news. When she tells me that I am to marry in the spring I dance for joy until I hear her next words. My groom will not be Pigat, but a stranger—a Hebrew named Er, the son of Judah. Until the wedding ceremony, I will live separately from the rest of my family on the far side of my family compound and learn Hebrew ways.

"I don't understand... Who is Er? I thought Pigat..."

"It's not for you to think. Hurriya could not match Judah's offer." Mother pushes aside the door flap and impatiently demands, "Come."

A girl, only a few years older than me, steps into our tent. I glance at her and turn back to my mother.

"Judah gives you this slave," my mother's tone implies that this is a great honor. "She will teach you Hebrew ways: how to cook their food, obey their laws, and prepare you to be a proper wife for Er. You will move your belongings immediately, and your slave will pick up all necessary supplies from now on. I will visit once a week to test your progress."

As far as my mother is concerned, her job is done. Daughters are destined to improve the family's coffers—it isn't prudent to become involved emotionally. Her efforts in beauty routines, wardrobe, and social presentation have been successful. My father may have been the negotiator, but my mother knows that it was her attention to detail that brought about such a large bride price.

My mother starts to leave, but turns back and gives me a rare smile of approval. "The bride price was a large one. Learn your lessons well."

It feels like I've been punched in the stomach—I find it hard to draw a breath as I begin to understand. "It was all just a stupid dream," I think. "Pigat will not be my husband. They sold me to the highest bidder—a stranger, a strange Hebrew. I don't even know what he looks like."

LESS THAN A WIDOW

The slave girl coughs apologetically, and I stare at her. A red birthmark starts on her cheek, extends down her neck, and disappears into her shift. She is about my height and age, but that is all we have in common. My oiled skin is soft and fragrant; hers is dry and tanned. My delicate hands and arms are covered with swirling henna tattoos; her plain hands are rough and sturdy. My henna-hued hair is elaborately braided; hers is dusty brown and pulled back under a scarf.

None of this matters when she smiles at me. I believe our sisterhood starts that very second as her loving heart shines into mine like a warm sunbeam.

"What is your name?" I ask.

"They call me Hedya."

"Hedya. I haven't heard that name before. What does it mean?"

She pronounces it slowly and clearly—in three syllables. "Hee-tee-ah. It means 'voice of the Lord.'"

And so the teaching begins.

יהוה

These short months are the happiest of my life. Our situations—Hedya's and mine—are not so different. We were both sold for the benefit of our families: she in payment of a debt, and me to increase the family's assets. Here in our lonely tent with no one else present to meddle or judge, we learn to know and love each other.

A gifted teacher, Hedya concentrates on lessons about Hebrew food—preparation of meals will be one of my main duties. Soups and stews are the main meals—that much is the same as what I've been used to—and Hebrews also eat from a common pot, using scoop-shaped pieces of bread. I am delighted to find out that I will not have to give up milk, yogurt, butter, or cheese as these are some of my favorite foods. Hedya even taught me to make Er's favorite treat: a sweet cake prepared by partially baking flatbread, smearing it with oil and honey, adding a sprinkle of anise seeds, and cooking it a little longer until it is glossy brown.

But she doesn't tell me what Er is like—maybe because she doesn't want anything to spoil our happy time.

יהוה

I learn scores of Hebrew rituals and how to say their prayers word for word. Those I memorize easily by repetition—the two of us saying them aloud to each other as we go about our daily customs. But I find it really hard to understand her teachings about the Hebrew's God Yahweh.

The carved gods of my family's household are given a special place in our tents. Even though they are capricious, vain, and vengeful, we continue to bring gifts and endure pain so that we may receive—in return—the changing of seasons and the bringing of life-giving rain. And we have many gods, each one with their own area of influence: seasons, health, protection, warfare... We constantly weave intricate dance-steps to try to please them all, and we never know for sure if we are heard.

On the other hand, Hedya tells me that the Hebrews have only one God, and He is so holy that they don't even say his name out loud. They refer to him as Yahweh, which means "He is." Hedya says he is a jealous God, and that means I must leave my household gods behind when I marry—He will not tolerate them in the tents, or the hearts, of his people. Yahweh demands obedience— just like our gods—but it's not the same, she insists.

"What's so different?" I ask this question so many times that I'm sure Hedya is going to throw something at me if I ask it again, but I still don't understand.

"Yahweh demands obedience because He loves us and has chosen us to be His people," Hedya says.

I just shrug my shoulders. Our ancestral gods have chosen us as well— they've been in our family line for generations. But Hedya won't give up. She concentrates so hard on her thoughts that the round loaf she is patting into a circle gets too thin and large for our baking stone. I take it from her with a grin, roll it back into a ball, and hand it back so she can begin again. Suddenly her face lights up, and she puts the ball of dough down so she can move her hands as she explains.

"Your father and Judah made a contract, a covenant, when they determined the settlement for your marriage to Er, is this not so?"

I nod my head, "Of course." For important matters, two men bring animals to be sacrificed, cut them up, and walk through the blood that gathers between the bodies of the slain animals to signify a binding agreement. This is a standard custom, a way of showing that a contract is equally entered and agreed to by both parties and that they promise to uphold said blood oath or covenant.

"Did your gods—your family's gods—make this kind of agreement with your ancestors?" Hedya grins as she asks this question—she is sure that this time her explanation will clear up my confusion.

"That's absurd!" I respond as Hedya knew I would. Everyone knows that gods don't lower themselves to the human level to make anything like a covenant; that would strip them of their power over us. It is up to us to strive to please them, to curry their favor, and to make sacrifices to meet their demands. Then, if they so choose, they will benefit us for a season.

"Having a god enter into a covenant with us only seems absurd because you don't know Yahweh," Hedya nods her head in affirmation as if what she just said makes any sense at all to me. "You see, Tamar, your gods don't love you, if, in fact, they are even capable of knowing you exist. Your ancestors

LESS THAN A WIDOW

chose the deities to be your family gods, but their responses are uncertain and willful."

I have to agree with that. I went hungry for months to give them offerings of grain, and they did nothing. Tears slip down my cheek as I think, "I will never see my beloved Pigat again."

Hedya's voice interrupts my musing. "Yahweh commanded Abram to prepare animals for sacrifice and lay them in halves, side by side. Then Yahweh caused Abram to fall into a deep darkness in which he saw a vision of a torch and a smoking pot passing between the carcasses. The great Yahweh, the God above all gods, made a covenant with Abram and his lineage and chose them to be His people."

If what Hedya is telling me is true, if there is a god who covenants—who makes promises, and keeps them—I will gladly leave my gods behind when I become a part of the Hebrew people.

יהוה

I learn the truth about the kind of man that Er is during our first night as husband and wife. He is cruel and revels in power, using that supremacy to cause pain. He is good at it, and he practices and refines his skills during the long year of our marriage.

I won't tell you the sickening details—they don't matter anyway. It was the ever-present pain and the hopeless efforts to avoid more that stick in my mind about that year.

I cried real tears for the entire week of mourning when Er died, but they were not caused by sorrow. Tears of gratitude rolled down my cheeks because Yahweh must have heard my prayers and brought me relief by killing him—wicked, evil man that he was. Moans of relief overflowed: no more beatings, no more trying to obey his every command to avoid punishment that was inevitable, and no more wild parties with their inescapable agonizing consequences.

I lifted my voice, wailing with the mourners, but found it hard to make my ululations of freedom sound grief-stricken. But Hedya is at my side, watching, listening, and helping me maintain a sorrowful countenance.

After that first week of relief, reality returns and paints such an ugly picture that I cannot ignore it any longer. I am a widow, an almanah. The root of this Hebrew word means "unable to speak," and that is a good description of my widow's status. Hard as my marriage to Er had been, I'd had a place in the world. Now I am on the lowest rung of the cultural ladder and hanging on for dear life.

As if that's not bad enough, it gets worse. "There are two kinds of women in this world—those who are mothers and those who are not," I think. "I am less than a widow—I am a childless widow."

This tragic turn of events is a catastrophe disguised as a rescue.

But Hedya urges me to have faith that Yahweh hears my cries, that He does love me. "Just wait and see," she keeps saying. "Wait to see what He will bring to your life."

So I wait, and not for long. Judah declares that this is a Hebrew household, and they will follow Yahweh's law to preserve the line of his firstborn. He stands up at the evening meal and instructs Onan, "Go and sleep with your brother's widow; it's your duty as a brother-in-law to keep your elder brother's line alive."

Hedya explains this to me when we return to our tent. "If a dead brother has no surviving children, male or female, from any relationship, at the time of his death, a brother can be required to perform yibum. Judah decided that Onan must discharge his responsibility as a go'el (kinsman redeemer) by fulfilling the yibum obligation."

"Perform yibum, what exactly does that mean?" I have no idea what she is talking about.

"Impregnate you."

"Oh." That I understand.

As Hedya helps me get ready to go to Onan's bed, she explains some more. "If you bear a child, it will not be Onan's child, but Er's."

"What about me? Will I be Onan's wife?"

"He may choose to marry you, but that is not required. In either case, the child will inherit Er's birthright, and you will be acknowledged as the child's mother."

יהוה

Onan does not brutalize me in the same physical way that his brother Er had done. In his tent, he baits me with his words, uses me as a plaything for his pleasures, and then refuses to plant any child seeds in my belly.

Imagining him as an animal helps me to endure. "If Onan was an animal, he would be a fox: sly, tricky, devious, and hard to catch."

Outside of our private encounters, when there is an audience, he plays the diligent Hebrew whose only concern is to fulfill the task set before him—a noble man putting aside his needs for the love of his dead brother.

I seldom talk any more, but I challenge everything about my life in my thoughts. "Cannot Judah see Onan's deceit? Is he really that easily fooled—this man who has practiced his own deception for an entire lifetime?"

I know why Judah left his family: he sold his own brother into slavery. Hedya had told me the whole story.

"How can he not see that his own son, Onan, is following in his father's footsteps with his lying and sneaking?"

And what will happen to me if Judah believes Onan's lies and insinuations about my unwillingness to cooperate and about my inability to con-

LESS THAN A WIDOW

ceive. Somehow, Onan even started a rumor that I have brought a curse upon his family.

"Maybe there is some truth in this rumor."

If I do carry a curse with me, it finally catches up with Onan. He is killed in a fall—"by Yahweh's hand," Hedya says.

Shelah, the only remaining brother, is still just a smooth-cheeked boy, too young to perform yibum.

Judah will not allow me to eat with the family any longer. I am banished to my tent with only Hedya to attend me.

"What will he do next?" I think as I chew the food I can't taste. "Does he believe I am cursed or that I have cursed them? Will he send me out into the desert to be killed by wild animals? Will he kill me himself?"

In the end he sends me back in disgrace to my family: "Live as an almanah at home with your father until my son Shelah grows up. Then I will send for you."

"Wait until Shelah is old enough to practice yibum, that's what he said, but is it what he really intends?" I am not fooled, but don't put my rebellious thoughts into words.

At least he allows me to take Hedya with me.

יהוה

A widow is of less use than a slave, although I work like one. We represent only two more mouths to feed, Hedya and I, and my father can find no loophole in the marriage contract to sell us for a profit.

"He must have missed something in his oh-so-shrewd bartering." If I could laugh, I would.

Years pass in this in-between life. We are both visibly thinner, dirtier, our tattered clothing worn and frayed. Without Hedya I would have lost hope, but she continues repeating her hymn: "Wait on Yahweh and see what he has for us." For my part, I am waiting for Judah to send word that Shelah is old enough, that it is time to come back to become the mother of Er's child. As time passes, it dawns on me that I may continue to wait until I am ancient, too old to conceive and bear a child.

I do my assigned tasks wearily and retire to our tent. Hedya, on the other hand—positive, gentle, loving, and capable Hedya—becomes a favorite of the whole household. Sometimes I feel a pang of jealousy, but it takes too much energy to keep that emotion going, and I barely have enough to get through each day. When I'm not working, I sleep the deep sleep of oblivion.

Hedya serves the evening meal to the men, works for and gossips with the women, and then brings something back to our tent for us to eat. If I'm already sleeping, she wakes me up. First we say our evening prayers, then she watches to make sure I eat everything that she's brought. While we eat, she tells me all the news about my family, which has grown with the addition of my brothers' wives and their babies. My father often hosts guests—travelers, shepherds, or priests—and Hedya recounts all their stories to me.

יהוה

I am tired of sleeping and hoping that my sorry life will end. The truth is, I am a widow, but after the husband and pretender I've endured, perhaps that fact is a blessing from Yahweh. I haven't had much to do with Yahweh except in reciting our evening prayers—Hedya insists I participate. My personal entreaties have been few, erratic, and full of lamentation and bitterness.

Instead of sleeping as I wait for Hedya to return to the tent in the evenings, I begin sitting outside to look at the desert stars—so bright and clear it seems like I should be able to reach out and touch them. To pass the time, I talk to Yahweh in the way I've heard Hedya speak softly to him from her bed at night—as if He listens, as if He cares.

At first, all that pours from my lips are complaints. "I'm a widow without a child—a nothing, a less-than-nothing. You gave me husbands, but no one would ask to be the wife of men like them. I endured so much pain, and still you did not let me conceive..." I cry the tears I have been storing deep inside me since my first night as a wife.

Gradually I grow as tired of crying as I am of sleeping, and my prayers reflect this change. I still begin in the same place of sadness and pain, but now I don't always end there. "I'm a widow without a child—my clothes announce my station to all who see me. I'm a lowly almanah, but I am fortunate to have a place to live and food to eat." Tonight as I hear the approach of Hedya's footsteps, I add, "and I have a friend. Thank you, Yahweh."

The night sky frames a full moon. I admire its glow and begin this evening's prayer with thanks: "for this tent, for food, for Hedya, even for these widow's clothes." My robe is in sad shape, torn and worn, but as I manage to utter gratefulness for the dreary garment, it occurs to me that I can't change the clothes that announce my station any more than I can change the fact that I am a childless widow. What I can change is their condition.

"Where did this thought come from?" That next day I ask my mother for needle and thread.

Mending progresses on more than just my clothes. Instead of waiting for an end—for so long death has been the only way out that I could envision—I come to a decision that as long as I am alive, I might as well get involved in the business.

יהוה

Tonight Hirah's nephews, on their way home from a visit to their uncle's house in Adullum, are guests in my father's tents. Hedya tells me their news:

LESS THAN A WIDOW

"Judah's wife, your mother-in-law, died, and the family is in a period of mourning." I can find no trace of sorrow in me for the death of this woman who raised such evil sons, nor can I bring myself to hope any longer that Judah will send for me.

Hedya sits across from me as I eat, watching, waiting for me to say something in response to this news, but I cannot dredge up any compassion for Judah in the darkness in my heart. I chew slowly to give myself time to think, "I don't want to speak ill of the dead woman—I have even stopped cursing her two eldest sons. And Judah always had a kind word for me..."

"Another death—Judah's mourning must be deep." It's the best I can do.

Hedya nods her head. "That's what the young men said; he's so grief-stricken that Hirah is concerned. He asked his nephews to go home by way of Judah's lands—that's where they're headed now. Hirah wants to make sure Judah meets him in Timnah for this year's shearing of the sheep and the festivities that follow."

יהוה

For two days my thoughts are filled with Judah and his journey to Timnah. He will have to take the trail that is less than a day's walk from here. I'm disgusted with myself for the spark of hope that keeps flickering in my usual gloom. "So what?" I think. "What does it matter if he is half a day's walk or a week's walk away?"

I can't snuff out the tiny flame, so I argue its uselessness with Yahweh as I sit in my customary spot under the stars. I begin with my perpetual lament: "Judah will never send for me. I will die as I live—an almanah without children who must depend on the dubious charity of her family. I will die here with no one to mourn my passing."

As if someone whispers in my ear, my mind fills with an idea. "If Judah won't come to you, go to him." My lethargic self, my angry self, my bitter self laughs—or makes the awful sound that would be a laugh if I could laugh.

I answer the voice in my mind. "Go to him? What good could come from that? He will never bring me home to Shelah!"

Again, the bark of bitter mirth grates out of my throat. I know Judah will never risk the life of his only son.

Hedya brings our supper, and we eat without conversation. But I can tell she has something on her mind by the way she keeps glancing at me and looking away when I return her gaze. Tired of waiting for her to gather the courage to speak, I ask her, "What's on your mind?"

"Judah will be so nearby, you should go meet him on the trail."

"I was...how did you...on the trail?" We were both thinking the same thing. "How could that be?"

Why would I want to do that?" I ask her.

TAMAR : CANAAN

Hedya shakes her head. "I don't know really, but I haven't been able to get the idea out of my head all day. Maybe if you talk to him, you can convince him that you mean Shelah no harm."

"I already tried that before he sent us here. I told him I had nothing to do with Er's death. Nor Onan's." I shake my head. "He wouldn't listen then; why would it be any different now?"

"I don't know, but I can't stop thinking that you should go meet him." Hedya shrugged. "It's probably just a silly idea."

"That's what I've been telling myself all day—it's a crazy idea—and then you tell me that you've been thinking the same thing." A shiver runs down my spine. "Maybe there's a reason we both can't get it out of our minds."

Neither of us can think of what that reason could be, however, so we follow our usual nighttime pattern: food, prayers, sleep. But once the idea is born, it won't die—I toss and turn trying to come up with a sensible reason for me to meet Judah on the road and get nowhere.

I must have fallen asleep, because suddenly I am awake with my mind full of a new question. I poke Hedya. "Wake up." She grunts and turns over, so I poke her again. "Hedya, this is important! Wake up."

I ask her the question. "The practice of yibum, does it only apply to brothers?"

I don't know if she is slow to answer because she is still asleep or if she doesn't understand my question. I rephrase it. "Can only brothers practice yibum?"

"I'm not sure," she finally says. "That's the only way I know of. A rabbi would know. Why do you ask?"

"While I was sleeping, I thought or dreamt—I guess it doesn't matter which one it is—but it occurs to me that while Judah would never risk Shelah's life by asking him to lie with a woman he believes may use her evil powers to harm him, maybe he would be willing to risk his own life."

Hedya's mouth falls open. "Judah? He wouldn't."

"I agree," I answered. "But then, he wouldn't have to know who it is exactly that he is lying with."

"What are you talking about? Are you well?" Hedya puts out her hand and feels my forehead, checking for fever, and that makes me laugh. "What's so funny?"

"I'm not sick, and I'm not crazy either," I assure her. "Admit it! Judah will never send for me. On the other hand, we know that it's important to Judah that he and his family follow Hebrew practices—he even sent you to teach me all about his people and his God before I married his son."

Hedya nods reluctantly, and I continue. "If his last remaining son dies, Judah's whole line will be erased. He can't take the chance of that happening—he won't let me anywhere near Shelah."

"Then what's the use of trying to meet him on the road to Himnah?"

LESS THAN A WIDOW

I interrupt Hedya. "Judah has to be the one to father Er's child—not Shelah. Judah will act as a go'el—a kinsman savior—instead of Shelah."

"He won't do that!" Hedya protests.

"He will if he doesn't know that's what he's doing," I tell her. "I'll pose as a prostitute just outside of that village, what it's called? Eni...En something... Enaem—that's it. He has a man's needs, and he will have been months without a wife. Judah won't be able to resist—he will visit my tent."

"That would be so dangerous," Hedya objects.

"So is staying here for much longer counting on my father's charity. He's not known for his generous nature."

Hedya needs more convincing. "Say you set up your tent and pose as a prostitute. What will he do when he recognizes you?"

"If I stay in the tent's shadows and wear a prostitute's veil, I don't think he'll figure out that it's me. And I will serve him wine laced with an herb that causes drowsiness, and no sooner will we have practiced yibum," I raise my eyebrows and grin at my word choice, "he will fall asleep. When he wakes up, I'll be gone."

"It might work," Hedya agrees reluctantly. "But if you do get pregnant, how will you prove it's his child? He could have you killed!" Hedya grabs my hand. "This is crazy..."

I give her hand a squeeze and let go. "Probably, but we're desperate. My father won't keep us here much longer, and Judah won't bring us back to his tents. We either do this or we accept as true what everyone believes—we're better off dead."

With a deep sigh, Hedya nods her agreement. "Maybe...maybe you could sneak something of his while he's sleeping and hide it, but it has to be something that he will recognize and can't deny belongs to him."

"That would work," I reply. "Then, if he decides to kill me, I will just send it to him by a messenger to say that its owner is the father of my child."

"Let me guess," Hedya says. "I get to be the messenger."

יהוה

We have only days to plan every detail and gather supplies. We know when shearing will take place and where they will go to sell the wool. The road that Judah must use in order to join Hiram goes straight through the small village of Eneam and curves as it heads uphill. Part of the way up, just out of sight of the town, there's a flat area sheltered by an overhang—that's where I will set up my tent. I gather the few things I will need and pack and repack them nightly, taking special care with the vessel of doctored wine.

Hedya comes up with a perfect solution for my absence. She and I have continued the Hebrew practice of a week's separation during a women's menstrual flow, followed by ritual cleansing. This practice is not so different from the henna purification symbols used by the women of my clan, and we have been allowed to continue the Hebrew tradition in the hopes that Judah will soon call for my return. "The timing's a little off, but I don't think anyone will question me. Plus, I'll get to eat your portion of the evening meals as well as mine," she tells me with a happy grin. Hedya is always hungry.

I leave early in the morning before anyone else wakes up. The sun hasn't yet made its way above the horizon, but the sky is lightening as I sneak away from the family encampment. The first part of the trail is smooth and runs slightly downhill. The pack doesn't feel too heavy until I climb the first hill; then with each step it seems to gain weight—pound by pound—all morning. When the sun reaches its zenith, I find a patch of shade where I can take a break during the hottest part of the day. Although my body tries to relax, my unstoppable, whirling thoughts are anything but restful. It's almost a relief when it's time to strap on my large pack again and continue the climb.

Just when I begin to panic that somehow I've gotten lost, I reach the peak of my climb. Crossing a small plateau, I find the trail on the other side and look down into the valley. Enaem is visible in the basin below, but the road leading to it has so many twists and turns that much of it is out of sight.

"Almost there!" I tell myself.

I start the descent, leaning back to balance the heavy pack, knees flexed, and place my feet carefully to avoid slipping on the rocky ground.

The clearing is just like I remembered. A flat area on one side of the road, half-shaded by a large overhang of rock, backs up to the mountain. To my relief, I hear the drip, drip of water trickling through a crack in the rock. It is just wide enough for me to push my drinking gourd into the opening, and I leave it there to slowly capture a few drops to wet my throat.

I set up the tiny tent under the overhang so that it will be shaded even when the sun is directly above it. As daylight quickly disappears, I sit in the darkness and nibble on a handful of parched grains and lentils, washing it down with a mouthful of water. Then I unpack my belongings by feel, spreading out the best garments that Hedya and I could secretly gather.

"The veil! Where's the veil?"

Anxiety grips me until I find it still inside the carrying pack. I strip down to my shift and, making a mat from my widow's garments—dusty from the day's hike—I lie down and attempt to sleep.

יהוה

The next morning I wash away yesterday's grime with a sponge bath, hide my widow's garments, and put on the clothes I had brought along.

"What a relief to get out of those appalling widows' garments!"

I make sure my hair is braided and oiled with a sweet-smelling concoction my sister-in-law gave to Hedya in thanks for her preparation of a sooth-

LESS THAN A WIDOW

ing balm that healed her baby's heat rash. The veil had been the most difficult clothing item to come up with—we had to steal two veils from my mother's stores and sew them together. A close inspection would reveal our deception, but it should do the trick. With no other preparations to be made, I begin the tedious, but most distressing part of the whole plan—waiting in the shade outside my tent for Judah to pass by.

יהוה

Judah trudges up the trail midafternoon. I recognize him immediately. As he draws near, I take a step closer and beckon to him. At the same time I offer a silent prayer, "Thank you, Yahweh, for this blessed overhang and its deep shadow."

Judah hesitates and looks around to see if anyone else is in the vicinity.

"It's cool in the tent," I speak in the seductive tones my mother taught me a lifetime ago. He just stands there looking at me, so I continue, "You look like a man who knows what he wants. Come, sit beside me and drink my wine."

"Well, it is a dry walk to the top of this mountain," Judah says as he takes a step closer.

"Careful," I silently remind myself. "Don't push too hard or he'll get suspicious."

"I have just the thing for a dry throat, fine sir," I reply out loud. I lift up my goblet of wine, smile an invitation, and step to the door of my tent. "Join me."

"I am interested," Judah says as I take his staff and help him remove his pack.

"What can you offer in payment for my favors?" I ask.

"I will send back a young goat from my flock—I'm on my way to join my shepherds for the shearing." Judah draws himself up into a posture of authority.

"How can I be sure that I will receive payment?"

As I expect, Judah bristles at the veiled insult. "I am a man of my word."

I softly run my hand up his arm. "Yes, I'm sure you are, but you must understand…a woman in my position needs something tangible in hand before pleasure begins. Is there some kind of guarantee you can give me?"

Judah frowns, but I feel a tremor of excitement under my hand that still rests on his upper arm. I place it softly on the center of his chest. "Perhaps you can leave your personal seal-and-cord and the staff that you carry. When your servant comes with the young goat, he can return your pledge items to you."

When Judah hesitates, I run my hands through my hair so he can smell my perfume and say in a low hoarse voice, "Or perhaps you would prefer to bring the young goat to me yourself."

יהוה

"Thank you, Yahweh, for men's passions," I think I look down at my father-in-law deep in sleep on the floor of my tent.

Judah wasn't interested in drinking any wine until much later. It was tricky to continue to conceal my identity, but his overwhelming fervor and the darkness of the tent made it possible. A few mouthfuls of doctored wine afterward made him so groggy he fell asleep quickly.

When he wakes an hour later—cursing the pain in his head and the fuzz in his mouth—I was already hidden in a crevice, along with his seal and staff. He calls for me, but I don't move. Muttering, he comes out of the tent and looks around. Finally he shrugs, shoulders his pack, and resumes his ascent up the mountain.

What for him had been a momentary satisfaction of his urgings, for me was the performance of yibum. As I watch him reappear and disappear up the winding path, I stay secure in my hiding place. When he reaches the top of the bluff, Judah turns and looks back down into the valley. At that moment, I know.

"I am with child. Praise be to Yahweh,

who hears and responds."

יהוה

Morning sickness is hard to hide from women who have experienced it themselves. Even so, I am almost to my fourth month before my mother puts her hand on my protruding stomach to confirm her suspicions. But we had planned for this day. Hedya quickly and quietly makes her way to our tent, retrieves a small carry sack, and disappears into the wilderness. My mother marches me to see my father, and when I finally am returned to our tent—now under guard—I have a split lip. A rope around my ankle is attached to a stake and allows limited mobility.

Father immediately sends a message to Judah, who returns within days to accuse me and personally supervise my punishment for the heinous crime of being a whore. "Bring her out!" Judah yells. "Burn her up."

I am led to a cleared area, stood up against a post, and my arms are tied around the pole behind my back. Servants gather dung, thorn bushes, and branches from white broom plants to make a fire large and hot enough to kill me. Under a canopy, Judah watches and drinks wine with my father and brothers. My mother and brothers' wives gather up their children and disappear into their tents, hiding from the horror to come.

I haven't been given anything to eat or drink since my grievous condition was discovered. I was so thirsty, I drank my own urine.

LESS THAN A WIDOW

"Stay alive long enough for Hedya to find a way to talk to Judah," I whisper to myself over an over until my voice gives out. Then, I continue to urge myself in my mind. I slide down the pole to a sitting position and try to remain conscious while I wait for rescue or death.

"Hedya will find a way to talk to Judah. Surely Yahweh won't desert me now!"

I want to believe that Yahweh wouldn't provide a child—for Er, for Judah, for me—just to kill the baby within me before it can even be born. But I see no sign of Hedya.

The door flap to my sister-in-law's tent is pushed aside, and her arm gently pushes her eldest son, only eight years old, into the afternoon sun. He approaches the men under the canopy from behind and whispers a message in Judah's ear.

My brother—he has never been able to hold his liquor well—grabs his son by the arm. "So you want to see what happens to loose women, do you? Sit beside me like a man, then."

Judah stands up and bows to my brother. "The boy brings me a message. Would you allow him to come with me so that I may hear what he has to say?"

My brother loosens his grip on his scared son's arm, and with the boy in the lead, Judah disappears around the side of the tent.

I have no idea how much time passes before he appears again. A fly crawls across my face and repeatedly tries to enter the interesting tunnel of my nostril, and I barely have the strength to shake my head in an effort to discourage it. My arms, bound tightly behind my back, no longer even tingle or hurt—they don't feel like a part of me anymore. Although the sun is blazing, I am no longer sweating, and I pray that if I am to die, I do so soon, before the fire is lit. If I were able to form tears in my dehydrated state, I would cry for the baby in my womb that will never have a chance to live.

Sandled feet approach and stop in front of me. I crack open my eyes enough to see that they belong to a man, and I try to lift my head to see who it is. I get as far as his belt before the effort proves to take more strength than I still have. My head falls to my chest. But my ears still work.

"This woman has been falsely accused." Judah's voice rings out in the officious tones he uses for pronouncements of importance. "What we called prostitution was, in fact, the performance of yibum. Therefore, I withdraw my accusation, for she is in the right. I did not send for her to marry my son as I said I would."

Judah turns toward the women's tent and beckons. Hedya steps to the front of the group of women who are watching from the tent doorway in disbelief. She makes her way to Judah, lays her carrying sack at his feet, and bows low to the ground.

"Cut Tamar loose, and care for her. Send a message to me when she is well enough to travel, and I will send a donkey to carry her to the tents of my people where she will give birth to Er's child." Judah's voice is choked and harsh, as if it hurts to push the words from his throat. When he is done, he walks away from the camp without another word. His servants hurry to gather their belongings and follow him.

יהוה

Judah is true to his word. He sends a donkey to carry me to his encampment and servants to guide and guard Hedya and me on the trail. We are given a separate dwelling in the family's home place—surrounded by people, but left alone. Like any man, Judah does not like to be reminded of his wrongdoing; he cannot bear to look at me or hear my voice.

Despite the ministrations of a skilled midwife, I labor long and hard to give birth to twins, and neither of them desires to leave the safety of my womb. When one sticks his arm out, the midwife ties a red cord around it; then he pulls it back inside. She and Hedya push on my stomach as contractions continue, encouraging me to push. I am spent and think I can't go on when I hear the midwife exclaim, "A breakout!" The second twin is the first to enter this harsh, unforgiving world of ours. I name him Perez, which means "burst forth." When Zerah finally makes his appearance, he cries as he waves his little fists almost as if he is declaring, "Look at this red string! I am first."

יהוה

The following years teach me that feeding and caring for twins is all-consuming, but for that I am thankful. Since their early years, the growing boys have been spending more and more time with their grandfather. But they are my sons, and because of them, I am no longer considered a societal outcast. I am the mother of Er's children, and as such I will always have a place here within this family.

My sons. My wild, loud, energetic sons—I watch as they run past me. Perez lives up to his name—"burst forth." He always leaps first and looks second. I shake my head as I watch him charge up the hill waving a stick, challenging his brother with, "You can't catch me."

Zerah watches Perez scrabble his way up the hill and chooses an alternate route to the top. The baby with the red cord that staked his claim as firstborn, the one who withdrew his arm and let his twin break out first, still watches and lets his brother lead the way—at least physically. But Zerah's name, which means "bright," also shines through in his character. He is seldom the first one to enter a room, but he is the one who shines so brightly that others are drawn to his side.

LESS THAN A WIDOW

Hedya comes and sits down across from me to help grind the day's grain. Two stone disks sit on top of each other between us, held together by an upright wooden peg which extends upward through a hole in the upper wheel. She tips a gourd, spills grain into the opening, and we take turns rotating the handle that turns the upper stone disk to crush the grain.

Instead of being castoffs, Hedya and I have been given a place here; we belong. I am the mother of sons, and Hedya is my loyal maidservant and friend.

"Praise be to Yahweh, who hears and responds." I say the words out loud, and Hedya echoes the tribute.

We listen to the brothers bicker, play, argue, and compete. The flour spills from between the stones to the cloth below, and I smile.

I am content.

NINE
(CONTINUED)

As Elimelech tells the story, Ruth sometimes hears Tamar's voice overlaying his deep tones as if she is saying, "Pay special attention to this part; it's important." And Ruth did. For the rest of the day, Ruth goes quietly through the motions of her work while her mind replays and processes what she had heard.

Sitting in the shade during the hottest part of the afternoon, Ruth cards wool and thinks. "I have to find out more about this Hebrew God, Yahweh. Why would he care about Tamar—she's not even a Hebrew? Chemosh never promises anything—not even to wake up for spring—unless we give him gifts: terrible, awful gifts." But that thought brings her too close to her recurring nightmare in which she watches Chemosh's wicked priest place Durha on the altar..."No! Chemosh bears no resemblance to Yahweh at all."

Gathering up the carded fibers and her spindle, Ruth moves closer to the loom where Naomi is working. Twirling this foot-long slender stick, using her thumbs and forefingers to draw out fibers caught in the hook at the spindle's top, Ruth spins a stone whorl to give momentum to the rotating spindle.

Once she gets her spinning rhythm going, Ruth's mind goes back to Tamar. "What if her father had kicked her out? Wouldn't it be less cruel to kill her quickly than sentencing her to slow death by starvation? There would be only one way women like her could earn a living, but prostitutes don't live pleasant or long lives."

"Why didn't Judah have Tamar killed anyway?" Ruth asks Naomi. "He could have said they were lying, that she stole his seal and staff—no one would have stopped him."

Naomi frowns and is slow to respond. "He wasn't really a bad man—Judah—not like his sons. And he had lied to his father before and found it hard to live with that all the time." She shrugs her shoulders. "And he wanted to obey Yahweh, I suppose."

"If he wanted to do the right thing, why didn't he?" Ruth had been puzzled about this question since she heard Tamar's story, but there are some things girls don't ask men about—especially slave girls and their masters. "Why didn't he just be the father right away, instead of going through the whole thing with the brothers?"

LESS THAN A WIDOW

Naomi passes the shuttle the entire width of the loom before answering, and she pauses to look at Ruth as she answers carefully. "This is a difficult question to answer, especially to one as young as you. Practicing yibum is meant for brothers, not fathers-in-law."

"Then why did Judah say Ruth was right, and he was wrong?" Ruth wasn't going to let Naomi get away with this half-answer—she never let any subject rest until she'd figured things out.

Naomi sighed and continued, "Not everyone would agree that Tamar's interpretation was right—this is not how yibum is usually practiced. Maybe it was because the idea was new to Tamar or because she was desperate, but she really stretched the understanding of yibum in a way that hadn't been done before."

"So, I was right. Judah really could have had her burned to death anyway." Ruth's view of Tamar's bravery increased.

"That was a very real possibility," Naomi acknowledged. "That's why I believe Judah was a good man. It took courage on his part to admit he was the father and honor Tamar as the mother of Er's sons—in a way, his support of her interpretation of yibum gave them life."

"But, why..."

Naomi laughed and held up both her hands, palms out. "No more questions, young lady. My head is spinning, and we have work to do. You need to go to the well to fetch water now, anyway." She waves at Orpah who is striking a pose in the entryway. Orpah returns Naomi's wave, but her eyes are focused on Killion kneading clay across the courtyard.

Ruth glances at Killion who is doing his own posturing, and speaks to Naomi in a voice just loud enough for the two admirers to hear, "Oh, I don't think Orpah will mind waiting for a few more minutes."

Naomi laughs again and gives Ruth a playful swat. "Off with you two!"

BOAZ
בֹּעַז

BETHLEHEM
2 YEARS LATER

TEN

Once again, Boaz puts his shoulder to the stone with the other men and pushes. It takes the strength of at least five men to roll it back along the groove dug in front of the entrance to the family tomb.

יהוה

    Just weeks ago, his mother Rahab had complained of a headache. She'd lain down to sleep and never woke up. All of her husband's strength and will must have gone to the grave with her. Propped up on cushions, Salma received visitors for the week of mourning. He refused to walk, a hard chore in the years since his collapse in the field, and within days he stopped talking and eating.
    Boaz tried in vain to encourage him not to give up, but Salma just looked at him with vacant eyes. Finally, in frustration, Boaz tried to put some food in his father's mouth, but most of it just fell from his slack jaw on the bed—the rest he choked on until Boaz rolled him on his side and Sarai cleared his throat with her finger.
    "Boaz, dear heart, you need to let him go," Sarai murmured into his ear that night as they lay close together, warming each other against the cold night air.
    "I know how much he loved Mother—we all did—but he's just giving up. He's never admitted defeat before, not even during the famine." Boaz's whole body is taut with frustration, choosing anger over fear of his father's death. "It's like he just wants to die."
    "I believe he does," Sarai speaks quietly. "You are up and out of the house early, so you haven't seen how hard it has been for him to get up, dressed, and into his chair in the mornings. Elon had been helping Rahab get him dressed and feed him breakfast for weeks, and then he would be so exhausted he'd have to rest before he could receive any visitors. I think he only stayed alive for Rahab, so he wouldn't leave her alone in this land full of Hebrews."
    "Why didn't you tell me how bad it was?"
    Sarai sighed. "You have been busy and working so hard, doing most of your father's work as well as your own—I just didn't want you to worry about one more thing. And your mother was caring for him…"

LESS THAN A WIDOW

When Boaz didn't answer, Sarai continued. "I think living is just too much hard work now that Rahab's gone. We need to tell him we love him, and let him die in peace."

יהוה

Facing the sealed tomb, Boaz feels the weight of all the responsibilities his parents had carried settle onto his own shoulders, and his leg muscles contract and tremble under the demanding load. Boaz attempts to stand up straight and drop the imaginary burden, but it won't budge and threatens to sink him into the sandy ground—his heart races and he finds it hard to breathe.

"Boaz."

"Daddy!"

Sarai and seven-year-old Aram stand in front of him, shielding him from the gaze of gathered mourners. Sarai lays a tentative hand on his arm. "Boaz, are you well?"

Boaz shakes off her arm and snaps, "Of course!" But his swirling thoughts betray his words. "My father and mother are dead, the whole of Bethlehem is waiting for me to do something foolish enough to gossip about, and my wife and son are looking at me as if I'm crazy. What else would I be?"

"Then we should go. They are waiting for you to lead them." Sarai half-turns and sweeps her arm toward the gathered family and friends, clumped together in small groups forming a line.

Boaz takes his place at the head of the procession. Sarai and Aram tread wearily behind him, followed by her maid carrying their young daughter Sheerah. As they trail back to Bethlehem, the mumbled conversations and wavering wails of sorrow float up from the mourners and wrap Boaz in a cloud of grief.

"I don't want to go home—it's not home without Mother and Father." He admits to himself that he does not want to carry the full load of being the family patriarch. "Why did you both die? I'm not ready for all of this."

The day is already heating up as the funeral procession enters the city gates. Automatically, Boaz glances toward his father's seat, half-expecting to see him there with the other city elders as they give spiritual and legal counsel, but the alcove is empty. The elders and many of the townspeople came to the tomb with his family. Salma, his father, was loved by many—some grateful for his compassionate care during the famine years and others for his wise counsel as a leader and city elder.

יהוה

The load on his shoulders grows heavier during the seven-day mourning period. A distant cousin—a man whose family had had food to eat during the famine only because of his father's sacrificial generosity—approaches Boaz and, while drinking his wine, lies and pretends immense sorrow over Salma's death. "Your father promised that when he died, all my debts would be forgiven."

Boaz clenches his fists and barely resists the urge to punch the lying man in the mouth. "It could be true," he thinks. "Father's heart was easily stirred to pity."

Elon steps to his side and bows to the man. "Thank you for bringing this matter to our attention, but now we are in the time of mourning. If you would be willing to return at another time with your request…" Elon takes the man's elbow and guides him toward the door.

City council members curry favor. Boaz will soon acquire his father's seat, and each faction is eager to bring him under the wing of their interests. Petitioners present their arguments to convince Boaz that their side of the story is the only one to hold merit. Merchants try to influence his opinion about the proposed raising of booth fees in the marketplace. Men with marriage-aged daughters are sure that such a young patriarch, in the fullness of his manhood, needs more than one wife. "She's young, beautiful, and knows how to please a man." One father is sure Boaz will hand over the excessive bride price he's demanding right then and there.

Uncle Imlah and his son Balak make their appearance on each of the seven days of mourning. Despite his increasing girth and difficulty in walking, Uncle Imlah shrewdly scans the crowd and directs his son toward anyone he thinks can be sweet-talked into entertaining a high-interest loan. Balak makes his way around the room, offering praise for Salma while insinuating that both he and his father are cut from the same cloth. Those naïve enough to be drawn in by his words are invited to join Uncle Imlah and sit at his right side, only to be ensnared by sticky filaments, imprisoned as tightly as a fly in a spider's web.

"Salma was an esteemed man of character, full of compassion, with a heart that compelled him to rescue those in need." Balak's sonorous voice, speaking to his back, startles Boaz. "He had been totally devoted to Rahab since she ensnared his heart in Jericho." Balak shakes his head mournfully.

Balak had followed Boaz as he escaped the crowd by climbing the stairs to the roof. Boaz reluctantly turns to find his cousin offering him a glass of wine. Making no reply, Boaz accepts the proffered glass, and they drink together.

Balak continues his two-faced talk masked as sympathy. "My father and I offered thanks just this morning to Yahweh for bringing back the rains and ending the drought before Salma reached the end of the family holdings in his rescue attempts during those hard times."

Again, Boaz offers no comment, at least not out loud, and Balak hurries to fill the silence. "We were remembering your father as a man steeped in Hebrew tradition in spite of his Canaanite wife."

Boaz holds up a hand. "I am no longer a little boy that you can taunt with your insults about my bloodlines. My mother Rahab worshipped the same God to whom you gave thanks this morning."

"No insult intended, I'm sure," Balak said quickly and bowed with a hand to his heart. "I meant only to give tribute to your esteemed father."

"Then I thank you. If you will excuse me…" As Boaz turns away in dismissal, Balak lays a hand on his arm.

"One more thing, please." Boaz stops and grimly turns back to face Balak.

Feigning deep sorrow, his hand again covering his heart, Balak goes on. "My father wanted me to convey to you that, in honor of your father's memory, he would like to extend an offer of financial assistance should you find yourself in need during this transition time."

"Thank him for his consideration and assure him that his offer, while valued, will not be necessary," Boaz replies mimicking Balak's heart-to-hand bow. "Now, I wish to be alone to grieve for my father."

"Most certainly, cousin." Balak makes his way down the stairs, meeting his father's inquiring glance with raised eyebrows.

יהוה

For seven days the family's home is filled with pipers and mourners wailing laments as visitors console Boaz and Sarai. Days pass, and the sweet smells of burial oils and spices slowly fade away. Distant relatives pack their belongings, and their home slowly empties of visitors. Everyday sounds return—children playing, mothers scolding, townsfolk hurrying down the road, merchants calling out their wares, donkeys braying, doves cooing—normal life.

Boaz finds it hard to make this transition—in fact, he resists entering its flow. He is caught in an eddy of churlish restlessness and an inability to sleep. Night and day his thoughts follow the same circular path. "Yahweh, if you hadn't stopped the rains, my parents wouldn't have worried themselves into an early grave. Father would still be here smiling through his white beard as he watched his grandchildren sitting on his wife's knee. How am I supposed to go on without their guidance and wisdom? How am I supposed to deal with all this…?"

But he has no words to describe "all this." And he has no desire to figure out what "all this" really is.

This morning he stands on the roof as the sun rises in the east, dons his prayer shawl, and recites the morning prayers, but they are just words memorized long ago. Boaz paces a well-worn route around the rooftop, fruitlessly hoping that constant movement will keep reality at bay.

"Boaz." Sarai's voice speaks his name over and over with increasing insistence and finally steps into his path before he even realizes that she is there.

Wrapping her arms around him, she tucks her head under his chin and pulls him close. Reluctantly giving into his wife's embrace, Boaz feels her ragged breathing against his chest and is overwhelmed with guilt as he realizes that Sarai misses Mother and Father as much he does, and he has done nothing to comfort her or ease her added duties.

"I'm sorry," he murmurs. Boaz kisses the top of his wife's head, breathes in the light smell of jasmine oil, and holds her gently.

After a few minutes Sarai pushes away and looks into her husband's face. "Have you slept at all?"

Boaz just shrugs and doesn't give voice to his thought. "Why do women always state the obvious as a question?"

Sarai calls down the stairs, "Aram, bring your father's staff."

Dragging the too-tall staff behind him, Aram climbs up the final few stairs to the roof, his little sister Sheerah tagging behind. Boaz kneels on one knee as his son approaches solemnly and wraps him in his arms. The staff clatters to the floor as Sheerah—who never wants to be left out—jumps on top of both of them.

Aram hugs his neck in a death grip, and Sheerah competes for her fair share of attention until she is distracted by the staff. Aram dives from his father's arms and grabs it out of her hands, but Sheerah won't let go, and they wrestle—loudly—for possession of the staff which is too big for either of them to handle until Sarai steps in and shushes their protests.

"What's this all about?" Boaz asks his wife with an attempted smile.

"Your pack is ready, too." She endeavors to return his grin, but bites her lip as betraying tears slide down her cheeks. "Go to the desert—talk to Yahweh—and find the answers you are looking for."

Boaz feels his face flush with shame. He knows that he will say "yes" to her suggestion–command. Even with Elon's help, the work she is offering to take on could drive her to her knees, and she is four months pregnant. Embarrassed by his eagerness to run away from his responsibilities, Boaz embraces his wife and hides his face in her hair. The children push their way between them to be a part of the loving, and they stand wrapped in each other's arms—all four of them—a smaller family without grandmother and grandfather.

Sarai pulls away first and takes each child by the hand as she steps back.

"There are too many distractions here, and you need to pray and hear Yahweh's voice." At his weak protest, she places her hand softly over Boaz's mouth. This time her smile starts with her lips and makes it all the way to her eyes. "It will be months before our baby will be born. Elon and I can handle things at home for a while."

"And me," Aram pipes up. "I can help."

"Of course," Sarai responds. "I depend on your help."

Aram's proud smile turns to a scowl when Boaz doesn't say anything, but only distractedly ruffles his son's hair.

LESS THAN A WIDOW

The family follows Boaz down the stairs and helps him shoulder his pack and waterskin. Aram and Sheerah grab the staff, pushing and pulling it, fighting over who is going to have the privilege of giving it to their father until Boaz settles the issue by taking it from both of them. Sarai gives him a little push toward the door. "Talk to Yahweh, listen to his answers, and come back to us when you are ready for life again."

"I have met wisdom, and her name is Sarai." Boaz kisses his wife on the cheek, lays his hand on Aram's head, tugs on Sheerah's braid, and turns towards the wilderness.

Sarai's whispered prayer floats on the air after her husband, "Yahweh, heal his heart and bring him back to me."

יהוה

Elon watches from a rooftop on the other side of the compound as Boaz makes his way toward the city gates.

With a frown he turns to his son standing beside him. "You have everything you need for an extended stay in the desert?"

At Jair's nod, Elon goes on. "Yahweh's hand was surely in the timing of your return home. Although your mother would prefer to keep you here, Boaz is not himself, and I would feel better if he had some protection out in the wilderness."

After years of soldiering, Jair had returned home when he heard of the death of his aunt and uncle. "I've done my share of protection assignments," he smiles at his father. "This is what I'm good at—don't worry."

"It's better if Boaz doesn't even know you are there, but if he sees you…" Elon says.

"He won't." Jair settles his pack on his back and hangs his water bag across his shoulders and checks to see he can still reach his knife hanging in a sheath on his belt. "We have been friends since childhood—if I do need to let him know I am there, it will be because he needs help, and he will be happy to see me."

ELEVEN

TWO MONTHS LATER

The days pass without anything to distinguish one from the other. By the time Boaz cares enough to wonder how long he has been holed up in this desert cave, he finds it impossible to determine how many days—weeks—it has been since he left home. "How long?" is the refrain in his brain as he drifts off to sleep.

He wakes up scratching and thinking an alternate refrain, "Why don't these lousy bugs find their own cave?"

Pushing back matted hair, Boaz groans as he rolls to a sitting position and uncorks his waterskin—one last drop of warm water falls on his tongue. Over the rumbling of his stomach, he focuses on the sound of a locust in flight, tenses his muscles, and waits for it to land. In one quick motion he grabs it, pops it in his mouth, and crunches its life-giving juices. Lying back down, he falls back into the half-doze that has consumed so much of his time in the desert.

It's nearing sunrise when Boaz wakes up and gropes his way out of the shallow cave. Feeling his way to his customary spot, he leans against a boulder high above a dark-shrouded desert valley and watches rays of light flicker on the horizon as the sun rises to announce another day.

"Your world is beautiful, Yahweh." Boaz begins the conversation with praise, but it isn't long before he's listing his complaints again. "Why did you let my parents die, Yahweh? They loved and served you faithfully. I wanted our firstborn baby to live. I wanted Aram and Sheerah to grow up learning from their grandmother and loving her as I did. Sarai and I wanted to lay our next child in my father's arms to receive his blessing."

Picking up a handful of stones Boaz tosses them, one at a time, over the ledge and listens to their passage as they rebound and tumble into the wadi below.

"Father and Mother worked so hard to give food and shelter to anyone who needed it, bought relatives' land, forgave debts…Now everybody is depending on me, watching me, measuring me against him…I had my life planned out—and it didn't include having to take on this responsibility so soon."

Grabbing another handful of stones he tosses one and counts the number of bounces until it reaches the bottom. "It wasn't your plan though, was it?"

LESS THAN A WIDOW

He digs a bigger rock out of the shallow dirt on the ledge and heaves it over the side.

"You expect me to carry his heavy load, but I'm not Salma. It would be easier to just die in this desert."

When he depletes the supply of pebbles within reach, Boaz is surprised to discover that he has also depleted his stockpile of whining, but not his anger. He stands up and shouts at the dawning sky, "I'm still here. What do you want from me? Do you even hear me?"

A voice floats down from the cliff above. "Oh, he hears you all right, and so do I. Maybe you should listen to his answers."

Boaz flattens himself against the cliff edge.

"Yahweh must have infinite patience, because I'm sick to death of your complaining, Boaz."

"Who are you?"

"You don't recognize my voice? I'm the cousin who pinned you in every wrestling match we ever had."

"Jair? Where are you?" Boaz strains to see the cliff above his head in the growing light, then spins when he hears footsteps on the ledge beside him. "What are you doing here?"

"Listening to a bad-tempered boy who refuses to grow up."

"What did I do to deserve this?" Boaz spits bitter words in his cousin's face. "I asked Yahweh to show me my guilt, to tell me what it is I did so that he has cursed me."

Jair shakes his head. "Yahweh has cursed you?"

Boaz angrily pounds his chest. "Yes, he has cursed me. My parents were too young to die, and now I'm left alone with not just a family to support, but a whole household—a whole city—full of people depending on me to work myself into an early grave like my parents did. For what? So I can leave the same legacy to my son Aram?"

Jair pulls his knife from its sheath, leans against the cliff behind him, and cleans under his fingernails. "Tough life."

"What do you know? You don't have to make any of the decisions out there. You have officers to tell you your every move. You can't even breathe without their permission."

Jair shoves Boaz up against the cliff, his forearm across his throat, and his knife under his chin. They glare at each other nose to nose. "Who are you to question Yahweh's wisdom? Do you dare to argue with the Almighty? You are Yahweh's critic, yet you have no answers."

Boaz tries to speak, but can only gasp for air.

Jair has more to say. "Life's not all about you—it's so much bigger than that." He steps back and points to a bird gliding on the air currents above them. "Is it your wisdom that makes the hawk soar and spread its wings toward the south?

BOAZ : BETHLEHEM

Is it at your command that the eagle rises to the heights to make its nest? No. It is Yahweh who made the universe, and it is Yahweh who rules all things."

Jair turns back to Boaz who is red-faced with a lack of air and a dawning realization of his selfishness. "You're not the only one who's hurting. Grow up. This is life—live it."

Boaz fingers the knife prick on his neck and licks the blood from his finger. "Pinned again."

Slipping the knife back into its sheath, Jair bends down to peer into the shallow cave. "Phew. You stink. Better wash up before you go home." He turns and heads up the hillside.

"Where are you going?" Boaz calls after him.

"Something I have to check on." And Jair is gone.

יהוה

Salma had sent his young son Boaz into the desert with the shepherds to learn about this part of the family business firsthand, so—twenty years later—he congratulates himself for finding this hidden well with only a few false tries. "Some things you just don't forget."

Wearing only a loin cloth, Boaz wrings water from his robe and spreads it on a bush near the water trough. Water drips from his freshly-washed hair onto the unkempt beard that hides his face. After scrubbing his skin with wet sand to rid it of weeks of grime, Boaz pours water over his head, and the flowing water triggers memories of his father.

"You are there to watch and learn," Salma had told him before he left with the shepherds. So Boaz had diligently studied geography and the care and breeding of animals, but the only question his father wanted him to answer months later was, "Why do the sheep trust the shepherd?"

"He must have been satisfied with my stumbling answers," Boaz thought, "because he told me that a responsible leader provides the same kind of love and care to his people."

The bleating of sheep brings his thoughts back to the present, and Boaz quickly moves behind a cluster of white broom plants and watches to see who is approaching.

Two shepherd boys and a large flock of sheep and goats head into the valley. Smelling water, the lead goat pushes forward bleating, and others crowd behind him.

Boaz returns to the well and lets his waterskin down into the well on a rope, hauls it up, and pours water into the stone trough. As he repeats his task, a stone whizzes past his ear. A shepherd is already twirling another stone in his slingshot. The other holds onto the horn of the lead goat blocking the animals from getting past him and brandishes his staff.

LESS THAN A WIDOW

Spreading his arms wide in an open posture, Boaz backs away from the trough. He gestures at his body, naked except for his loin cloth. "As you can see, I have no weapons. I mean you no harm."

The boys look at each other, and the one with the staff is the first to speak. "I hear by your accent that you are Hebrew."

The slingshot stops its twirling, but the boys still block the flock from approaching.

"Yes, I am. When I heard you coming, I filled the trough for your animals." Boaz grins and asks, "Would it be safe to get dressed now?"

Slingshot boy grins. "You'd better or you will get an ugly sunburn."

The older shepherd steps aside to let the thirsty flock crowd up to the trough as Boaz puts on his still-damp robe. "Who are you, and why are you here?" Still gripping his staff, the shepherd is polite, but his tone sends a faint challenge.

"I am Boaz, son of Salma from Bethlehem. I've been on a sojourn in the desert...mourning the death of my parents."

The two boys look quickly at each other and away. "We didn't recognize you, sir." The young boy clamps down on a snort of laughter while his older brother dips his head in respect. "Please pardon my brother's jest, sir."

"Can't deny the truth when you hear it." Boaz laughs, then asks, "Whose fine animals are these?"

"They belong to Hiram, son of Simcha."

"Give him my regards when next you return home." Shouldering his light pack, he waves and makes his way up the hill. Squinting at the position of the sun, Boaz decides he might have two hours of daylight left and realizes he's anxious to go home.

יהוה

Sunlight and shadows play across his face as he wakes up beneath the breeze-blown branches of the scrub bushes under which he'd spent the night. Shaking out his dew-damp robe, he spreads it over the bushes to dry. Rubbing the sleep out of his eyes, Boaz is disappointed to see that he'd slept longer than he had meant to this morning, then smiles when he realizes how eager he is to return home.

Facing the already-risen sun, he raises his arms to the heavens and prays:

"Blessed are you, HaShem, my God and God of my ancestors,

Master of all works, Lord of all souls,

Who bestows good things upon the unworthy,

and has bestowed upon me every goodness."

Eating a handful of parched grain and legumes from the sack that Jair had left for him, Boaz turns back toward the hidden well, looking to see if the two young shepherds and their flock have grazed their way through the valley yet. "I wonder where they are?"

Boaz wraps his almost-dry robe around him, cinches his belt, and shoulders his pack. Climbing up on a rock to get a better view, Boaz looks again for any sign of movement in the valley behind him. "There! No it's only a shadow—a moving shadow."

He looks to the sky—buzzards make their slow circling descent from great heights. Loosening his knife in its sheath, with walking stick in hand, Boaz scrambles down from the boulder and trots back the way he came to investigate.

Sure that the boys would have come through the valley where there's good forage for the sheep, he hurries toward the mouth of the canyon. Just ahead buzzards fight over something on the ground—the carcass of a dead lamb. Throwing rocks and swinging his staff Boaz manages to drive off the lumbering birds, and he crouches down to examine the grisly body.

Grabbed from behind, Boaz finds himself on his back with a knee pressed into his chest and a knife at his throat. Jair sees his face, grunts, and lets him go.

"Again!" Boaz spits out as soon as he can breathe again.

"Heard you coming." Jair speaks quietly.

"Thought you must have."

"Had to make sure it was you. If it wasn't…" Jair shrugs and scans the surrounding hilltops.

Boaz gestures at the dead lamb. "What happened?"

"Ambushed. I was on the other side of that ridge, but I was looking in the other direction." Jair points across the valley. "I'd seen signs of people in the area and have been looking for them for the last few days."

"You knew there were thieves nearby and didn't tell me?" Boaz challenges his cousin. "It might have been a good thing to mention."

"Suspected someone was out there; didn't know who," Jair said. "By the time I found out, it was too late."

Boaz looks at his cousin sharply. "Too late for what?"

Jair just turns and walks away. Boaz follows.

A little further into the narrow valley Boaz sees Jair's robe spread out on the ground and stops—he doesn't want to see what—who—is under it. Holding his breath Boaz lifts the robe to find just what he feared—the bloody bodies of the two shepherd boys, straightened out as if asleep with arms folded over their chests. "I talked to these boys yesterday at the well. You laid them out here?"

LESS THAN A WIDOW

"When I found them, they were starting to get stiff. I thought to bury them here, then I heard you coming." Jair shows no emotion, his words flat and evenly spaced. Only someone who's known him since childhood would know how tightly he was holding himself inside.

"So, we really don't know what happened or who..."

Jair interrupts. "The flock spent the night just down there—see that rock wall? This must be one of their favorite spots. There's a little curved indentation into the hill and the shepherds built a half wall. They'd made a fire last night and looks like they were cooking this morning when they were interrupted—their cooking bowl was still on the coals, broken in half."

"Sheep-stealing murderers of children!" Boaz looks down to see that he has drawn his knife and is holding it in his hand. Trembling with anger and grief, he slides it back into its sheath. "And we have no idea who they are or where they went."

"One of them had a sword—looking at the boys' wounds, I'd guess it to be of Moabite make." Jair continues to scan the valley and surrounding hills as he talks. "Now that they have what they came for, they are probably pushing for the border, but we can't be sure. We need to bury the boys and then find a defendable place to spend the night."

"Do you think they'll come back?" Boaz follows Jair's gaze.

"Best to be prepared."

The two men work to dig a shallow hole in the rocky ground, lay the boys gently side by side, and scrape a thin layer of soil over them. Next they roll and carry heavy rocks and stones, building a small cairn to protect the bodies from scavengers. By the time they have finished, the sun is on its downside slide toward the horizon.

"I'd like to spend the night high on a rocky tor so we can see or hear anyone sneaking up on us." Jair pulls a strip of dried meat leather from his pack and hands it to Boaz. "If we push hard we can reach there before nightfall. It will give us a good view in every direction."

יהוה

Jair sets a fast pace, but after the long steep climb out of the valley, he takes pity on Boaz and takes a brief rest. After he catches his breath, Boaz asks, "If I hadn't come back looking for the shepherds, what would you have done?"

"Gone after the thieves."

"What do you think you could do alone?" Boaz goes on quickly, not wanting Jair to take offense at the question that he was asking in all seriousness.

"Kill them." Jair's voice is matter-of-fact. "Get the sheep back."

"How? There have to be a number of them."

"Six, maybe more."

Boaz shakes his head in disbelief. "And you would take them on by yourself? How?"

"One at a time."

"That's a little crazy, isn't it? I don't see how…" Boaz thinks he is calling his cousin's bluff.

Jair just shrugs. "Got you, didn't I?"

Then he's off, setting a faster pace than before. The two tired men arrive at their destination before nightfall. Eating the last of the parched grain and a few dried figs, the two men stay in the shadow of tall boulders as they scan the surrounding land in all directions until Jair is satisfied that they are not being pursued.

The men wrap their robes tightly around them as the night wind whistles around and through the standing rocks. Once the sun goes down, the hilltops are cold.

"Can you teach others to do that?"

Jair is quiet so long, Boaz thinks he may have already fallen asleep. "If they want to learn."

Boaz nods—that's what he wanted to hear. "It's time to drive these murdering thieves out of our hills. You can lead us."

"Lead who?"

"I've been thinking…All of Bethlehem's flocks graze in this region. We could ask for volunteers."

Jair snorts. "Nobody will volunteer."

"No, not today," Boaz agreed. "But when we get back to Bethlehem and tell them about what has happened here, mothers will cry and fathers will wonder how they will feed their families without their sheep. They will want revenge for their dead sons. That's when they will volunteer."

"I'd like to see that."

Fatigue finally wins out—Boaz's body demanded sleep while his brain was still fully engaged—but the thoughts continued in the abstract images of a dream:

> Salma's voice comes out of the mouth of a bloody lamb
>
> propped up on its forelegs. "People resist changing the way
>
> they have always done things," Salma's voice says. "Even
>
> though your actions are meant for good, there will
>
> always be those who oppose you."

"That's dumb," Boaz snaps impatiently. "Are you trying to tell me that I shouldn't try to find a better way to do things?" A buzzard swoops down and pecks at the Salma-voiced lamb until Boaz drives it away with a stick.

"Of course you should. It's just that this conversation reminds me of one I had with your mother," the lamb continues. "My cousin Imlah had been staying with us for a few weeks, and he was constantly criticizing your mother Rahab's accent, the way she spiced the food, and just about everything that she did. I managed to ignore him until he referred to her while speaking to the servants as 'that shameless heathen.' I head-butted him across the room. Baaaaa!"

"But mother wasn't a heathen—she worshipped Yahweh!" Boaz thought of childhood taunts he himself had endured about his "mixed heritage" and slammed the stick he was still holding over a rock, breaking it in two.

The lamb laid down, its head on its stretched-out forelegs. "When I was still fuming that night, your mother said, 'People don't know what to expect from anything or anyone new or different—they get frightened, and their responses can be cruel or dismissive. You must learn to not take it personally.'"

The lamb lifts his head. "Can you believe that?" Salma's voice was full of admiration. "'Don't take it personally!' she said. But she was right. She knew people—your mother did."

The lamb didn't seem to expect an answer, which was good because Boaz couldn't think of anything to say.

"Rahab always said, 'Never be afraid to see the opportunities that Yahweh puts in front of you—just grab them and hold on.'" Salma's lamb-face smiled at me. "You're like her, you know—she was always looking for ways to make things better, too."

The lamb coughed deeply, and blood trickled from its mouth. With a deep shuddering sigh, it rolled over on its side and died.

יהוה

LESS THAN A WIDOW

Boaz woke up thinking about his parents and wishing he could talk with them about his idea and how to get the citizens of Bethlehem to work together to form an ongoing volunteer patrol.

Jair was adding some greens he had gathered to a bowl of water, grain, and dried meat he had cooking over a small fire.

Boaz sniffed in the aroma and smiled. "Remember Mother always saying, 'Worries go down better with soup than without.'"

Jair smiled—he'd been a favorite of his aunt. "She had a saying for everything. When we were fighting, she'd tell us, 'First mend yourself, then mend others.'"

"When we didn't want to get up, she'd scold, 'Quit meditating on whether the flea has a belly button.'" The men laughed at the memory, and Boaz went on. "My favorite is the one she told me when I was upset about something, 'Draw close to Yahweh, so when the walls fall down, you are held up.'"

Jair pulls the stew off of the fire to cool and kicks sand over the flames. "Two more days of hard walking to get home. We'd better eat."

INTERLUDE

RAHAB

JERICHO
1 GENERATION EARLIER

RAHAB'S STORY

I will live with the consequences of this question until the day I die: Am I a traitor or a savior?

Truth resides in both alternatives, but most people choose one side or the other.

What do I think I am? Listen to my story and when it's done we'll talk again if you still haven't made your own judgment.

One of my earliest memories is of taking a nap beneath the counter in the roughly-constructed inn near Jericho's city gates. My mother cooked vast quantities of stew and flatbread, and my father sold it alongside wine, parched grains, and figs. Father won this dilapidated building in a game of chance and, as he always told me, that moment is when life began for him and my mother and I—no longer one mouthful away from starvation, but sellers of food to others. They developed a flourishing business selling good food to soldiers guarding the city gates, traders hungry for home-cooked food after months on the trail, and locals visiting the marketplace.

Father, however, wasn't satisfied with the success of his small eatery. "Isn't Jericho the strongest city-state in the region? Doesn't it sit at the center of all the trade routes? Isn't our crescent-shaped valley more beautiful than any other with its fragrant balsams and palm trees? Hasn't the great goddess Ashtorah chosen Jericho as her home?" Father had a big dream—a dream that matched the size and importance of the great city-state of Jericho—his inn, The New Moon, would be the gathering place for all citizens of Jericho and beyond.

It wasn't long before Father hired others to do the cooking, cleaning, and animal care. He moved his wife into a home inside the inner city walls where she happily had babies and cared for them. I refused to join her, as did my brother Elon—both of us unwilling to leave the excitement of life in the inn for the boredom of crying infants and runny-nosed children. Besides, Father needed us.

As Father's business grew, so did the establishment as well as the amenities it offered: sleeping rooms, stables, and entertainment. My childhood growth was marked by the many additions to The New Moon. It was here I changed from a ungainly and awkward youth into a beautiful and desirable young woman. When the captain of the guard—who had been trying to lure me to his bed for months—finally offered to pay my father a princely sum for the services of "the graceful gazelle who serves my food," my father knew what his next expansion would be.

I was ready for him—I had known this day was coming long before my father did and had gone to Elon with a plan. After weeks of arguing with me, he finally gave in. I would agree to offer these services that Father requested and find others to join me in my new line of work, if—and only if—the money we earned was ours to keep. We would pay a small rent for private rooms that Father would add to the inn, and he would benefit from the paying customers that our services brought in. Elon would handle our money and guarantee the safety of all those involved in this new business venture.

Father swore and threatened to throw his ungrateful offspring out into the street where they belonged, but I sat quietly waiting for the storm to pass—I knew my own worth and was well acquainted with his bluster. We'd grown up listening to my father barter his way to wealth and status, and both Elon and I were quick learners.

When he finally exhausted his foul vocabulary and his anger at being bested in a bargain, I asked him quietly, "So, do we have an agreement, Father?" How he laughed—this big bear of a man—as he wrapped us in a smothering hug. "You have made me proud today, my children. You have learned your lessons well."

And so a new chapter of life began.

יהוה

I chose to enter this life, not because I wanted to be a prostitute, but to gain control of our lives—my life and Elon's. It would have been my lot anyway because Father was never one to turn down a business opportunity. The argument that finally brought Elon to agree to my scheme was that if Father agreed to our proposal, we would have our own source of income, and with it, a degree of freedom.

It wasn't hard to find others eager to enter our employ. Jericho's streets were full of women with too many mouths to feed at home, or unlucky recipients of male attentions thrown out when the men tired of their fun, or orphans, or runaways—soliciting customers on the street was how these women survived. Having a safe place to sleep, enough food, protection from unsavory customers, and small weekly payments was a better life than any of my women—and their dependents—had experienced before. Our customers appreciated our amenities as well.

Business grew quickly, and being my father's daughter, I looked for ways to expand. When a customer—a local farmer—couldn't pay his debts, I paid them. In return he repaid me with the flax that he grew each spring. He planted, weeded, and soaked the harvested flax in special processing ponds to decay the hard outer stalks. The half-rotted plants were then carted into town, and I hired women to spread them on the roof of my building to dry. Once they were dry, these same women beat them to break away the outer stalks from the grayish interior fiber. The resulting material was combed and straightened with a hackle, then separated into short fibers (used for making coarse, sturdy goods) and longer fibers for weaving into more luxurious linen cloth. We added a shaded courtyard workroom where the women spent the falls and winters spinning the raw fibers into thread and weaving the thread into linen.

Elon and I shared these duties as well: I oversaw the women's work, and he managed the sales—the customers of The New Moon provided an ample network of local and traveling merchants. We did well, and soon Elon had saved enough to marry and add rooms to our mother's house for the newly married couple.

Father—who prided himself on never missing a day at the inn—became very ill. First he insisted on staggering around, sweating profusely, until I convinced him it was bad for business. As he grew weaker, I assumed more and more of his duties, the most important of which was as a collector and disseminator of information. When he no longer had the breath to speak, I translated his whispers, until I feared that he would not recover. Elon bartered the use of an oxcart to bring Father home where Mother could nurse him.

From then on, I became the holder of secrets, of knowledge, of the latest news, and privy to the gossip of the streets, the marketplace, and the court. If the saying "Information is power" is to be believed, then I grew to be one of the most powerful people in Jericho—surely the most powerful woman.

Jericho was situated in the center of all the major trade routes, and The New Moon's early growth had come from catering to the needs of those who had been long on the road. Anyone who wanted to learn what was going on outside of Jericho, would come to the inn to hear the latest news—eventually everyone found their way to our inn. Some stories were told to all, others whispered to a select few.

Ever since I was a small girl, I had been fascinated by the tales of an unusual tribe of people, the Israelites. I perfected the art of hiding in dark corners and under tables, invisible to most, and listening to some amazing tales: how the Israelites revolted against their Egyptian masters, their escape and near slaughter by the Red Sea, how Moses called on their God to save them, and how their God separated the waters and let the Israelites through but drowned Pharaoh's army. This should have been old news—the Israelites had kept to themselves out in the desert for forty years since that event—but we continued to hear some pretty amazing reports: water suddenly flowing from a rock when the Israelites were dying of thirst, flocks of birds veering off of their migration routes just when the people needed meat, and—strangest of all—a sweet bread they called manna which they found on the ground each morning to keep them fed.

Most people laughed at these stories—saying only fools would believe them—but I was convinced they were true and hungry to hear more. About the time of Father's illness, all of the news brought into Jericho was somehow connected to the Israelites, and people were no longer laughing and scoffing. These Israelites were making their way towards Jericho and on the way had wiped out the mighty Amorite kings Sihon and Og on the other side of the Jordan River.

Everyone in Jericho was afraid that we would be the Israelites' next target, but it wasn't really their army that terrified everyone. After all, our king's army was well-trained, battle-tested, and had the finest weapons money could buy. The great city of Jericho boasted a double-walled defense, a water supply inside the city, full granaries, and capable troops prepared for an attack—we thought Jericho was impregnable.

No, it wasn't the Israelite army that everyone was afraid of, it was their God—at least that was the lesson I'd gleaned from all of the stories. It wasn't the skill or equipment of the Israelite armies, it wasn't the expertise of their military leaders, and it wasn't sheer numbers that made them victors wherever they went—they were a rather ragged, simple bunch, after all. But the Israelites didn't posture and boast about their own strength. Listen to these words that came from the mouths of the Israelites themselves, "Blessed is Israel, a people saved by Yahweh! He is the Shield who defends us, the Sword who brings triumph. Our enemies will cower before us, and we will march on their backs."

The question on the lips of the people of Jericho was, "When are they coming to annihilate us?" Not, "Will they come?" but "When will they come?"

The question in my mind—that never reached my lips—was, "How can I learn more about the Israelite God who is greater than any of the other gods?"

יהוה

They were just two more unwashed merchants in town to sell their wares—pots made for common use, not lovely design. After a successful day in the marketplace, they made their way to The New Moon for a meal and a room for the night—at least that was the story they told me, although one of them rarely said a word. The tall man—the one who did the talking—had an erect posture and distinct speech that didn't quite match his rough clothes or his stated line of work. This aroused my curiosity.

"If they're potters, then I'm Ashtorah's high priestess," I thought as I watched them sitting at a corner table, backs to the wall, eyes down, but aware of everything around them. I brought a meal to them myself, and we chatted about the recent harvest, the busyness of the marketplace, and the heavy security at the city gates.

I was not the only one who noticed them. My suspicions were confirmed as I was making the rounds through the main room from table to table greeting people—following in the footsteps of my father—and one of the off-duty guards made a less-than-stealthy exit out of the side door without finishing his wine.

The unlikely potters also noticed his hurried exit, and made their way to the door where I intercepted them. "Leaving so soon?" I asked loudly as I walked with them to the door, and the tall man nodded without looking my way. Once out the door I pointed in the direction of the gate while speaking quietly so only they could hear, "You have been recognized as Israelites—soldiers will be here soon." Both men looked at me sharply, and at the tall man's gesture, the other backed away down the street leading to the city gates.

"You might make it through the gate, but the soldiers will catch you before you've gone far. I can help you." I smiled and continued to gesture as though I was giving them directions.

"Why should we trust you?" Although his voice was quiet, the challenge was clear in his voice. His eyes never left my face, as though he would see the truth written there.

"Go past the second building to the alley and climb the stairs to the roof—don't let anyone see you. I will meet you there as soon as I can." With a smile, I stepped back and waved as they turned, shouldered their packs, and headed toward the gate. "You'll have to hurry," I called to their retreating backs. "The gates close at dusk."

I wanted to brush past the inn's guests and hurry through the kitchen courtyard to my room, but I made myself chat with more guests, even sitting down at one table for an extended conversation. Finally I left Elon in charge and strolled through the courtyard where the cooks prepared food, and beyond to my personal living quarters. Once inside my bed chamber, I clambered up the ladder that led to a trapdoor which opened onto the roof.

The smell hit me as soon as I pushed the trapdoor open—a musty, overwhelming, tickle-in-the-back-of-the-throat odor of stagnant water and rot. Just a few days earlier, the women had stacked the wet and decaying flax plants on the roof to dry, leaving only narrow walkways. With a scarf pressed over my nose and mouth, I looked around—unsure whether I hoped the men had followed my instructions or had taken their chances at making it out of the gate.

"Is anyone here?" I spoke softly. There was no answer, but I waited anyway, surprised at the strength of my disappointment. Just as I finally admitted that they hadn't trusted me and turned to go back downstairs, a hand grabbed my arm and spun me around. There, just inches from my own, was the face of the tall man. "Now what?" he growled.

"You will need to lie down here and cover yourselves with the flax," I said when I recovered from my fright. "I need to get back to the inn—I don't want people to notice my absence—and the king's soldiers will be here soon. I will tell them that you left Jericho, and perhaps they will believe me. If not, they will search all our rooms for you, but they will not want to spend much time looking around up here."

"Nor would I," the Israelite said with the hint of a smile.

"I will come back after we close for the night," I told them as I made my way through the trapdoor and down the ladder. After stopping in my room to remove any traces of flax from the hem of my garments, I made my way back to the inn.

I was talking with a silk merchant when they arrived—soldiers blocked every exit before the captain entered. He sat down across the table from me and laid his hand palm up on the table, watching me with a smile on his face until I placed my hand in his. As he closed his fingers around mine, he said the same words that began every conversation we ever had, "Rahab, you are as beautiful tonight as you were the first time I saw you."

I patted his hand with my free one. "My dear Captain, what brings you to my inn this evening? Would you like your usual room?"

Letting go of my hand, the burly man rose to his feet. "I'm afraid not, for I am here on official business for the king."

I stood up and widened my eyes with surprise. "Official business! For the king!" It wouldn't be easy to fool the captain. He was a shrewd man who had achieved his rank early and held on to it by being extremely good at his job—but artifice was a skill I practiced every day.

With the ghost of a smile at my attempt at impressed naiveté, he spoke in his official voice. "The king sends this message: 'Bring out the men who came to you to stay the night in your house. They're spies from Israel, come to spy out the whole country.'"

"I thought there was something strange about those two. They said they were potters, but, I don't know, they just didn't seem like potters to me…"

"Rahab," the captain interrupted forcefully. "Where are they?"

"Captain, I'm so sorry, they paid for a room for the night, but they left just before dusk," I frowned as I shook my head. "I didn't think they were who they said they were, and I should have said something to one of your men who were here tonight, but it never occurred to me that they might be spies. Israelites, you said?" The gooseflesh that covered my arms was real—I'm sure that fear had also caused that same reaction in many others who were sitting quietly straining to hear our conversation.

"They didn't leave that long ago—shortly before dusk, I think." I looked around the room for confirmation. "Yes, that's when it was. I remember telling them that they would have to hurry because the gates would be closing soon."

The captain met the glances of my customers with eyebrows raised. When many nodded their heads in agreement, he turned back to me. "Did they say where they were going?"

I thought for a minute. "No, I don't think so. They really said very little—oh, wait. They asked where they could fill up their waterskins, and I told them where the well was, but I don't know if they stopped there or not. They seemed anxious to be on their way."

The captain signaled to his men and headed to the door. "They can't be too far ahead of us. We'll find them before the night is over."

The room erupted with noise as the soldiers hurried down the street toward the city gate. "Israelite spies!" "That's what the captain said." "What do you think they were doing here?" "What do you think, you empty-headed fool! They're coming here." "Who's coming here?" "The Israelite army! Why else would their spies be in the city?"

The people whipped each other into a frenzy—the attack we had all been dreading was about to happen—and it didn't take long for our inn to empty. Anyone who had a place to stay inside the interior wall rushed up the hill, through the gates, and into the city proper. The less fortunate who lived in the poorly-built structures between the two city walls, locked themselves into their hiding places.

For the first time that I could remember, people left food on their plates and wine in their glasses. Elon stepped to the door and whistled. A few minutes later a few ragged boys appeared on our doorstep. "Bring your friends," Elon told them and gestured toward the tables. "Tonight they will have full stomachs." As more ragged street children crept silently in the front door of the inn to wolf down the leftovers, I patted my brother on the arm. "Elon, you have a good heart."

I slipped out the back door, made a stop in the storeroom off of the empty courtyard, and then into my room where I bolted the door. I didn't know if it was excitement or fear that made my legs shake and my palms sweat as I climbed the ladder to the roof.

יהוה

"Stay hidden," I whispered as I walked around the roof looking for anyone who might be able to see us. As I suspected, extra soldiers were patrolling the inner walls above us—the spies would have to sneak unseen down to my room. "I'll distract the guards while you climb down the ladder."

Going to the far corner of the roof, I slowly pulled my outer dress over my head. Clad only in my shift, I stretched my arms over my head, lifting my hair from my shoulders as if to cool off in the night breeze. Extending my arms to the sides, I spun in a slow twirl as I listened for the scrape of feet on the ladder rungs. I shook out my overdress and folded it slowly, pausing to stretch. With a languid wave at the leering guards, I strolled to the trapdoor and pulled it shut behind me as I descended.

LESS THAN A WIDOW

Crouched in the corner, knives at the ready, the two men relaxed as I closed the trapdoor. I stopped halfway down the ladder, and moved my hand in a spinning motion. Flushing, they turned their backs to me as I made my way to the floor and redressed in my outer garment.

"Wine?" I poured three glasses, and the men waited for me to drink before tasting theirs. Although they had sheathed their knives, the men remained alert and ready to bolt at any sign of betrayal. When the tall man finished his wine, he asked, "Why are you helping us?"

How could I answer this question, the one that had been screaming in my mind ever since I impulsively warned them when they left the inn? I closed my eyes and tried to organize my whirling thoughts. "I know that your God has given this land to you. We're all very afraid—everyone in the whole country feels hopeless."

I glanced up, and the taller of the two met my gaze in the dim lamplight. He gestured for me to continue. "Since I was a little girl, I've heard how your great God dried up the waters of the Red Sea before you when you left Egypt and drowned Pharaoh's armies right behind your people. And now, everyone is talking about what your God did to the two Amorite kings east of the Jordan, Sihon and Og—that you put them under a holy curse and destroyed everything. Are these stories true?"

At his nod, I continued. "When we heard these things our hearts melted in fear—the wind was knocked out of us. Who can find the courage to fight after hearing such tales? And all because of you Israelites, you and God, your supreme God, God of the heavens above and God of the earth below."

I stepped closer, and just inches from his face I made my plea. "I showed you mercy; now show my family mercy. Swear to me by God—your supreme God—and give me some tangible proof that when you conquer Jericho, you will guarantee the lives of my father and mother, my brothers and sisters—everyone connected with my family. Please, sirs, I ask you to save our souls from death!"

"Our own lives will act as a guarantee for your safety," the man agreed. "But, I warn you, don't tell anyone our business. If you don't betray us, we will keep our promise and be kind to you when the Lord gives us the land."

"I won't betray you." I whispered.

"Then we will keep our promise," the tall man replied.

"Never show fear or weakness" had been the code I've lived by, the rule for behavior that had kept me alive and helped me grow my business, but suddenly my body chose that time to betray me. Black spots appeared in my vision, and I couldn't catch my breath. I wasn't aware of being held up, until my heart resumed its steady rhythm. I pulled away and briskly told them my plan.

"My rooms are on the outside wall, and that window opens to the outside of the city walls. We can tie this rope, and you will be able to escape through the window." I showed them the food I had retrieved from the storeroom, and

RAHAB : JERICHO

they stowed it in their packs. "The soldiers will be searching by all the shallow fords across the Jordan, so you must run for the hills instead so they won't find you. Hide there for three days—that will give your pursuers time to return to Jericho. By then it should be safe to get on your way."

We secured the rope, and the quiet man stuck his head out the window looking for any observers. After the guards passed on the wall above, he swung out of the window and lowered himself to the ground.

"What is your name?" The tall man's question startled me. "I would know whose family it is that we have promised to keep alive."

"I am called Rahab."

"And I am Salma, of the house of Judah," he replied gravely. "In order to keep this oath you made us swear, here is what you must do."

Salma removed a red cord from around his waist. "Hang this red rope out of the window through which you let us down. When our army comes against Jericho, you must gather your entire family with you in your house—it is important that they all be in this house. Any who go out the doors of your house into the street and are killed, it's their own fault—we aren't responsible. But for everyone within the house we take full responsibility. If anyone lays a hand on one of them, it's our fault." He held my arm in a strong grip. "You understand?"

I nodded, and he continued with a final warning. "If you tell anyone—anyone—of our business here, the oath you made us swear is canceled—we're no longer responsible. Their deaths will be on your head."

"I accept your terms. I will do all that you have said." Salma released my arm and looked out the window, waiting for the guards to pass before he joined his companion below.

When he made it safely to the ground below, Salma looked up and waved before disappearing into the darkness. I untied the rope and replaced it with the red cord he had given me.

יהוה

I was used to keeping secrets—a skill I had learned from the cradle tucked into a corner in the inn, growing and serving, running errands for my father and his customers, and later as I ran my own business and gradually took over running the inn. But this was different. If anyone discovered my dealings with the Israelite spies, I wouldn't live until the Israelites came to destroy our city—the punishment for treason was a cruel and prolonged death. But how would I ever be able to persuade my family members and others in my household that they needed to stay in my house when the attack finally came unless I told them the truth about why they couldn't leave?

Street people are suspicious, independent thinkers whose abilities to escape have been key to preserving their lives. My family started out on the street, and while the youngest children hadn't experienced that terror and hunger, they had been raised by parents who knew danger only too well. The same was true of those who came from the streets and now worked for me in the inn and in my flax business—they, too, were part of my family. I spent anxious days wondering how to convince them to hide in my house—and my thoughts spun in the same circle over and over again. "I will need to play on their terror, maximize their fears, and manipulate all the people that I love. I can't think of any other way to save them."

As it turned out, the inhabitants of Jericho—including my family—didn't need my help to imagine their destruction and feel their hearts and spirits melt with terror. There was only one conversation on everyone's lips from the time the Captain of the Guard returned without capturing the spies until we saw the Israelite armies for the first time.

Imagine being an inhabitant of Jericho for the five weeks prior to being surrounded by the Israelites. Imagine hearing how their God sent plagues from heaven upon the Egyptians but spared the Israelites. Imagine the retelling of the stories of their God parting the Red Sea and completely destroying the most powerful army on earth. Imagine hearing how this God brought water out of a rock and put food on the ground to keep this people alive in the desert for forty years. Imagine hearing that this God now brought this people—the dreaded Israelites—closer to Jericho and the tales of the few survivors from the complete destruction of mighty kings and their cities on the other side of the Jordan. And now—our scouts reported on what they saw with their own eyes—this God caused the Jordan River itself to stop flowing just long enough for two million people to come across on dry ground. The dreaded Israelites built their latest camp three miles away from Jericho and were eating from our fields, vineyards, and flocks.

Jericho's city gates were locked—in both the outer and inner walls. Soldiers maintained positions on top of the inner twelve-foot-high wall, which was wide enough for five soldiers to march abreast. All of Jericho was in siege mode even though there were no enemy armies in sight. The people—from royalty to beggars—cowered behind the city walls and prayed to our gods that somehow this terror from the desert would pass us by.

My invitation was given this way. "If we are to going to fight for our very lives and most probably die, then let us gather with those we love to fight and die together."

Acceptance came quickly—when the Israelite army came into view, my friends and family agreed to take refuge in the inn. They believed that we would end our days together. The distress I felt at not being able to reassure them that their lives would be spared was mistaken for anguish at our impending doom.

יהוה

RAHAB : JERICHO

The city of Jericho was prepared for a siege—for battering rams, raining arrows, rocks and pots of burning oil lobbed into the city by siege engines, wall-scaling ladders swarming with soldiers, and the terrifying battle cries of an invading army. We knew how to fight that kind of battle, and had it been any army except that of the Israelites and their almighty God, we would have fought confidently, sure that we would be victorious as we had been so many times before.

The sentries yelled at the first sight of the approaching army, and warning bells sounded the alarm. Shutters were closed, doors were slammed and locked, and soon the streets were empty of people. We all squeezed into the inn—my father and mother, brothers and sisters with their spouses and children, and my workers who sometimes felt more like family to me than my own blood kin. And we waited for the noise of battle.

All we heard was the unending bleating of rams' horns. We coughed as the feet of hundreds of thousands of marching feet filled the air with dust. But nothing else except the yells of our soldiers as they taunted the Israelites—there were no responding cries.

My curiosity finally overpowered my caution, and I ventured out onto the roof and peeked over the bulwark. Confused, I called Elon, and he joined me on the roof. We watched as the smell of decaying plants mixed with the dusty air and saw soldiers marching by—row after row, battalion after battalion—all dressed for battle, but never looking at the city or uttering a word. The only sound was the muffled beat of their feet on the earth and the eerie blasting of the horns that grew farther and farther in the distance.

We kept watch on the roof until the last of the soldiers marched out of sight. Our family peppered us with questions when we rejoined them, but Elon and I had no answers. The strange sounds of the horns and the silence of the soldiers, who seemed so intent on marching that they ignored the city they surrounded, was peculiarly unnerving to all of us. I'd watched the Captain of the Guard at his station on the inner wall above the city gates. He was surrounded by other military officers, and their body language spoke of confusion and frustration. How can you fight an enemy who doesn't approach, doesn't speak, and doesn't fight?

The second day was the same as the first, as were the third and fourth, and the citizens of Jericho displayed the full gamut of reactions to this outlandish attack—if that's what it was. By the fourth day, only half of the townspeople locked themselves in their homes while the Israelites paraded around our walls. It wasn't life as usual—tensions were high, and bickering and fights erupted in the streets as people worried about the underlying intentions of this strange parade.

Armed Israeli soldiers led the way. Next paraded seven priests continually blowing rams' horn, and they were followed by more priests carrying a carved box with golden statues of winged men on top of it. Rings on the box were threaded with long poles, and the priests carried these poles on their shoulders—no one touched or went near the box. And the procession repeated itself, the armed men quietly marching behind this strange box—day after dusty day until six days had passed.

Keeping all of my extended family in the house almost proved to be an impossible task. If my father had been able to make the walk up the hill to his home, he would have been the first to leave the inn. I found myself giving thanks under my breath to the God of the Israelites for the illness that had weakened him or he would have taken my mother and my siblings who still lived at home with them. Without Elon's strong support, many of my brothers and my sisters' husbands would have insisted on going back to their homes as well. But Elon was the eldest son, and so his words carried much weight. However, of my work crews, only those women with children and no husbands remained with us. Even so, we were crowded, tempers were short, and everyone kept asking, "How long can this go on?"

The alarm bells rang their warning shortly after dawn on the seventh day. After six days of the same routine, the people of Jericho grew alarmed when the parade of soldiers and priests kept on marching around Jericho. By the third time the ragged, silent soldiers marched around the perimeter, the streets started to empty again.

Jericho's soldiers—weary and bad-tempered after days of readying themselves for a battle that never happened—began to taunt and jeer the marchers.

Just when we thought the lines of quiet marchers would never end, the sound of rams' horns stopped briefly and then sounded together in one long blast. This must have been the signal the Israelite army had been awaiting for seven days—they shouted, beat their swords on their shields, and caterwauled their most horrifying battle cries. Our soldiers responded in kind until the ground began to shake and the bricks and rocks from both the inner and outer walls rained down on the cities.

I can't talk about what happened after that, for we huddled in fear in the inn—crying and moaning in fear. All I know is what I heard, buildings caving in, people screaming, soldiers yowling their battle cries, swords clanging against swords, the crackle of fire, running footsteps... Finally, a pounding on the door and a voice yelling my name over and over.

I crawled to the door, and the pounding came again. "What do you want?" I managed to yell.

"Rahab, open the door," the voice yelled. "It is Salma of the house of Judah. The fire is getting close—you all need to come with me now or you will burn to death."

Herding frightened people to safety when they believe that soldiers have come to kill them almost proved to be an impossible task. Finally, I convinced Elon to pick up his children and pull his wife out the door into the soldiers' arms. When the others saw that they weren't harmed and that the soldiers were actually leading them safely out of the city, there was such a great rush to the door that we almost trampled each other to get out and away from the horror that had once been Jericho.

I was the last one to leave, and I almost didn't make it. I looked around, and there was nothing left standing that wasn't engaged in roaring flames. Choking, stunned by the devastation, I ran back into the inn—I didn't know what I was doing. But Salma chased after me and tried to talk me into coming with him. When he realized that all my reason had fled with my family, Salma picked me up, threw me over his shoulder, and ran out of the inn and out of Jericho.

יהוה

I opened my eyes for the first time two days later, and I was with my family in a tent near the Israelite camp. My family has made their homes with the Israelites ever since that day.

My home was with Salma, of the house of Judah. We settled in Bethlehem.

ELEVEN
(CONTINUED)

During the long dusty miles Boaz and Jair grow the patrol idea from a possibility to a plan.

In order to winnow out any weaknesses, Jair plays the role of a city elder asking questions, while Boaz defends the plan. "How will you get everyone to participate?" Jair demands. Boaz replies, "Every family that has sheep or goats will be required to volunteer one able-bodied man per every ten animals they send out to graze. The volunteers will be trained and take their place on a rotating schedule for patrol duty. If for some reason someone cannot fulfill the volunteer requirement, they can pay another to take their place."

"Is there anyone in Bethlehem can possibly organize and train these volunteers?" Jair asks with a sly smile.

"I'm so glad you asked," Boaz answers sweeping his arm toward the man plodding next to him. "Jair, a fine man who is well-regarded in Bethlehem, has only recently returned home after serving as a soldier for ten years. Surely Yahweh has brought him home to us at a time when we really need a man of his experience and leadership abilities."

"How will he be paid?"

Boaz claps his hands together once. "I was waiting for this question, because my mother had just the perfect saying: 'Do not be wise in words—be wise in deeds.'"

Boaz clears his throat, and speaks in the deep, sonorous voice of an important man. "We can no longer stay safe behind our city's walls while our sons and daughters are murdered and our flocks are stolen. I firmly believe that having trained men patrol our grazing lands is the right thing to do, so not only will I volunteer to be part of the first group to go out to protect our animals and people, but for the remainder of this grazing season, I will pay Jair a fair wage and offer him the hospitality of my home. After that the city elders will meet again to develop a fair means of payment from those who have flocks."

Jair applauds. "How can anyone say no?"

That afternoon they top the last ridge on their journey and see Bethlehem spread out in the valley below. "We will be home before nightfall," Boaz notices and spends the remaining hours planning. "Tonight our people will mourn.

LESS THAN A WIDOW

Tomorrow morning will be the right time to meet with the city elders to share our plan. It has to be tomorrow—if I wait any longer, I will lose momentum."

He practices his speech. "Mothers are crying out for their children. Fathers wonder how they will feed their families without their sheep, and they call for retribution. I propose that instead of empty revenge, we provide protection for the living. If we all work together, we can drive these murdering thieves out of our hills. If a man from every household will volunteer in turn, we can share our weapons, polish our skills, and protect our loved ones, our flocks, and our lands..."

RUTH
רוּת

MOAB TO BETHLEHEM
2 YEARS LATER

TWELVE

Mahlon's muscles bulge as he drags the heavy bag of clay soil into the courtyard. His wavy curly hair sticks to his forehead, which is streaked with red mud from pushing his hair out of his eyes. He frowns toward the doorway where Ruth is watching from the shadows, and she quickly steps into the sunlight with a water jar.

"Slaves shouldn't keep their masters waiting," she giggles to herself.

Mahlon points at a large open bucket. "Not quite half full."

Mahlon's in charge of mixing the clay, and he takes his work very seriously. He really doesn't have to tell Ruth what to do—she's been his assistant since Elimelech turned this important step in pottery-making over to him—they work well together. Ruth adds clumps of clay soil into the water as Mahlon stirs it with a wooden paddle. Ruth watches Mahlon closely to see when he's ready for more soil, but that's really just an excuse for something she finds herself doing all the time anyway.

Ruth fits a loosely woven, flat-bottomed basket over an empty bucket, and Mahlon pours the clay slush through this sieve. After emptying each dipperload, they move the excess debris from the top of the sieve to an extra bucket. There are too many rocks in this batch—Mahlon's not happy with the small amount of watered clay.

Tired from working at his potter's wheel in the shade of a bower, Elimelech straightens and stretches his back as he absently rubs his chest, streaking his shift with wet clay.

"I can't keep going all the time like I used to," Elimelech thinks disgustedly. He signals for his youngest son to take over. Killion makes most of the simple bowls and plates now—a job that matches his impatience with prolonged, meticulous hours at the potter's wheel. He prefers the marketplace full of noise and plenty of people to bargain with. Mahlon is a creative perfectionist, so Elimelech depends on him to do any specialty designs.

Elimelech continues to rub his chest and grimaces as he looks into the full debris bucket.

Sitting back on his heels, Mahlon points to the bag of clay soil. "This is the best of what we have left in the storeroom—a lot of rocks and a little clay. We're going to have to find another site soon with better quality clay.

LESS THAN A WIDOW

The pain hits hard and fast. Elimelech groans, clutches his chest, drops to his knees, and vomits. Mahlon drops the dipper, hurries to his father's side, and eases him into a sitting position.

"Abi, are you hurt?" Mahlon kneels and puts his arms around Elimelech's shoulders. The rhythmic hum of the spinning potter's wheel dies out as Killion stops his foot in alarm. "Abi?"

Naomi steps into the doorway, still holding the grinding stone. "What's wrong?"

Elimelech groans again and falls to his side on the ground. Mahlon puts his arms under his shoulders. "Help me move him."

Ruth moves to pick up his feet, but Killion lets the potter's wheel fall and pushes her aside. They lay Elimelech gently on a mat in the shade. Naomi's hands cradle his face as she calls out. "My husband—Ba'ali. Answer me. Ba'ali."

Ruth dips a cloth in clear water and hands it to Mahlon. He smoothes his father's face. "Abi. Father. Wake up."

There is no response except for one last shuddering breath.

"No!" Naomi reaches her hands up to heaven. "Yahweh, let him live." She smothers Elimelech's face with kisses. "Ba'ali. Stay with me."

Mahlon puts his arm around his mother and hugs her to him. "Mother, he is gone."

And the wailing begins.

יהוה

Everyone is trying to adjust.

Months pass, and Naomi is no longer wailing, but she doesn't sing any more—and she barely talks. At least she is eating again. She grinds the grain, makes the bread, and cooks the food. She does all of her usual tasks, but it's as if the part of her that contained joy died with Elimelech. Ruth feels as if she has lost both of them, and the bad dream returns to torture her sleep more often than it has in years.

Most days Killion sells pottery in the booth in the marketplace. He has a real talent for sales, and the business is growing. His happy smile disappears as soon as he enters our gloomy household—it feels wrong to him to smile when his mother is nearby.

Mahlon's face has gone from serious to grim. He seldom looks up from his work as he spends most of his time at the potter's wheel now. Even so, there is a gracefulness to even the most useful pottery that he crafts. He's making oil lamps today, reciting the Torah as he works, his feet spinning the wheel in rhythm to his chanting voice.

Ruth prepares clay—a dirty, lengthy process—thinking, "I wish you could just dig it out of the ground, and it would be ready to make into a pot.

A few days ago she had added water to it, put it through a sieve, and set it out to dry. Today, stripped down to her shift, she works the clay with her feet—dancing on the slippery mound. The clay slime itches as it dries white on her brown skin and molds her dress to her body. Fold; mound; dance. Fold; mound; dance. Ruth closes her eyes, feels the clay under her heels and digs in her toes. Stomp, jump, and twist—she moves to the rhythm of the wheel and Mahlon's chanting voice until the clay feels just right.

Ruth dances the clay dance to the rhythm…that has stopped. Keeping her eyes closed, Ruth stands still and moves her focus from her toes back to her ears. The wheel isn't moving; Mahlon isn't chanting. She peeks through slitted eyes—he is just sitting there staring at her. The lump of clay on his wheel is lopsided and drying out.

Ruth doesn't know what to do, where to look, what to say. She drops her eyes. "He must think I'm a fool!" she thinks to herself as he gets up, lays down his potter's wheel, washes his hands, and climbs the stairs to join Naomi on the roof top.

"What's wrong? I don't understand. Is he mad at me? Did I do something wrong?" Ruth has no more answers to her mind's questions now than she has for the last few weeks. "We've worked well together since I came to this house. Now when I come into a room he either won't look at me or won't stop looking, or he leaves or tells me to go do something somewhere else. Is he angry because I watch him? I am a slave—a slave who watches her master. Have I offended him?"

"The clay won't take care of itself." Ruth tries to distract herself from worrying by forming it into balls to dry in the sun, large and small and some in between. Then she goes to the storage room and cleans it top to bottom.

Naomi is still on the roof with Mahlon, and they signal for Killion to join them as soon as he gets home. Ruth makes the evening meal hoping the smell of food will bring them down the stairs, but only Naomi makes her way down from the roof. Without saying a word she gathers up the food and puts it onto a tray. When Ruth moves to help her, she shakes her head, and carries the evening meal up the stairs.

Ruth sweeps the courtyard, lays out the sleeping mats, banks the fire, and locks the gate to the street. Finally it is too dark to do anything more, and she wraps herself in her blanket and pretends to sleep. Pretense eventually becomes reality, and thoughts become dreams:

> The man-monster's face, chest, and arms are painted
>
> red and black in ghastly swirls that look like winking eyes
>
> as he moves. He throws himself to the ground in front

LESS THAN A WIDOW

of the blazing altar, then leaps to his feet and points a

large knife to the sky, an inhuman scream coming from

his open mouth. The gong sounds again as he cuts

his chest and lifts the dripping knife to the east,

to the west, to the north, and to the south.

The drums begin the rhythm, and the people

chant, swelling louder and louder:

"Chemosh. Chemosh. Chemosh. Chemosh."

The priest steps to the table where the little girl lies.

"Noooo!" My screams are enveloped

by the roar of the crowd.

When Ruth struggles back to consciousness, Naomi's arms are around her, and she croons as she smoothes the unruly dark curls off of Ruth's sweaty forehead. "Hush, now. It's only a dream. Don't be afraid."

Ruth can't stop shaking as her heart continues to beat to the drum's awful rhythm.

"Lie down now and sleep." Naomi covers Ruth with the blanket and sings a lullaby—one she has sung to soothe her during so many dark nights:

"Numi numi yaldati, numi numi nim:

Sleep, my little girl, sleep."

"Numi numi chemdati, numi numi nim:

Sleep, my darling one, sleep."

RUTH : MOAB

Love and security flow through Naomi's voice, and comforts Ruth as it did when she was a child. Gradually she slips back into a deep sIeep and doesn't wake again until Naomi touches her face early the next morning.

Sitting next to her, Naomi's lips are smiling, but her cheeks glisten with moisture. Ruth sits up quickly.

"Did I sleep late?"

"You didn't. But get up now; there is much to do."

"Is something wrong?"

Naomi hesitates and then pats Ruth's hand. "No, nothing's wrong. But we have much to prepare for."

"Why? What's happening?"

"My sons are getting married next week."

Ruth chokes and gasps for air. Her mind screams, "Mahlon is getting married! And Killion. Did everybody know about this except me? And their wives won't want me here; I know how that works. Are they going to sell me? Will I have to get everything ready, serve at the wedding, and then be sold?"

"Ruth." Naomi's sharp voice seems to be coming from a long distance. "Ruth!"

"I can't stay and talk to her. I can't!" Without speaking, Ruth grabs the empty water jar and runs all the way to the well. To her surprise, Orpah's waiting for her there. Ruth doesn't want to talk to her either, but when she turns to leave, Orpah grabs her arm.

"Ruth, what is the matter with you?"

"Leave me alone."

"You're crying! Are you crying?"

"Let go." Ruth tries to pull her arm out of her friend's grasp, but Orpah hangs on.

"I thought you'd be happy. Don't you want to marry Mahlon?"

"Let go of my...what did you say?"

"Don't you know? Mahlon paid my bride price this morning, and..."

"Wait, what? You're marrying Mahlon?"

"Ruth, come and sit down." Orpah starts to laugh but stops when she sees the look on Ruth's face. "You really have no idea, do you?"

"Orpah, just tell me what you're talking about."

"I will if you will listen. Come sit down with me."

So Orpah tells Ruth the whole story. "Killion wants to marry me, but Mahlon is the oldest so he needs to get married before Killion does. Another problem is money—the family doesn't have enough to pay for two brides—so Killion told Mahlon to marry you because everyone can see that he's in love with you anyway. All the two of them had to do was convince Naomi. Mahlon talked with my father and negotiated a bride price so I can marry Killion, and it was settled."

LESS THAN A WIDOW

"I'm not going to be a slave any more," Ruth marvels silently. "I will be a bride."

And everything happens just the way Orpah said it would.

THIRTEEN

TWO YEARS LATER

Business is good—too good for Mahlon whose days at the potter's wheel stretch longer and longer. He groans as he sits down on his sleeping mat, flexes a stiff arm, and rotates his neck back and forth. Ruth fetches the small bowl she's been warming by the fire and kneels beside him. Dipping her hand into the bowl, she rubs the warm oil into Mahlon's shoulders, her hands dark against his freckled skin. Under Ruth's skilled hands, Mahlon's muscles slowly release their tension.

"Mahlon means weakling—Naomi told me how afraid she was that her tiny baby, born too early, wouldn't live long. But he's no weakling any more…" Ruth stops that train of thought firmly. "Don't get distracted yet," she tells herself. You still need to tell him your idea."

Moving in front of him, Ruth takes his hand in her lap, dips her other hand in the oil again, and kneads the stiffness from his strong fingers, palm, and up his arm. She does the same thing to the other arm.

"Lie down so I can work on your neck."

Mahlon's eyes close and his body relaxes as she works.

"Feel good?"

"Unhh."

Ruth gives a tight neck muscle a little extra squeeze.

"Ow."

"Oh, good, you're still awake." Ruth bends over and kisses the tip of his nose. "Don't you want to know what this is?"

"I know what it is: pleasure." Mahlon pulls her face down and kisses her.

"That, too, but I meant the oil I'm using."

He grins. He's teasing, but at least he's listening.

"It's my grandmother's recipe." Ruth holds up her oily fingers and wiggles them.

"Can't be—it doesn't smell like old goat."

"I've never heard you complain when it stops the pain."

"That part's great. It's the sheep following me around that gets a little annoying."

Ruth playfully slaps his shoulder. "Well, if you don't want to know…" She gets up and picks up the bowl of oil.

Mahlon reaches out one hand and grabs her ankle. "Where are you going?"

"I'll just put this away if you're not interested."

Mahlon groans as he sits up. "Oh, I'm interested, all right." He raises his eyebrows and rubs his thumb up and down her leg.

Ruth stamps her foot. The other foot—not the one he's holding onto.

He laughs and pats the mat next to him. "Come, sit down, and tell me about it. Is this the secret project that you sold one of my pilgrim flasks for?"

"I needed to buy the ingredients." Ruth moves the bowl out of harm's way and sits down beside her husband.

"How much did you get?"

"Enough. Killion isn't the only one who can barter, you know. Don't you feel better?"

Mahlon moves his shoulder and arm and rotates his neck. "And here I thought it was it was just your skillful hands."

"Of course, that's part of it."

If her mind had a foot, she would stamp it. "It's so hard to have a serious conversation when he's like this."

Ruth takes a deep breath and blows out the irritation, choosing her words carefully. "I used the same ingredients for grandma's balm, but put it in a different base and added some spices that…"

Mahlon laughs and kisses her nose. "You are so much fun to tease. There's more to your plan, so tell it to me."

Ruth is thinking, "Finally!" but what she says is, "I think we should sell it as healing balm, and put it in your pilgrim flasks."

"Your oil? In my flasks?"

"When people are hurting, they want something to take the pain away. This works, and the flasks are just the right size."

"And now it smells good."

I rub my finger against my thumb near his nose. "People will buy it, and I bet they'll pay more for it if it's in one of your beautiful flasks. Like this one."

Mahlon takes the flask from Ruth and turns it in his hands, studying it. "Maybe a little smaller with a longer neck. A tapered stopper and a flat bottom to sit on a shelf…"

Ruth smiles as she thinks, "He's forgotten I'm even here," and watches his face as the design develops in his head. Eventually, the picture implanted in his brain, Mahlon leans over and taps her forehead with his index finger. "I'm in trouble now. What other plans do you have for me rolling around in that head of yours?"

"Now that you mention it, you could add a dipper to the top of the water jars. And how about a lamp that…"

RUTH : MOAB

"Stop! Stop!"

Mahlon pulls Ruth to him and kisses her full on the mouth. "Would it be possible for you to only tell me one new idea per week?"

"How about two?"

Mahlon rubs his arms to get some of the oil on his hands and rubs her neck. He kisses her eyelids and sighs.

"Abi knew."

Even though Ruth is ready for the kissing to continue, her curiosity wins out. "What do you mean?"

"I was supposed to be wedging clay, but Killion threw some at me, and we started wrestling. We smashed a pot. Father was so angry. He grabbed my arm, and I thought…I don't know what I thought, and then he just left."

Ruth waits quietly—Mahlon is a slow, careful talker, and there's no rushing him. He hasn't told her this story before, so Ruth swallows her questions and waits.

"Abi didn't remember taking his money pouch, but it was in his hand when he saw your father beating you. He only had the four gold coins, and he threw them on the ground right next to you. Abi said Yahweh meant for him to be there in time to save you, that Yahweh must have had a special reason for bringing you to us."

"Do you believe that?"

"I do." Mahlon pulls his wife to him and kisses her again—slow, long, and hard. "And I think this is part of it."

Ruth leans into his embrace. "I have to agree," is her last clear thought for a while.

יהוה

THREE YEARS LATER

Mahlon and Killion are thrilled by the expansion of their business. The whole family works hard to keep up with the growing demand, and Naomi responds positively to their enthusiasm. Orpah and Ruth love their husbands and are loved in return, but as the years pass without the addition of babies, their contentment is threatened.

"I see less of Killion than I did before we got married." Orpah has been complaining since the men went into the hills to dig for clay two days ago.

"I'd say you see more of him now, if you know what I mean." Ruth wiggles her eyebrows and grins, but her attempt at humor falls on deaf ears.

"And now I'm stuck doing all your work, too." Orpah puts her hands on her hips and glares at Ruth. "I don't see why you get to be the one to sell our pottery in the market."

"Because that is what Mahlon decided." Naomi's voice is sharp; her patience growing thin with the constant bickering of her daughters-in-law.

"Orpah, I'm sorry." Ruth stops talking when she sees the tears in Orpah's eyes and realizes that there is more to this than who will be selling pottery in the market.

Naomi notices, too, and puts her hand on Orpah's shoulder. "I can bake the bread myself. Why don't you take the day off and go visit your sisters?"

"That would be great, wouldn't it? I could play with their children, and listen to Sabeen complain about how uncomfortable it is to be with child in this heat." Orpah can't hold back the pain in any longer. She covers her face and sobs, and Naomi put her arms around her.

"Do you think we are cursed?" Ruth gasps.

When Orpah says the words out loud that she's been too afraid to even think in case they are true, Ruth's mind races with possibilities. "Maybe Yahweh is jealous of the idols Orpah has hidden in her things. Maybe Mahlon wasn't supposed to marry me—that wasn't part of Yahweh's plan—and He is angry enough to have cursed both Orpah's womb and mine. No. I won't believe it!"

"If we are cursed, why is the business going so well?" Ruth reiterates the question Killion had asked Mahlon. She'd overheard the brothers talking just a few weeks ago when Orpah miscarried again. To her shame, Ruth has never even missed a monthly cycle.

"Sometimes it just takes time." Naomi uses the same soothing voice as when she coaxes the goat to quit kicking and give us her milk.

Ruth bridles at her tone. "I am doing everything right, working hard, saying the prayers, obeying all the laws. What else can I do?" As the words leave Ruth's mouth, she sees the look on Orpah's face.

Ruth blushes and looks away thinking, "She knows I blame her and her worthless idols. And she blames me, because she thinks her useless idols actually have the power to curse us."

"Of course it couldn't be her fault—not "Ruth-Who-Knows-All!" Orpah is ready to fight, and so is Ruth.

"Daughters, I will not listen to this any longer." Naomi's face is red and her hands are clenched. "Orpah, go for a walk and come back when you're ready to be civil. Ruth, you are late for market. Out, both of you!"

Orpah steps into the courtyard, looks back at Ruth, and spits on the ground before she flounces out into the street.

"Hamot, I'm sorry." But Naomi doesn't want apologies, and she motions for Ruth to go. She does, but not before she sees the tears in her mother-in-law's eyes. Ruth lingers in the courtyard wondering whether she should go back in and apologize again until she hears Naomi's voice, cracking and full of tears.

"Yahweh, why do you bring us this misery? The famine was so bad we had no food—we had to come to Moab to eat. Then you took Elimelech. Isn't that enough? Do not turn your anger on my sons and their wives."

Naomi chokes back a sob. "We should never have left Bethlehem."

"She blames herself, but what if it *is* my fault?" Ruth shakes her head to deny the thought, attaches the harness to her shoulder, lifts the legs of the cart, and clatters over the stony courtyard to the street. "Is it me? Are we cursed because of me?"

FOURTEEN

ONE YEAR LATER

The city of Kir-hareseth goes mad at the end of every winter. The marketplace in the temple square is empty except for sellers of love potions and drinks. Priests and priestesses hustle about in their red robes getting ready for the three days of insanity that they call the awakening of spring.

Orpah helped Killion take down the pottery stall yesterday—the whole square in front of the temple is cleared out for the festivities—but Ruth refused to help. When Ruth volunteered to bring home a large supply of water instead, Mahlon reacted with impatience.

"He knows I can't go anywhere near Chemosh's wicked altar at this time of year," Ruth mutters under her breath on her fourth trip to the well today. Even with four large jars full, the family will have to ration water for the three days of the celebration—it won't be safe for any foreigners to be on the streets and worse for those who married them.

"Ruth, wait." Orpah calls out, and Ruth turns to see her hurrying behind her with another full water jar.

"Where'd you get another jar?"

"I convinced Killion that we'd need more water, so I borrowed a jar from my mother." Orpah is panting—whether from excitement or hurrying, Ruth can't tell. "Wait up, and let me catch my breath."

"Just for a minute." Ruth is eager to get home and barricade the doors, but Orpah hates being cooped up for the festival. She misses the parties and all the excitement. Ruth shakes her head, thinking, "Not me. Not since Durha."

Ruth's anxiety makes her impatient. "Come on. We need to get back."

The minute the women enter the courtyard, Mahlon and Killion close and latch the gate. They drag the cart in front of it and start piling heavy bags of clay soil into it.

"Bring Mahlon up on the roof with us tonight." Orpah whispers in Ruth's ear so Naomi won't hear her. "It'll be fun."

"I won't have anything to do with Chemosh and his bloodthirsty festival!" Ruth feels like her friend plunged a knife into her heart. Anger floods

LESS THAN A WIDOW

her mind and she fumes silently to herself, "She knows what happened to Durha. How can she even suggest…"

Orpah makes the sign to ward off the evil eye—pinky and pointer finger up while middle fingers are held to the palm by the thumb.

"Shh. Don't say such things. Chemosh will hear you!"

Hurt and angry, Ruth's voice drips with scorn. "Orpah, why should I be afraid of a god who can't even wake up or remember how to plant seeds and bring the rain without all this awful craziness?"

"You never think about anyone but yourself. Maybe Chemosh does hear you and is angry. Maybe that's why we don't have any babies in this house."

"He can't hear or do anything!" Ruth almost screamed the words, and Mahlon and Killion watch as she stalks out of the storeroom. Orpah follows, her hand still formed to ward off the evil eye.

יהוה

Mornings are the only time it is quiet during spring festival. The city comes alive again in the afternoons, and the nights are full of firelight and revelry.

Locked in their self-imposed prison, it's hard for the family to stay out of each other's way. Killion and Orpah spend most of their time on the roof. Mahlon typically works at his potter's wheel, but he won't let Ruth prepare the clay each day as she normally does—she's messed it up too many times during previous festivals. When Ruth helps Naomi prepare meals, she tends to burn the bread and her fingers, too.

Tonight is the final night, the culmination of the celebration—the night of sacrifice. Ruth sits on her sleeping mat in the gloom of the main room. There's no more work left to distract her—she's reorganized the storeroom, swept and cleaned everything, and carded all the wool.

"I'm so tired, maybe the dream will leave me alone," she thinks and closes her eyes, but the back of her eyelids come alive with dancing flames and flashing knives. She jerks her eyes open, hugs herself, and rocks back and forth.

Mahlon stands in the doorway, and his shadow fills the rectangle of light with an eerie, elongated shape. "Ruth, you need to stop doing this."

"I'm not doing anything."

Ruth turns her back to him, thinking but not saying, "Does he think I choose this delerium?"

"I've been patient, but it never changes."

"What do you want from me?" Ruth stands up.

"Look, hiding in here doesn't work—it's never worked. Tonight we'll go up on the roof. We'll watch the parades, and we'll…"

"You know I can't do that!"

"You can't or you won't?"

"Mahlon, please."

RUTH : MOAB

Ruth's mind screams, "He doesn't hear me. He doesn't want to hear me." She can't say the words that would help Mahlon understand her pain, so instead she asks accusingly, "You want to join the rest of the city in their insanity? Is this really the way you want to make a son?"

Ruth covers her mouth to stop the angry words, steps closer to Mahlon, reaches her arms out to him, and pleads, tears streaming down her face. "Don't you understand what's going on out there?"

Mahlon backs away from her touch. "Spring is coming, so people party. They go overboard; that's why we stay locked up in here just to be on the safe side. And you—you are always a little crazy."

Ruth mind fills with flames as priests lead Durha to the altar. "Tell him why," Ruth argues within herself, eyes closed, lips moving without sound.

"It's evil," she forces out of her mouth in a whisper.

"That's not what Orpah says."

"Did she tell you it's my fault we don't have children?"

Mahlon avoids the question. "Orpah's sisters conceived during the festival. She was conceived during the festival. It's what this time is all about—planting seeds—making babies."

"It has nothing to do with life," Ruth yells, her voice cracks with fear and anger. "It's about Chemosh—and he's all about death. Blood, and pain, and murder."

Mahlon pulls Ruth close and kisses the top of her head, but she stands stiff as a board. Still, Mahlon doesn't give up.

"Don't you want a son?"

"Of course, I do, but this is not…"

"I'm not asking." He takes Ruth's hand, and she follows him up the stairs to the roof.

יהוה

As evening falls, Killion and Orpah lean over the wall at the edge of the roof watching people swarm toward the temple square. Eddies of revelers flirting, dancing, and drinking disrupt the mob's progress. When Orpah leans too far, Killion grabs her. She throws her head back laughing, then pulls him to her and kisses him passionately.

Ruth stands a step behind Mahlon with her eyes closed, wishing she dared to plug her ears.

Temple guards push through the crowded streets below bellowing, "Make way!" Parading closely in their wake are chanting priests and priestesses.

The head priest—the monster of Ruth's nightmares—strides in front of an oxcart looking neither right nor left. His face, bald head, and chest are painted in fierce patterns of red and black. Burly slaves surround him, roughly pushing aside anyone who doesn't get out of the way fast enough.

LESS THAN A WIDOW

When Ruth hears the rumble of wheels and the heavy clopping of the oxen, her feet seem to step forward of their own accord, her head tilts down, and her eyes open. Her brain screams a warning not to look, but it's too late.

"Is it Durha?" Of course, it's not; she knows it's not, but the girl in the cart is wearing the same white robe and her face...Ruth strains to see the girl's face and realizes she can't even remember exactly what Durha's face looked like—that brings such sharp pain that she gasps.

Two little children ride in the cart, eyes black, faces pale and blank with drugs above their simple white robes. A priestess stands behind them, her claw-like hands gripping their shoulders.

Somehow a woman from the crowd slips past a guard and lurches toward the cart, arms outstretched, screaming, "My baby. Don't take my baby!"

The guard shoves her aside, and she falls hard, banging her head on the rough road. A man fights to pull her limp body out of the surging crowd and finds an empty doorway to shelter in. As he cradles her bleeding head in his lap, tears run down his cheeks.

Ruth licks her lips, tasting the salt of the man's tears. "Or are they mine?" a part of her mind wonders.

"Stop! You can't have them!" Ruth doesn't recognize her own voice as her shrill scream joins the noise made by the revelers below. She grabs whatever is nearest to hand—a bowl of figs—to throw it at the priests, but as she brings her arm back, Mahlon wraps his arms around his wife and pulls her away from the edge of roof.

Ruth beats on his chest and screams in his face, "Let me go!" But Mahlon holds her in a bear hug until she quits struggling.

"Enough, Ruth! Stop acting so crazy," he pants. "Are you finished now?"

Gasping for air, Ruth shakes her head. She's afraid to look at her husband's face, to know the answer to the torturous questions in her mind: "Is he angry with me? Does he still love me? Will he send me away?"

"Just be still. I'm going to let you go." Mahlon lowers Ruth to a mat and sits down beside her. "This was a mistake."

Ruth nods, but when he puts his arm around her shoulders, she doesn't pull away.

"When you're ready, I'll bring you downstairs," he murmurs in her ear.

יהוה

Mahlon—in his usual gentle, caring manner—covers Ruth with a blanket as she lies on their sleeping mat and leaves the room without speaking. Naomi is in the courtyard, and Ruth hears her tell him, "We need to leave this place."

Afraid to close her eyes, Ruth's exhausted body finally betrays her, and with sleep comes the dream:

People everywhere. The fire and smell of incense. The drums and the chanting of that evil name: Chemosh. Chemosh. Screams. Fire. People pushing. Agony. Fear.

A quiet voice speaks in my ear with great authority.

"Peace; be still."

In the sudden stillness, I ask, "Who are you?"

"We need to leave this place."

"I don't know how."

"Take my hand."

"Who are you?"

"You know me. We've been talking for years."

I take his hand and follow in his footsteps.

And dream of the sun breaking through storm clouds.

FIFTEEN

TWO YEARS LATER

Every muscle in her body protests as Ruth bends over to wrap the clay Mahlon and Killion have already gathered into manageable chunks. Digging clay is hard and dirty, but Ruth loves the sense of accomplishment and the freedom being out of the city brings. "I remember the first time Elimelech brought me along to dig clay," Ruth smiles at the thought. "Naomi objected, but he just winked at me and said, 'Many hands make light work.' I still miss him—he bought me as a slave but treated me as a daughter."

The work on this trip, even with Ruth's extra set of hands, has been anything but light. Ruth straightens slowly and looks around the campsite.

This deposit yields the perfect clay for the fine pottery that is Mahlon's specialty. That's the only reason they have kept coming back to this site and then only during the dry season—the clay pit is located in a narrow wadi that fills suddenly with rushing water during rains. The men have to squeeze through a narrow opening, but then the cliff walls open up enough to allow both of them to dig. Ruth's job is to cut and wrap blocks of clay in manageable chunks and prepare it to be carried back to town.

Mahlon told Naomi and Orpah that they would return today, but yesterday afternoon Killion discovered that the clay seam unexpectedly continues into the side of the cliff—made visible by the rushing waters during the latest rains. Last night around the fire the two men argued about whether or not they should stay an extra day to gather as much as they could carry home.

"This clay is too valuable to leave any behind."

"It won't be easy, but we can dig into the hillside…"

"I don't know…it's pretty dangerous."

"But it's so hard to find clay of this quality, and who knows how deeply it goes into the hillside? If there's a lot more, we may not have to search out another source after all."

In the end, both men agreed that it would be a shame to leave any of this precious clay behind, so they're digging again today. Ruth is repacking everything—filling the donkey's packs with as much as the beast can carry and making room for some wrapped blocks of clay in each of their carrying baskets.

"You won't be the only one with a heavy load on this trip," Ruth tells the donkey blinking in the shade of a sycamore tree. The donkey is a welcome addition to their clay mining expeditions, although Ruth is sure he doesn't enjoy them as much as she does—his idea of a perfect day is sleeping in the shade. He lets out a long bray.

"Quit complaining. You have a few more hours until your work starts. Be glad you can't help me pack." Ruth stands with her hands on her lower back, stretching her tired muscles.

The donkey brays again and jerks back against its tether.

"What's your problem?" Ruth spins around when she hears a rumble and feels the ground shake. A cloud of dust shoots out of the fissure. "No! Oh, no! Mahlon. Killion."

The earth jumps under her feet, the dust cloud spreads, and it's hard to breathe. Ruth runs, falls, crawls, toward the fissure, but it's blocked—she can't get in. The narrow opening is filled in with boulders, stones, and dirt. She attacks the slag heap that buried Mahlon and Killion, screaming their names. She cries and digs, but it's hopeless. Ruth can't move the boulders, and the more she digs at the gravel and dirt, the more it fills in the cracks. Her hands are scratched and bleeding—fingernails ripped and missing. But Mahlon and Killion are buried deep—half of the hillside collapsed filling the wadi.

"Could they still be alive?" That thought starts her screaming, "No, no, no!" Her screams soon turn to a prayer she repeats over and over as she digs, "Oh, Yahweh, help me!"

יהוה

It is dusk when the donkey's soft lips tickling her face rouses Ruth. But when she reaches up to touch his nose, he doesn't like the smell of blood on her hands and nervously backs away. Hands, arms, legs, feet—everything is covered with scrapes, dirt, and crusting blood. The donkey is agitated, but stays close to Ruth, cropping and chewing whatever vegetation he can find. When something crosses Ruth's hand, she automatically closes her fist. "His tether!" Ruth rolls to her side and holds on with two hands.

Holding tightly to the rope, Ruth hauls herself up, using the donkey's legs for balance. Amazingly, he doesn't kick even when she grabs him around the neck to stop from falling. Leaning heavily on her four-legged rescuer and stopping often to rest, Ruth staggers back to camp just as the sun is setting. The donkey stops by a low rock that has a natural trough and won't budge another step. Ruth sinks to the ground and closes her eyes, but once again his tickling lips and whuffling breath on her face bring her back to consciousness. He's thirsty, and Ruth realizes she is, too.

Once again Ruth climbs up the donkey's leg, rests leaning on his back, then stretches and tugs repeatedly at the waterskin propped on the rock. Finally, it tumbles to the ground and she plops down next to it. Pain shoots through her torn fingers as she tries to pull out the plug, until water finally spills into the natural trough. Dropping to her hands and knees, Ruth laps up the water, the donkey's head right next to hers, and they both drink their fill. Leaning against the rock trough in the dark night, exhaustion overtakes her.

יהוה

The morning sun makes it above the horizon and shines full on Ruth's face. She opens her eyes to see neatly stacked blocks of clay—they're piled everywhere.

"Horrible, beastly clay. You killed my husband." Ruth kicks and throws the blocks, screaming as if these lumps were responsible for Mahlon's and Killion's death. "I can't even bring their bodies home," and that thought renews her anger. Soon the campsite is a wreck, covered with flung hunks of clay.

Ruth looks at her red-stained hands and thinks, "This is the clay they died for. The clay that will never be shaped into beauty by Mahlon's hands."

Exhausted by her outburst, Ruth's only desire is to lie down and die. "My husband…I don't want to live without you," she sobs, but she can't quiet the persuasive voice in her head. "Naomi and Orpah will never know what happened if you die in the desert too. Besides, you can't leave our men alone and unremembered."

Ruth picks up a wrapped block of brick that somehow escaped her rage-induced frenzy and turns it over and over in her hands until it occurs to her, "The clay…I can use it to mark the place of their death."

Retrieving the scattered clay block by block, Ruth stacks it near the sycamore tree under which they shared their last meal. Every part of her hurts as she lifts, carries, and stacks the wrapped bundles of clay until she has a waist-high altar. Ruth drapes Mahlon and Killion's sleeping robes over it and places her precious cooking bowl, etched with Mahlon's mark, on top.

Using a stick, Ruth digs up the grain and figs she had buried yesterday—it seems a lifetime ago—under the coals to roast. The delicious smell tickles her nose, and her stomach shouts its hunger. Ruth wraps some in a cloth for the trip home, shares a double-handful with the donkey, and puts the rest in the altar bowl. Digging through the firepit, Ruth finds a still-glowing ember and fans it, adding dry leaves and dead twigs until she has a steady flame.

When Ruth picks up the jar of cooking oil—"delicate-looking, but sturdy as only Mahlon could make it"—anguish threatens to take over again.

"Yahweh, give me strength."

She pours the olive oil over the grain and watches it overflow down the side of the altar until every drop is gone. She holds a broom brush stalk to her small fire until the end burns with a bright flame and carries it reverently to the alter and lights the oil. The men's robes, the food they would have eaten, and

LESS THAN A WIDOW

the clay they would have made into useful and beautiful shapes catch fire. As fragrant smoke drifts up to the heavens, Ruth falls to her knees and sings:

> "In the rising of the sun and in its going down,
>
> I will remember them;
>
> In the blowing of the wind and in the chill of the winter,
>
> I will remember them;
>
> In the opening of buds and in the rebirth of spring,
>
> I will remember them;
>
> In the rustling of leaves and in the beauty of autumn,
>
> I will remember them;
>
> In the beginning of the year and when it ends,
>
> I will remember them;
>
> When I am weary and in need of strength,
>
> I will remember them;
>
> When I am lost and sick at heart, I will remember them;
>
> When I have joys I yearn to share, I will remember them.
>
> So long as I live, they too shall live,
>
> for they are now a part of me as I remember them."

Ruth holds Mahlon's prayer shawl to her face, breathing in the scent of him, and picturing him getting ready for morning prayers. Rising to her feet, Ruth closes her eyes and mimics the actions she has watched him perform every morning as if she, a woman and now a widow, were standing in for him as he offers up his last prayers to Yahweh.

With both arms outstretched at shoulder height she holds the tasseled shawl in front of her. Her voice sings the blessing, but it is Mahlon's deep tones that she hears in her mind and heart:

"Baruch atah Adonai, Elheinu melech haolam..."

Lifting the shawl high above her head, Ruth lets it settle down onto her shoulders. She pictures Mahlon's strong hands as they grip the ends of the shawl, lift it over his head, and drape it over his shoulders. Her scraped and bleeding hands match the picture of him in her mind, motion for motion.

"Worshipful are you, O Lord, our God, King of the Universe..."

יהוה

Ruth stumbles through the desert, empty basket on her back, and a black hole in her heart. The donkey, anxious to get back to his shed and bag of grain, chooses the path toward home. When they wearily stumble through the city gates, Ruth grabs his mane. She doesn't notice the questioning stares from those who pass her on the street; it takes all her concentration to continue putting one foot in front of the other as the donkey leads her home.

Orpah, watching for their return from the roof, screams when she sees Ruth coming down the street alone except for the donkey at her side. Naomi runs into the street from the courtyard with Orpah close behind.

"Where are they?" Naomi looks up and down the road. "Where are my sons?"

"What is that?" But Orpah won't accept her husband's prayer shawl from Ruth's outstretched hand. "It's Killion's—why do you have Killion's prayer shawl? Where is he?"

Naomi sinks to the ground and covers her face with her hands.

"I'm sorry," Ruth says. "I tried, but I couldn't get them out. The hillside came down on them, and I couldn't find them."

Naomi doesn't answer. I'm not even sure she heard me, but Orpah did.

And the wailing begins again.

SIXTEEN

"This is my last night in this home where I have been so loved and happy," Ruth thinks as she climbs the stairs to sleep on the roof, but doesn't bother to lie down on her mat. "I'm afraid. What will become of us?"

"Almanah," Ruth said the word out loud, hating the feel of it in her mouth. *Almanah*, the word for widow, with its root word meaning "unable to speak" repeats itself over and over in Ruth's head.

"But I can speak. Somebody listen to me; somebody help me." Only Ruth hears the words she speaks out loud as they are carried off into the wind. There is no response up on the roof, for she speaks only to herself. "It doesn't matter if I speak, because no one hears, no one cares. And we are even less than almanah for we have no children." Without children to inherit what belonged to their fathers, widows have nothing—no economic or social support.

"We are less than widows," Ruth murmurs. "Less than widows..."

Orpah's family hasn't abandoned her, even though many people thought they should. "She left to join her husband's family—there is no coming back," her uncle announced to Orpah's father before the others shushed him.

But Orpah always was a bright light in their family, and they want her to stay in Moab. Ruth overheard Orpah's brother try to convince her again this afternoon. Orpah told him it wouldn't be right to stay, but when he said that he had already spoken to a potential husband for her, she cried.

He held her hand and told her earnestly, "You don't have to leave and neither does Ruth; she would be a great second wife for someone—nice to look at, bright, and a hard worker even if she can't bear children."

Orpah has a second chance for happiness in Moab, but loyalty is one of her strongest traits, and all Naomi has left is her two daughters-in-law. Ruth has no idea what Orpah will do—for all the time they have spent crying together since her fateful return alone to the city, they avoid talking about the future.

Ruth has no illusions about staying in Moab. She shakes her head at bitter memories, "I've seen what it means to be second wife, and I won't willingly do that again! My only other option would be to become a temple prostitute for Chemosh or Ashtorah. No!"

"I would rather die first." As Ruth spits out these words, she knows they may well be true. Even so, she repeats them. "I would rather die."

LESS THAN A WIDOW

Ruth stands at the edge of the roof and looks down at the street below. "I could jump," but she dismisses that thought immediately. "That would leave no one to care for Naomi."

The only reason Naomi hasn't already laid down, refused to eat, and die is that she doesn't want to die in Moab—she wants to die and be buried among her own people in Bethlehem. Ruth steps back from the wall around the edge of the roof with a growing realization. "I don't want to die at all—not here in the shadow of that awful temple or in Bethlehem. In the desert I wished that I had died with Mahlon and Killion, but then I had to come back for Orpah and Naomi."

Sobs wrack her body, and she sinks to the floor and cries until there are no tears left.

Everything except the donkey is gone—traded to buy their passage with a trade caravan leaving in the morning. The caravan leader agreed to take the long route to bring the women to Bethlehem, but Ruth suspects that was just a part of his bargaining to wring every last thing of value from them—such an easy thing when there are no men to stand up for them.

Ruth shrugs her shoulders and thinks, "So be it. There's no way we can travel to Bethlehem on our own—the caravan master can demand whatever he wants."

What he wanted was more than Ruth had to give. She had hoped to bring the last of the healing balm in Mahlon's beautiful jars along to Bethlehem and sell them there. Instead, the precious jars are the final payment that will allow the women a place in the caravan to Bethlehem, but only "if we can keep up."

Ruth's face flushes with anger remembering her inability to barter for better terms. "Naomi wants to die, but not until she's back in her precious Bethlehem," Ruth sighs at the thought. "At least the caravan master didn't know about Naomi's death wish."

It was enough that he is well aware of the unspeakable dangers for women without protection on the road. Part of her refuses to accept their plight, and the argument continues in her mind. "We have no choice—the caravan is our only hope, but I'm not sure about how safe we will be with them either."

Ruth pulls Mahlon's prayer shawl from the top of her pack and holds it to her face, breathing in what little fragrance of him remains—it's almost gone. "Oh, Mahlon," but she clamps her jaw shut against the grief that threatens to drag her back into its clutches.

"I can't torture myself like this," she thinks. "We'll die for sure if I drown myself in grief like Naomi." So Ruth drapes his shawl over her head and shoulders and looks in the direction they will travel tomorrow and laughs at herself. "I don't know what I think I will see in the dark—just the stars."

In her head, Ruth hears Naomi's voice telling her favorite story:

RUTH : MOAB

"...Yahweh spoke: 'Let there be a space above the waters!'

Yahweh made the sky. He separated the water

under the sky from the water above it.

And there it was:

he named sky the Heavens..."

"Yahweh," Ruth whispers his name before retreating back into her mind. "Everything we do in this house revolves around Yahweh—what we eat, what we do, who we pray to. Naomi is convinced that Yahweh took his favor away from her family when they came to Moab—this is why Elimelech, Mahlon, and Killion are dead—and now Naomi wants to die, too."

"Yahweh, I want to live." Ruth utters these choked words aloud and hardly recognizes her own voice. "Do you still hear me when I cry to you? Do you still care for this useless widow? I have nothing left if I can't trust in the God of my family."

Ruth looks again at the stars, and tries to hold onto the assurance of Yahweh's promises as Elimelech and Mahlon had always done. "Elimelech said you sent him to rescue me—he said you had a reason for bringing me into this family. Mahlon believed it, too. But now, they're all dead. Naomi's the only one left—with no children to carry on the family line—and she wants to go to Bethlehem. Is that the reason you saved me? Do you want me to help Naomi go home just to die?"

"That can't be it!" Ruth's whole self yells her protest in her mind.

Exhausted, but too restless to sleep, Ruth takes everything out of her carry-bag and starts to repack it: a flint, a knife, and the last one of Mahlon's pilgrim flasks. She checks—again—the hem of her good shawl for what she had hidden there—Naomi's wedding jewelry that she had also worn when she married Mahlon. She smiles in satisfaction at what the caravan master would say if he knew about the jewelry.

"We'll need something to buy food in Bethlehem—if we expect to live," Ruth thinks as she places dried figs and popped grain on top of the packed items. "Yahweh, you rescue me in my dreams. Will you rescue me—us—in life, too?"

Ruth stands up, arranges Mahlon's prayer shawl and chants a formal prayer. "Blessed are you, HaShem, our God, King of the Universe. Please, Yahweh, save us."

יהוה

LESS THAN A WIDOW

Full waterskins are really heavy. Ruth is glad the donkey will be carrying them. Tents are being packed up in the caravan's camp just outside the city gates as Naomi waves with one hand and keeps a firm hold on the donkey's rope with the other. He's not looking forward to this journey any more than the women are.

Ruth hesitates to rush Orpah's good-byes, but gently touches her arm. "We have to go."

Orpah's mother hugs her and won't let go until her sisters gently untangle their arms. Sabeen hangs a bag on Orpah's shoulder and gives her a gentle push. Orpah's face is streaming with tears as she catches up with Ruth.

"Fresh figs." Her attempt at a smile wavers as she pulls one out of the bag and hands it to Ruth. "Eat this. We can't start our journey on an empty stomach."

Ruth heads right for the donkey and adds the waterskins to his pack, careful to balance them evenly. Naomi talks quietly to Orpah, and Ruth hears only the last part.

"...stay here with your family."

"I can't...I love you."

"And I love you. That's why I want you to stay in Moab."

"But Killion..."

Naomi almost shouts as she interrupts Orpah. "Is dead! Both my sons and my husband are dead. We are nothing—women without power or protection—how can I love you and want that kind of a life for you?"

Naomi calms herself with a deep breath and touches Orpah's cheeks with her worn hand. "Look at me. I'm too old for any man to want me. I won't bear another son, and even if I did, you'd be too old for childbearing by the time he grew up. I have nothing to give you."

"But it wouldn't be right to leave you."

"Orpah, dear darling Orpah, you have a future here in Moab—your family is here. There is nothing for you in Bethlehem. Yahweh has emptied my life of all that is good. Stay here, marry again, have babies, be happy. Do this for me, because I love you."

Orpah looks back toward the city gates where her mother and sisters are still waving good-bye. The war inside between loyalty to Naomi and common sense are tearing her apart.

Ruth put her arms around Orpah and whispers in her ear. "Don't worry about Naomi. I'll look after her."

"No, Ruth! What's true for Orpah is true for you, too." Naomi's voice is hard and angry again.

"I'm sorry, Mother, but it's not. Orpah's home is here with her family, her people, her gods. My heart left Moab a long time ago, and now my body will follow it. Your people are my people; your God is my God. I swear in Yahweh's name that where you die, I will die, and that's where I will be buried."

The caravan leader bellows at the women, "You didn't pay enough for us to wait for you!"

Ruth waves at him. "We're coming!"

Naomi points to the crying women at the city gates. "Your mother and sisters are waiting for you, Orpah, my child."

The three of us hug one last time, hating to say goodbye. Naomi pulls away first. "Go on, dear one. Be happy."

Orpah takes the bag of figs from her shoulder and hangs it on Ruth's. She kisses her on both cheeks, then kisses Naomi. Her first few steps toward her family are tentative, but soon she's running, and they move to surround her.

Naomi grabs my arm—hard. "Ruth..."

"I can be just as stubborn as she is," Ruth thinks and draws her thumb across her throat as if cutting it with a knife. "May Yahweh do this to me if I break my vow."

Naomi tries to glare at Ruth, but relief shows in her eyes. The caravan starts to move. Ruth puts her arm around her mother-in-law's shoulders, pulls on the donkey's lead, and follows.

"Shall we go, Mother?"

יהוד

Ruth leads the donkey, and Naomi trudges alongside with her hand tangled in his stiff mane. Her body is there, but her mind is somewhere else. Most days she barely speaks.

The women's usual spot is in the middle of the caravan—dusty, but safe. Well, safe from bandits anyway. The camel drovers are another story.

"Was that you in the boss' tent last night or was that his camel?"

Ruth rolls her eyes. Scarface asks the same question every day, and for some strange reason his cohorts think it's hilarious—every day. Of course, his name isn't really Scarface, but giving them nicknames passes the time. Every day they trudge across the desert under a blazing sun. It's brutal; it's dangerous. But it's the repetitiveness of step after step after step when all one wants to do is find a spot of shade and rest that wears one down.

"Maybe these filthy men are doing me a favor by annoying me all the time—it keeps me alert and moving," Ruth's mouth curves into a smile at this thought.

"The god of death walks in your shadow." One-Eye steps closer and hisses at them.

Naomi waves her hand in One-Eye's face as if brushing off a fly.

"Boss' greed will bring the wrath of the gods on us all." The man has been trying to get the other drovers to kill us or at least drive us away. According to the augury shown in the bones he tosses, bringing women on a trade caravan brings bad luck.

Ruth covers Naomi's hand on the donkey's mane with her own and swerves off of the path to get away from him, but trips in the soft sand. Ruth loses her balance and falls right into the arms of Fleabite, who catches her with a lot more enthusiasm and physical contact than the situation calls for. "Don't worry, *Habibi*. I've got you."

"That's what worries me!" Ruth thinks as she jerks away and hurries the donkey and Naomi back to the path. Fleabite acknowledges the leering encouragement of his fellows with a bow.

"They get bolder every day—I have to do something," Ruth thinks as she notes where each man is.

That evening the men laugh and drink around a campfire as they do every night on the trail. Naomi and Ruth have their own evening ritual: the two women move out of the firelight and donning their husbands' prayer shawls and chant:

"Hear O Israel! Yahweh is our God, Yahweh is one!

And you shall love your God with all your heart,

And with all your soul, and with all your might."

As usual, the ribald suggestions and jeers get louder while they pray, but Ruth has planned a surprise ending tonight. She raises her hands to the heavens and howls. The men grope for weapons and face the night, searching for danger. Finding none, they focus their attention on Ruth who is swaying in the dark. "Now!" her mind yells at her.

Ruth moves nearer to the fire so eerie planes of light and shadow move across her face. She mutters, moans, and sinks to the ground just long enough to make the men anxious, then draws her knife from its sheath and leaps to her feet.

"Ana Adonia hashia na."

Four times Ruth screams the words as she circles around the fire, slashing her knife skyward in all four directions before thrusting it toward them.

"She curses us." Many of the men make the ward sign to protect themselves from the evil eye. "The woman is crazy."

Still muttering and swaying as if in a trance, Ruth presses the knife into her thumb until it draws blood. With everyone's eyes following her every move, she draws her bleeding thumb across her neck as if cutting her throat, leaving a line of blood. She points her knife toward the men by the fire one by one as she licks the blood dripping from her thumb.

Blinking rapidly, Ruth focuses her eyes, slowly puts her knife in its sheath, turns, and walks back to the small tent where Naomi is waiting. Before closing the flap, Ruth places the knife within her reach, pointing its tip toward the men by the fire.

At last Naomi speaks, if only to scold. "I have never seen Yahweh worshipped in such a Moabite way."

"No, but this time His message wasn't for you—it was for my countrymen. Now everyone in the whole camp understands that we have a mighty protector, greater than any man!"

But Naomi's words sting, and it's a long time before Ruth can sleep.

SEVENTEEN

"Go." The camel-mounted caravan master herds the two women and their donkey out of line and points at a faint track.

Ruth looks around and sees no sign of a village or habitation. "What is this? We paid you to take us to Bethlehem."

"Not enough."

"It was enough when we were in Moab." Ruth feels fear hit her in the stomach.

"And now it's not." He leans forward as his eyes undress Ruth. Ruth sidesteps to put the donkey between her and danger.

"I knew this was coming," she tells herself. The man had been leering at her the last few days as they drew nearer to their destination. Ruth pulls her knife from the sheath hanging from her waist.

 "Do you really think you could stop me with your puny blade?"

Offering a silent prayer to Yahweh, Ruth settles the knife in her hand and prepares to defend herself, but Naomi moves forward in front of her daughter-in-law. "It's all right, Ruth." Raising her hands she slowly turns in a circle, her walking stick raised high. "We are in Hebrew country and under the full protection of Yahweh the Almighty Warrior and Ruler of All."

The caravan master raises his voice so the gathering drovers can hear. "Of course, they will be safe in Hebrew country where the sorry creatures that pass for 'men' are afraid of Ruth's tiny little knife." But he makes no move to dismount from his camel and nervously scans the surrounding hills.

"I think I know where we are. We can find our way home from here," Naomi whispers to Ruth under the cover of the men's jeering laughter.

Ruth hands her the rope, and Naomi urges the reluctant donkey to follow her down the steep hill. Knife still in hand, Ruth follows slowly, turning in circles to watch as the caravan moves on, drovers spitting and calling insults after them.

יהוה

The truth was, Naomi had no idea where they were, but she had been counting the days traveling with the caravan and knew how long it took to arrive in the land of her countrymen.

LESS THAN A WIDOW

Ruth shakes her head and laughs in disbelief. "You really don't know where we are?" She's never known Naomi to lie before and is amazed that she could do it so convincingly.

"Well, no, but I know we are in the land of my birth." Naomi shrugs her shoulders. "What did you want me to say? We had to get away from that filth before anything happened. I just followed your example." With a pat on Ruth's cheek, Naomi signals that rest time is over. She leads the way around a brown rocky hill where green plants push their way through dried brush signaling spring.

As far as Naomi is concerned, the conversation is over. Ruth shakes her head and tries to sort out her feeling as they pick their way on the rocky path. "Why didn't I ask Mother more questions? I never used to hesitate. Since the day Naomi found out her sons were dead, she's only thought about one thing—returning to Bethlehem. Nothing else matters. She makes no decisions and does little or no planning."

Ruth thinks of words that would describe the woman Naomi has become: quiet, listless, sad, disheartened…and despairs of any hope that the gentle, loving Naomi who is always ready with a smile or a story is gone, driven so far away by pain and bitterness that she will never return. But as she follows the woman walking ahead of her she feels a glimmer of hope, "Still, look at what she just did! Maybe Naomi is still in there somewhere."

יהוה

Even though Naomi's fears are eased because they are in Hebrew country, Ruth knows that two women without protection can never be too careful. Although she sees no sign of people nearby, she keeps a nervous watch.

"The old lecher was telling the truth about my knife—it won't scare anybody—but it's all I have," and she mutters as she checks to make sure it is secure in its sheath. Ruth looks at Naomi serenely plodding along and thinks, "She's right—Yahweh is with us—but that doesn't mean we shouldn't be careful."

So when the sound of fighting erupts on the trail behind them, they run away as fast as they can looking for a place to hide. Stumbling around a curve in the path, they almost collide with a man who blocks their way with his sword drawn.

"Who are you?" His question is as menacing as his weapon.

"He's Hebrew!" Naomi claps her hands together and once again steps in front of her daughter-in-law. That shocks Ruth almost as much as finding an armed man blocking the path.

"I am overjoyed to hear the language of my countrymen again. I am Naomi, wife of Elimelech of Bethlehem."

"And who is this with you?"

"My son Mahlon's wife."

"Where are your husbands?"

Naomi breathes in and out before she answers. "We are widows. My husband and sons died in Moab, may they rest in peace. We are on our way home... to Bethlehem."

"Do you expect me to believe that you've come all the way from Moab alone?" The man with the sword points it at me.

"We weren't alone—not until today." He raises his eyebrows at my accent as he notes my dark skin and work-hardened hands. "We paid a trader's caravan to take us to Bethlehem, but this morning they told us to take this trail and just...left us on our own."

"If what you say is true, then why is this piece of filth following you?" He points behind Ruth and Naomi to two men who approach dragging someone between them.

"She speaks the truth. We are alone." Naomi voice is quiet but steady.

As the men get nearer it is obvious where the sounds of fighting came from. All three men are bruised and bleeding. The one being dragged in the middle has a lump over one eye, and blood from his split lip trickles down his chin. He looks up, and Ruth gasps.

The man with the sword has been watching us for a reaction. "You know him, then. Who is he?"

The captured man speaks up before Ruth can answer, but his Moabite accent and damaged mouth make him hard to understand. "Please, noble sir, I am just a simple camel drover from the traders' caravan. These women have been traveling with us, and I was told to follow them to protect them, you understand? They paid for safe travel to Bethlehem..."

Ruth's knife is in her hand as she steps toward him. "Protect us? You filthy liar..." Naomi grabs her arm.

"Put that down!" At the swordsman's stern command, Ruth calms herself, bends over, lays her knife on the sand at her feet, and slowly backs away. She quietly looks at the man giving commands, waiting for him to speak.

"I will ask you again, who is he? And this time, tell me the truth."

Ruth can't decide how to answer his question. She shudders with disgust at the thought of what the drover's intentions were, but seeing him on his knees shaking with fear, Ruth feels something close to pity. Fleabite notices the slight change in her expression and holds out his hands in supplication to Ruth.

"Stop that," Ruth snaps at him in his tongue. "I know why you followed us. Why would you think I would want to protect you?" As she hears herself say this out loud, her mind and conscience get into an argument. "Even though he's scum, he is a Moabite, same as me. Will they kill him? And would that make it easier for them to kill me?"

Ruth shakes her head to clear her thoughts and answers the swordsman's question out loud. "He is a drover from the caravan that we were traveling with."

"What is his name?"

Ruth looks at Naomi, who lifts her shoulders slightly. "I—we don't know."

"Are you telling me that you traveled together from Moab, and you don't know his name?"

"We didn't mingle with the drovers." Naomi's voice is haughty.

"I called him Fleabite." Hope jumps in Ruth's chest when the men laugh, and she attempts a smile in return. "But unless you are greatly bothered by fleas, he's not a threat to anyone."

"He is with you, then?" asked the swordsman. "You are bringing this scum to Bethlehem?"

"Of course he's not with us! He must have followed us to..." She stops speaking at that disgusting thought—probably not a good idea to say that out loud. "He has no place with us—he eats and sleeps with camels. Send him back, for the fleabags will miss him."

Evidently, this is funny, too. Hoping to gain favor, even Fleabite joins in with his captives' laughter.

The leader turns to Naomi. "Do you also wish that we should let this 'man' go free?"

At her slow nod, he puts his fingers to his lips and whistles. Two more men appear, and the leader points toward Ruth's countryman. "Escort this flea lover back to his caravan."

"Surely you're not going to let him go?" One of Fleabite's captors can't contain his indignation. Even angry, bruised, and dirty from the scuffle, this young man makes a good first impression.

The swordsman ignores him and continues his instructions to the latest arrivals. "Once you have determined that they are really traders and are heading for the coast, let him go." Turning to Fleabite, the swordsman addresses him in the Moabite dialect. "You may keep your sorry life a little longer because the women have asked that we let you go, but don't enter our country again. We'll be watching, and we won't give you a second chance."

As Fleabite and his escorts leave, Naomi calmly fans herself. Ruth feels ready to burst out of her skin, so she busies herself with adjusting the donkey's pack that had slipped during the short-lived escape attempt. Strong young hands lift the load from the other side of the donkey, and bright blue eyes look into Ruth's brown ones. His appraising stare makes her suddenly aware of what she must look like after so much traveling. Ruth drops her eyes and turns her back to the young man, tucks a stray hair into a braid, and tries to brush accumulated dirt from her skirt.

The young man offers the women a drink from his water bag, and Ruth glances at him while she takes a sip and notices that he is still watching her. Embarrassed, she hands the water to Naomi.

RUTH : BETHLEHEM

"I am thankful for your protection." This self-assured Naomi has not made an appearance since the death of her sons. "Are you and your men traveling to Bethlehem?"

"Let me introduce myself. I am Jair, son of Elon, Retainer to Boaz." Jair gestures at the men who accompany him. "We are on patrol."

Noticing Naomi's confusion, the swordsman explains. "Raids on our flock and attacks on travelers have increased, so Boaz and the other city elders organized patrols made up of volunteers from every household. We are patrolling."

"I am pleased to hear that Boaz, my kinsman, is an elder now. He is truly a man of Yahweh." Naomi gracefully bows her head.

"It has been many years, but I remember your husband. He was a fine potter." The leader returns her bow. "Naomi, widow of Elimelech, may you find comfort in Bethlehem, and may your return in springtime be a sign of new hope in your life."

Naomi bows once more. "*Ani mode leha*. I am grateful to you."

With a gesture to the helpful young man, the leader continues, "Tola, also in the employ of Boaz, will continue to show his concern for your safety by escorting you until Bethlehem is in sight. It is just a half-day's journey."

Authority replaces the kindness in his voice as he addresses his subordinate. "Never again question my authority on patrol. You will escort the women safely to Bethlehem, and retrace your steps to meet up with us in the morning."

Between wondering at the change in Naomi and enjoying the scenery—Ruth is not bored walking through the desert on this leg of the journey. "All right, I admit it," she smiles to herself. "Tola is pleasant to watch, even from behind."

יהוה

"Ladies, your destination." Tola sweeps his arm toward Bethlehem and ends with a deep bow. "I regret I cannot tarry to escort you to the gates, but I must return to my patrol."

Ruth almost laughs out loud at the words that he has obviously been crafting carefully as they walked, but Naomi saves her from embarrassment with a dignified thanks. Tola turns and hurries back the way they came in a distance-eating trot.

The sight of Bethlehem gives Naomi a burst of energy. Even the donkey plods a little faster as he senses the end of the journey, but Ruth's legs feel like lead weights as she drags herself toward this new, unfamiliar life.

Naomi and Ruth squint at the women and children visiting by the well near the city gates.

"The well is a social place here, too." The familiarity of the scene calms Ruth's nerves a little. "Right, Naomi? This looks just like Moab."

Naomi continues without responding. The children are the first to notice strangers, and they come running. The donkey brays—it smells water and wants some *now*. An elderly woman shades her eyes and walks toward the travelers.

"Do my old eyes deceive me? Naomi, is that you?"

Naomi embraces her. "Shalom, Zebidah, my old friend. It is good to see you again." Naomi sways a little, overcome with emotion, and Zebidah leads her to a nearby bench.

"Look everyone!" Zebidah motions for the other women to come closer. "This is my dear friend Naomi, back from Moab."

Naomi covers her face and rocks back and forth on her seat, wiping tears from her cheeks. Finally she speaks in a husky voice, "I'm back home, but I should change my name from Naomi—the name "pleasant" no longer has anything to do with my life. Mara—bitter—would be more suiting."

The women make sympathetic sounds, and Zebidah sits and puts her arm around Naomi. "Oh dear, I'm so sorry. Tell us what happened."

"I left Bethlehem with a husband and two fine sons, but I return cursed, empty, and alone."

"Alone! What does that make me?" Ruth thinks and isn't sure what spiteful thing may have made its way out of her mouth if the donkey hadn't chosen that minute to try to knock her over to get at the water.

Zebidah motions to a girl to pour some water from her jar into a trough for the donkey. "Who is your traveling companion, then?" she asks Naomi. Everyone stares at Ruth with unsmiling wariness.

"That is Ruth, widow of my dear son Mahlon, may he rest in peace."

Eyes widen, then turn away. "I think I liked it better when I was invisible," Ruth thinks but hides her thoughts by busying herself with the donkey as the curious villagers quietly voice their judgments among themselves.

"Mommy, why is her skin so brown?"

"She's a Moabite."

"Poor Naomi. How could she let Mahlon marry such a woman?"

"It would have been better to stay here and starve."

Their whispers are loud enough to be overheard, but Ruth pretends not to hear. She straightens up and smiles, "Shalom."

Only Zebidah returns her greeting. "Shalom."

Mothers call their children, gather their belongings, and hoist their water jars to their heads. Soon only Zebidah is with them at the well.

"It is nearly Sabbath. Do you have a place to stay?"

Naomi doesn't look at Ruth as she shakes her head.

"My son will not welcome a Moabite in his house, especially on Sabbath."

"But she is my son's widow. And she worships Yahweh."

"Then perhaps he will agree. Hurry; it's nearly Sabbath."

Zebidah helps Naomi to her feet, and they leave the well together. His thirst quenched, the donkey has taken advantage of the inactivity to take a nap, and Ruth has to grab his ear to get him moving.

People are in a hurry to get home before the daylight is gone, but that doesn't stop them from staring at Ruth and whispering to each other as she trails along behind the two old women.

Although she says nothing, Ruth tries to think her way out of feeling miserable and unloved: "What did I think Naomi would say—that 'she only made it back to Bethlehem because of my help?' The way these women acted isn't any different from what Naomi experienced when she moved to Moab."

Ruth keeps her face expressionless as she continues her inner argument. "You would think she would know how I'm feeling having been in the same situation in Moab…but what do I want her to do? Hold my hand? No…but she didn't have to say she was alone."

EIGHTEEN

Ruth is the energetic one this morning, and Naomi drags her feet. Zebidah's young grandson Nahshon leads the way.

"Here we are." Nahshon steps through a doorway leading into a small courtyard. Four rooms surround it, but only one of the rooms has a functioning roof. The walls are still standing for the most part, but timbers, mud, and straw from the ruined roofs litter the interior of the rooms.

Ruth leads the donkey into the courtyard as Nahshon drops his pack of tools with a loud thump. Naomi stands in the doorway with her hand over her mouth.

"What a mess. Did you really live here?" At ten years old, Nahshon's curiosity outweighs his tact.

"It was beautiful once." Naomi smiles as she looks around.

"But that was a long time ago, before you went to Moab, right? Why didn't someone else live here while you were gone?"

"Nahshon's mouth is always in motion," Ruth thinks. "He reminds me of Orpah."

"We didn't think we would be gone so long…" Naomi drifts around the neglected courtyard, lost in memories.

Ruth steps into the only room with a functional roof. "Oooh, what a smell!"

"Phew." Nahshon backs away squeezing his nose.

"Something's been living here, but I don't think it was human." Ruth kicks at some debris and, as if to prove her point, a rat scutters away to hide somewhere else.

"At least it has a roof," Nahshon chirps.

"It sure does. It's amazing that it is still functioning after so many years—what a blessing." Ruth inwardly chides herself for her own negative reaction. She offers a silent prayer to Yahweh, "Adonia, I am sorry that I doubted you. I've been worried finding a place to live, and when I find out we have a home, I'm unhappy that it needs a lot of work. I should be thanking you."

Ruth turns to Naomi. "Mother, shall we bless our new home?"

LESS THAN A WIDOW

"It's not new to me, remember. All those years in Moab, my heart was always in this place. But, yes, let's say a blessing." Naomi holds out her arms and prays:

> "Please allow light and gladness, peace and companionship,
>
> to dwell in this home and bestow abundant blessings
>
> and holiness in all of its rooms and corners.
>
> Please bless, Yahweh, this abode.
>
> Amen, may it be your will."

Naomi begins to wander again—her mind seeing scenes from long ago. Ruth grabs a rake and shovel and holds them out to Nahshon. "I guess we'd better get started."

He chooses the shovel, and the two attack the piles of debris left from fifteen years of neglect. Naomi sometimes joins in, but more often she sits rocking in the shade dreaming about how things used to be.

"Did you eat your children?" Nahshon's question shocks Ruth out of her worry about Naomi.

"Of course not! What kind of question is that?"

Nahshon cringes at Ruth's sharp tone, but it doesn't dampen his curiosity. "Mother says Moabites roast their children."

Ruth thought, "These are just the kinds of questions I'd hoped I wouldn't have to answer." Out loud, she replied, "Your mother is talking about the priests of Chemosh—a very blood-thirsty and useless god. I wish it wasn't true, but although the priests do sacrifice children, they don't eat them." Ruth hopes in vain that her answer will prevent any more questions.

"Did you see them do that—the priests I mean?"

"It's an awful thing, and I have nothing to do with Chemosh. Naomi and Elimelech taught me about Yahweh, the God of the Hebrews, and I worship Him now."

"Then where are your children?" Nahshon can't get his questions out fast enough.

"I don't have any. My husband died before we had children."

"Was he sick?"

"No, it was an accident—an awful accident."

"Did you see it?"

"Enough!" Ruth tries to stop more irritation before it erupts from her mouth and continues with as much patience as she can manage. "We'd better save our breath for digging through this pile of garbage, don't you think?"

"I can work and talk at the same time." Nahshon's cheerful grin tells her that he's heard this comment before.

Ruth tries to change the subject. "So I've noticed. You are a hard worker, aren't you? Your father must be very proud of you."

Ruth finds that she is grateful for his help as the chatter—and the work—continues for days.

יהוה

Ruth quickly becomes a master scavenger. Today she found a clump of last fall's sycamore figs that had never been picked—probably because no one else was desperate enough to shimmy out on that limb to get them.

It's nearing sunset when she enters Bethlehem's gate and navigates the maze of shadowed streets and alleys toward home.

"Ow." Something hits her in the shoulder. A dirt clod careens off the wall just inches from her face and another explodes on her carrying pack. Running to the other side of the street, Ruth crouches and picks up a few stones of her own. One arm up to protect her face, she creeps toward the alley where the attack came from. Hearing the scuffle of feet, Ruth throws a stone and then two more in quick succession. Running footsteps and jeering laughter erupt.

She tells herself, "It's only some kids trying to scare me," but her body responds with a burst of energy, and she starts to trot.

Naomi is waiting for her in the doorway watching the road. "What's the matter? Are you hurt?"

"No, I just hurried to get home so you wouldn't worry—I had to go a little farther than usual today, but look what I found." Ruth pulls the wrapped bundle of figs out of her carrying bag, opens it, and hands it to Naomi.

"What a treat!" Ruth hands her the knife from her belt, and Naomi slices a piece off and pops it into her mouth. "And so sweet ..." She slices a piece off for Ruth who savors it in her mouth, sucking the sugary juices before chewing and swallowing.

"Supper is ready."

The women wash their hands—three times as the law demands—and they pray. Before the meal begins, they recite the blessing over the bread:

> "Blessed are you, HaShem, our God, King of the Universe,
>
> Who brings forth bread from the earth."

Tearing off a piece of the flatbread, Ruth uses it to scoop a mouthful from the bowl of roasted grains and greens her mother-in-law had prepared. Naomi nibbles while Ruth eats ravenously—she finds it hard to leave any aside for morning. Ruth reaches for just one more fig, cuts it into small pieces, and the two women make the small bites last as long as possible.

It's dark inside the sleeping room as the two women grope around preparing for sleep, but they have no oil to burn and don't have a lamp to put it in anyway. Ruth lays on her mat listening to Naomi's occasional snores, and when sleep finally comes, she dreams:

> Stones fly at me—thrown by shadow people.
>
> They laugh and jeer as they hurl their projectiles.
>
> And I have no place to hide. No protection.
>
> And then He speaks in quiet authority.
>
> "Peace; be still."
>
> The stones stop in mid-air;
>
> arms remain cocked mid-throw.
>
> "Take my hand."
>
> I hear his voice, but I can't take my eyes off of
>
> the shadow people and the stones hanging in the air
>
> inches from my head. I don't dare leave my head
>
> unprotected by reaching out my hand.
>
> I am petrified—unable to move.

Gasping for breath, Ruth fights her way out of the paralysis that gripped her during her dream, and slowly movement returns. "He was there," Ruth thinks. "Why didn't I take his hand?"

Feeling her way out of the dark room into the moonlit courtyard, Ruth can't stop shivering even though she is wrapped in her blanket, so she fans the banked embers in the fire pit. Her stomach grumbles loudly.

Sitting on a rock with her feet close to the fire, Ruth hugs herself, lays her head on her knees, and lets the tears flow. "Oh, Yahweh, I'm so tired of being afraid all the time, and hungry, too. We're almost out of grain, and I had to go so far to find anything we could eat today. I'm trying hard, but I don't think we can live much longer on the little food I can scavenge."

Ruth lays her head on her knees and hugs her legs close to her body. "The people hate me here—the kids throw rocks. And Naomi—I never know what to expect from her any more—and she hardly eats anything. I feel so alone."

Eyes closed, Ruth isn't sure if she is asleep or awake, but Yahweh is there holding out his hand, just as he does in her dreams. "Shalom—peace." This time when she hears his voice, she reaches up and takes hold of his hand; her tears slowly dry up, and her shivering stops.

"I'm not alone—forgive me for forgetting," Ruth prays softly. "You were with us in Moab, with us when we traveled here with the caravan, and you are still with us. Yahweh, I promised that you—Naomi's God—would be my God and I would come here to Bethlehem to live among her people—to care for her and love her. I will die with Naomi now if that is what you want. But I ask for life, for myself and for Naomi. Yahweh, give me strength and show me a way to live."

Ruth curls up next to the embers, and, finally sleeps.

יהוה

"I'm going to the well," Ruth calls to Naomi the next morning and mutters to herself, "At least I can keep us well supplied with water."

Ruth has gotten into the habit of getting up with the sun in order to have the well to herself and is surprised to find the streets busier than usual this morning. A seedy-looking group of men mill about, blocking off half of the narrow street. Ruth looks down and away as she walks quickly past them, trying not to draw any attention to herself.

"You don't need water, nekava. Right here—this is what you're thirsty for." The speaker, tall, with greasy hair and piercing eyes, steps toward Ruth and holds out his arms.

"Bet you couldn't find a real 'man' in Moab," a cohort chimes in and the others roar with laughter at his disgusting wit.

"You came to the right place, habibi. Here I am." The first man takes another step toward her.

Biting replies are screaming in her head, but Ruth knows better than to let them leave her mouth. She keeps walking quietly, but the men, egging each other on, follow her. "Don't run. That's just what they're waiting for," she tells herself.

"Is anyone looking for work today?"

The men turn to see who's offering work, and Ruth ducks into an alley, peeking back to see what's happening.

"I'm looking to hire workers. Who's interested?"

The tall ringleader turns, and the others follow on his heels.

LESS THAN A WIDOW

"Who's asking?"

At the familar-sounding voice, Ruth shades her eyes, but with the sun behind his back, all she can see is a silhouette. When the speaker looks at Ruth and nods, and she finally recognizes him. "It's Tola—our handsome rescuer on the trail," she tells herself with relief.

Tola turns his attention back to the men. "I am Tola, one of Boaz's foremen. We are looking for some men to bring water to the fields for the harvesters."

The men laugh. "Fetching water is women's work."

"Why don't you ask that sweet little morsel?" The gang's leader turns to Ruth peeking around the corner from the alley and purses his lips in a loud kiss.

Tola holds his hands up and waits until they quiet down. "Boaz needs strong men to carry water to the fields, enough for his workers. He offers a fair day's pay."

"Simon." The ringleader never takes his eyes off of Tola. "Simon will accept your offer to work for such an important man as Boaz."

"What?" But Simon backs down immediately at the leader's warning glare and follows Tola. Then the man turns to look at Ruth, still standing foolishly by the alley. "We will meet again." He spreads his ams wide and bows with a cruel grin.

Ruth ducks back into the alley, and as soon as she is out of their sight, she runs the rest of the way to the well.

Ruth pretends to herself that she is standing in the shadows to catch her breath, but the truth is, she's afraid to join the women and children gathered around the well.

"Those blasted men made me late!" she thinks with a blast of anger. "Now I'm going to have to face all these people." Ruth concentrates on slowing her breathing, and as her heart beat calms, so does her anxiety. She breathes a silent prayer. "Yahweh, you are still holding my hand, aren't you? Thank you for sending Tola at just the right time—again—for another rescue."

Zebidah sits on her favorite bench near the well gossiping with some old friends, and Ruth scolds herself silently. "Zebidah's here and so is Yahweh—you're not a helpless lamb facing a lion." Smiling at the picture in her mind of her wool-covered and cowering self, Ruth puts her empty jar on her head and steps into the sunshine of the crowded square. A little girl returns her timid smile with a saucy grin, and Ruth's confidence increases.

"Shalom, baba," Ruth greets Zebidah. She shades her eyes with her wrinkled hand to see who is speaking.

"Ruth, shalom, come sit with us in the shade." Zebidah moves her bulk over and pats the bench next to her. "Adah and Chava, this is Ruth, Naomi's daughter-in-law—the special young lady who is taking such good care of our friend."

"Naomi and I grew up together." Adah leans forward and whispers conspiratorially. "Of course, she is a few years older than I am."

Chava nods at Ruth and folds her arms across her chest.

"She's not too friendly, but at least she's not leaving," Ruth thinks as she bows her head respectfully to both of them before sitting next to Zebidah.

"How is Naomi this morning?" Zebidah asks.

"She is well, thank you for asking, baba." The women take up their conversation right where they were when Ruth interrupted, and she's soon forgotten. Sitting quietly, Ruth lets the words flow past her as she remembers visits to the well in Moab until Zebidah reaches over and pats her hand.

"…says the barley harvest will be good this year." Startled, Ruth brings her mind back to the present and catches the end of Adah's remark.

"There's enough barley to leave plenty in the corners and some dropped stalks in the fields for the poor to pick up." Zebidah gives Ruth's hand a squeeze to make sure she's listening.

"It hasn't come too soon for Rebekkah. Have you seen how poorly she looks?" Adah sighs and shakes her head. "My husband always remarks on what a beautiful child she was."

"How good would you look with a new baby and that good-for-nothing husband of hers sitting around the house?" Chava's hands clench on her lap.

"My husband says the wheat will be ready early this year also." Adah nods her head.

"Do you think Rebekkah will have to glean this year, with the new baby and everything?" Zebidah looks at Chava. "Surely not!"

"She'll have to. I brought some barley cakes to her yesterday afternoon, and that lazy man of hers was just sitting there with a jug. There was no food in the house, but plenty of wine."

"She doesn't have to go far—Balak's fields are right next door." Adah nods again. "My husband says…"

"No woman in her right mind would glean in Balak's fields!" Zebidah squeezes Ruth's hand very tightly this time.

Ruth squeezes the old woman's hand in response and thinks, "I'm listening, Zebidah."

"My husband says he sweeps the fields clean, even the corners," Adah voices her husband's opinion *again*. "Balak is such a stingy man."

"And don't forget those filthy men that work for him. Remember what happened last year?" Chava dabs at her eyes with a corner of her headcloth.

"Hush," Zebidah shakes her head. "Let her rest in peace."

The three old ladies bow their head, so Ruth does as well. After a moment of silence, conversation begins again.

"I'll visit Rebekkah again," Chava said, "and tell her to glean in Boaz's fields."

"Boaz is a good man, even if he is too generous for his son's liking," Adah puts in. "My husband thinks he has strange ideas now and then, especially for a man who is a city elder and a judge."

LESS THAN A WIDOW

"Maybe so, but women are safe in his fields." And Zebidah's hand patting begins again.

"Boaz is a good man—no doubt about it." Chava looks around as if daring any of us to challenge her opinion.

Adah smiles a sly smile, leans forward, and whispers to Ruth again. "And he's good to look at, too." She smoothes her skirt and winks.

"And what does your husband say to that?" Chava laughs as she asks the question, and Ruth joins in.

The three old women stand up and hug each other before they head for home, and Ruth is surprised to notice that the crowd around the well has dispersed. As she draws water, she thinks about what the women said and tries to remember what Nahshon told her about the barley harvest.

"Zebidah could have just told me about gleaning, but she loves to be clever," Ruth thinks affectionately.

"Shalom, Ruth." Nahshon self-importantly leads a donkey into the square. An older man with a crippled arm starts loosening bands from the donkey's carrying pack which holds two large waterskins.

"Nahshon. Shalom." Ruth had been so deep in thought that she didn't even hear him coming. "Your grandmother was just here for water..."

Nahshon rolls his eyes. "Women fetch water for their homes. I work for Boaz during harvest, remember?"

"Yes, I remember." Ruth can't help but smile at the disgusted look he gives her. "I just was confused because I heard Tola asking for workers to carry water this morning, so I thought..."

"There are water carriers for each of his fields." Nahshon points toward the waterskins. "Boaz keeps large water jars at all of his fields, and the workers get pretty thirsty. It's an important job."

"I bet the workers are glad to see you!"

The old man loses patience with our prattle. "They won't be so happy if we're late because you two were chattering like magpies."

Nahshon makes a face at Ruth behind the old man's back, and she has a hard time keeping a straight face.

Ruth stashes her full water jar and furtively follows Nahshon and the old man out of the city gates to one of Boaz's barley fields. Hiding in the shadow of a large boulder, she watches the harvesters at work.

Men grasp handfuls of standing grain stalks with one hand, cut them off at the base with a sickle, and lay the cut stalks in piles. Women gather and bind the cut grain into large standing bundles. Men then load the bundles into an oxcart and take them away.

Rivulets of sweat tickle as they run down Ruth's chest, and her damp clothes stick to her skin. "If it's this hot in the shade, it must be like an oven working in the fields," Ruth thinks sympathetically.

RUTH : BETHLEHEM

A raggedy group of men, women, and children wait by the side of the field. At the foreman's signal, they rush to a corner of the field where grain has been left uncut. They grab as much as they can, shoving those who are smaller and weaker to the side. When a loaded cart leaves an area of the field the foreman signals again, and the frantic gleaners compete for any stalks missed by the harvesters. A man cuffs a boy who grabs for some stalks he'd claimed as his own, and Ruth doesn't want to watch any more. "Oh, dear! This shadow's almost gone already," she thinks. "It must be almost midday—Naomi will be worried."

Trying to keep out of sight Ruth hurries back toward Bethlehem and chafes with impatience when she has to hide in a gully while a group of men with scythes pass by.

"The old women's warnings this morning scared me," Ruth realizes, but finds it hard to focus on being watchful when her mind is running in circles around this gleaning idea. "It is just like you, Yahweh, to come up with a law to help people who are always hungry—like Naomi and me."

To her relief, Ruth's water bottle is still where she hid it and she splashes some now-tepid water on her face and into her parched mouth before heaving it to her head. It's the hottest time of the day, and her sweat barely has time to glisten before it dissipates. "If I glean, we will have food to eat now, but not enough to last any length of time. And do I want to grab barley away from kids who are probably hungrier than I am?" Ruth thinks as she walks.

Naomi calls from the door to our courtyard. "Ruth, where have you been?"

"Sorry I'm late." Ruth puts the water jar in its place and is surprised by her mother-in-law's strong hug.

"I don't know whether to hit you or hug you—I was that worried." Naomi holds Ruth's shoulders at arms' length and looks her in the eye. "Where were you?"

Naomi has been so absorbed in herself and her sorrow for such a long time that Ruth is shocked at her attention to the real world. "There were a lot of people at the well, so I had to wait. Then I got talking to Zebidah and two friends—you know them—Adah and Chava."

Naomi nods and waits for more, and Ruth doesn't know where to start. "I'm so hot ..."

"Wash up, and then we'll talk."

As Ruth strips down to her shift and pours dippers of water over her head, arms, and legs, she wonders how her mother-in-law will react. "Naomi won't want me to glean—I don't really want to either. But how else will we eat?"

Ruth glances over at her mother-in-law who spreads an eating mat and places a full bowl in the center. "Are those barley cakes?" And Ruth realizes how hungry she is—not only for barley cakes but for a real conversation with Naomi, something the two women haven't enjoyed for a long time.

LESS THAN A WIDOW

At first they just eat, relishing the sweetness of the honey, the chewiness of the cake, and the nutty crunch of seeds. It's not until they are picking the last crumbs out of the bowl that Ruth asks, "Where did you get these?"

Naomi laughs, and her laughter is as refreshing to Ruth as the barley cakes. "I wondered how long it would be before you asked that question. And I was right."

"When they were gone." Ruth joins her laughter.

"To the last crumb." Naomi pours something in a cup and hands it to Ruth. "Sweet tea."

Ruth sips the hot liquid and swishes it around in her mouth, unwilling to swallow until she has tasted every hint of flavor. "Did Yahweh send an angel visitor this morning?"

"Perhaps, but she looked very much like Zebidah with a large basket."

Ruth smiles. "She had a busy morning."

So they talk about gleaning—the Hebrew law which allows the poor to follow the reapers to collect grain left in the fields after harvesting. And about how the generosity of each landlord determines how much remains and who gets to glean.

"It's not only grain, but grapes and olives in the orchards. Elimelech always left more than what the law requires." When Naomi speaks her husband's name, it's almost a caress.

"I'm going to glean for barley tomorrow."

"You went out to the fields today to watch, didn't you?" When Ruth nods, Naomi lets out a long sigh. "Then you know how hot, dirty, and tiring the work is."

"Yes, I do."

"And how dangerous it is for women like us."

"We have to eat, and our grain is almost gone."

"Ruth, you know that no matter how hard you work, you won't be able to gather enough to make a difference for very long."

"Maybe not, but I need to try."

RUTH & BOAZ
רוּת & בֹּעַז

BETHLEHEM

NINETEEN

Ruth is up before dawn, too nervous to sleep. As soon as it is light enough to see, she makes her way through the twisting alleys and streets of Bethlehem and out of the gates to the fields. Stopping by yesterday's shade-giving boulder, Ruth prays as she settles down out of sight to watch for the man in charge. "Yahweh, give me the courage and strength that I will need today. May your loving heart swell up in Boaz so that he will listen to my request."

A group of men and women make their way to the fields. As they get closer Ruth recognizes Tola walking at the head of the workers, deep in conversation with a man just a little older than him.

"Could that be Boaz?" Ruth wonders. "Surely he is too young."

Tola moves to the back of the cart and passes out tools to the workers. The other man walks through the stubble left after yesterday's harvest and surveys the barley that is waiting to be cut. He bends, cuts off a few stalks, and examines them before lifting his arm in a signal. Tola returns the wave and directs the men to begin work. The other man continues his walk past the gleaners who are arriving at the field, and smiles as he drops the stalks next to a young boy. That act gives Ruth courage.

Ruth makes her way to the young man in charge and waits to be noticed. When he is alone, Ruth approaches. "Excuse me, sir. Are you Boaz, the owner of these fields?"

"I am Boaz's son Aram, and I am in charge of the harvest."

"Oh, I beg your pardon…"

"The old women didn't mention anything about his son," Ruth thinks. "Do I talk to him or wait and hope that Boaz will show up? If I wait, I'll lose my nerve, and Aram did notice the gleaners with kindness. I have to say something soon or I will lose my chance. But he is the one who speaks first."

Aram speaks first. "You're the Moabitess, aren't you? The one who came home with our cousin Naomi."

"Yes. My name is Ruth. Naomi is my mother-in-law."

"If you are here to glean, we welcome you."

Ruth nods, but before she can say anything more a worker approaches with a question. Stepping back, Ruth waits until their conversation is concluded before she approaches Aram again. He frowns when he sees that she is still there.

"Is there something else?"

"I had hoped to talk with Boaz."

Aram waits with growing impatience for her to go on, but Ruth silently continues her internal argument. "You know about Boaz and his reputation. This is his son, but that doesn't mean they are the same."

Aram notices her confusion and points to the other gleaners waiting by the field. "All you have to do is follow the other gleaners there and do what they do. You can wait with them for your turn to enter the fields." He starts to turn away, so Ruth blurts out the first thing that comes to her mind.

"I understand how to glean, but I wanted to ask Boaz..." Ruth stutters to a stop realizing how brash that sounded when he was trying to be kind.

"Look, I am in charge here, and I give you permission to glean." Aram scowls at Ruth and waves his hand toward the hungry people waiting their turn. Looking at their tired faces, hopeless already before the day's work has even begun, Ruth decides to take a chance.

"May I work in the field, right behind the women?"

Aram's snort is not encouraging. "We leave the corners and the edges for the poor to glean."

"And that is very kind, but there are so many poor people and not a lot of grain. If I could glean among the women..."

Aram cuts Ruth off mid-sentence. "We follow the law—corners and edges are left for the poor. You enter the field after we are finished." Aram turns his back on Ruth.

Ruth doesn't budge and breathes a silent prayer. "I need him to hear the rest. Yahweh, open his ears and his heart."

Ruth talks to his back, and Aram reluctantly turns to face her again. "The whole village speaks of the generosity and fairness of the house of Boaz. It is for that reason that I dare to ask, and I beg your pardon for my boldness. You spoke of the law about gleaning. Will you tell me where this law came from?"

Aram's searching gaze is unnerving, and Ruth looks down and remains as still as she can, still praying. "Please, don't let him be offended. Please, Yahweh, let him explain it to me and in the explaining speak your truth and love."

"Yahweh, our God, King of the Universe, gave the laws to our forefather Moses when he led us to this land. Leaving food for the poor is one of these laws, and we are very careful to live rightly as He commanded." Aram speaks proudly in much the same manner that Elimelech used when teaching the Torah to his sons.

"This is a strange law—one we don't have in Moab. What is its purpose?"

"As Yahweh cares for us, we Hebrews care for each other so that our poor do not go hungry."

Aram's pride—oblivious to reality—makes Ruth angry, so she turns and looks at those waiting to glean while she calms herself, thinking, "Is he blind? How can he say those people aren't hungry"?

While Aram waits for Ruth's response, he follows her gaze, and his frown deepens.

"But, look at them, sir. They are still hungry. They barely gather enough for today and maybe tomorrow. And they have to fight each other for every stalk of grain. Is that what Yahweh intended when he gave this law to Moses?"

Aram doesn't say anything for a long time.

Ruth opens her mouth to speak, but instead covers it with her hand and looks at the ground. "Yahweh, our God, King of the Universe, pour your love into his heart."

When Aram finally speaks, Ruth jumps. "You may glean among the women. Now go. Don't bother me with any more questions."

Ruth bows low to the ground. "Thank you, wise sir, for your kindness." But she is bowing to an empty field, for Aram strides away and begins a conversation with Tola who is working alongside the harvesters.

Adjusting her carrying shawl, Ruth enters the field. The conversation has drained all of her energy and a full day of work is waiting for her. The best she can do is a slow, methodical rhythm of stooping, picking up dropped stalks, and pushing them into her shawl. The sun is hot and burns the moisture from her body. The only water she brought with her is in one of Mahlon's pilgrim flasks, so she stops only occasionally to stand up, stretch her back, and take a small sip of water. While she works, she worried, "Any minute Aram might change his mind. Or Boaz might get angry and reverse his permission."

Step, bend, pick up, stow away—the rhythm becomes automatic and it takes all Ruth's strength to maintain it. She loses all sense of time and surroundings, except for once when she hears the cry of a tiny hungry baby. She is at the end of a row, and a startlingly thin young mother puts the crying infant to her breast. Without thinking, Ruth pulls a double-handful of grain stalks out of her shawl and lays them next to the nursing mother before turning back to the field.

TWENTY

Once out of sight of Bethlehem's gates, Boaz grabs a handful of stones and hurls them one at a time into a patch of green vines along the path. A gourd breaks open with a splat, and he flexes his shoulder.

"The old arm still has it," Boaz thinks and stands still listening—birds chirping, the scurrying of a small animal among the leaves, puffs of a breeze rattling the vines—and he smiles. "This is what I miss during those long hours in city council and sitting as the judge for those in the Bethlehem area." Instead of listening to wildlife and natural sounds, he listens to people talk—raging, complaining, debating, crying, promoting, selling, whining—and every once in a great while he hears a creative idea.

"Wait, there is at least one weasel I get to hear on a regular basis—good old Balak plays the role quite well." Boaz smiles at the thought and stays quiet as he enjoys nature for a few more minutes.

It's after elders' meetings to rule on complaints such as the one he just sat through that Boaz realizes how much he still misses Sarai. She was a good listener who kept things to herself, and a wise advisor when asked. "And sometimes even when not asked," Boaz smiles at the picture of Sarai sitting nearby with her head cocked to the side. "I could always tell when she had something to tell me. And she never let me get by with feeling sorry for myself too long before she told me to 'get to work.'"

"Hard physical work untangles many knots." Boaz quotes out loud the saying he first heard from his mother Rahab—one Sarai was fond of repeating.

Acting as an elder at Bethlehem's gates means listening to complaints and guiding the people through their differences—and what can't be resolved there comes before the judge. "And there I sit again. It's the same old thing—just on a grander scale." Boaz's thoughts transition to a prayer, "Yahweh, sometimes I wonder if you are sorry you chose us to be your people. It's surely not because of our loyal observance of your laws and ways." Boaz shakes his head as if that would clear it. "I'm out here to forget about all that for a while."

This has always been his favorite time of year: harvest to threshing. Of course, he doesn't have to be in the fields anymore because Aram has taken over those responsibilities, but Boaz can't stay away. He heads down the trail toward the barley fields, impatient to be a part of a group of people working hard together.

Boaz reminds himself why Aram is in charge of the crops now. "I don't have time to do it justice, and someday all that I have will be his. But I can't resist." Boaz flexes his shoulders and stretches his back as he walks—impatient to feel a scythe in his hand. "See, Sarai," he mutters with a grin skyward. "I'm still taking your advice."

Tola sees him coming and signals his men to take a break from cutting grain. They gather around the water jars in an open-air pavilion by the side of the field.

"The Lord be with you." Boaz claps one man on the shoulder, and nods at another, until he has greeted each of them. Surrounded by these sweating men, Boaz takes pleasure in two of his favorite things: working alongside others and the challenge of pushing his body—at least pushing it as hard as it will still go.

"The Lord bless you," the men return his greeting.

Boaz realizes he is superfluous and not really one of the workers any more, but he also believes that being with the men in a different environment than a courtroom, joining them, and renewing acquaintances as they labor side by side helps him immensely in his governing roles. "I'm not sure Aram agrees or understands—he does all the work, and I get all the fun," Boaz muses. "I probably drive him crazy, but the truth is, I'll be out here at harvest time even when they have to wheel me in a cart."

Tola hands Boaz a dipper of water. He takes a sip, pours the rest over his head, and shakes it off of his hair and beard, splashing the young man. He looks at the cut grain and stretches to his full height with a smile. "Not a bad morning's work for a bunch of young pups still wet behind the ears."

Tola grins at him and teases back, "It's a good thing those of us who are young and strong can work hard so our elders can have time to sit at the city gates." Tola's like a son to Boaz—he's lived with the family since his mother, Boaz's distant cousin, died in childbirth and Sarai, already nursing, was willing to feed two babies. When Tola's father died, his older brothers weren't interested in another mouth to feed, so he became a permanent member of their family.

"Who are you calling old?" Boaz pretends offense. "What you see is experience, not old age. Let me show you how it's really done."

Boaz makes a big show of taking off his coat and stripping down to a belted sleeveless shift. The men whistle and cheer as he flexes first one arm, then the other, and stretches his back and legs. They know what's coming, and they're more than happy to extend their water break. "Up and back?"

Tola picks up his scythe and hands one to Boaz. "Fastest or most grain?"

"Let's go for speed."

RUTH & BOAZ : BETHLEHEM

Boaz gets the jump on Tola, who makes a show of scrambling to catch up. The men lay down bets and call out encouragement. The women also cheer and laugh from the field as they wipe sweat from their faces and tuck stray hairs under their scarves.

The two men are neck-and-neck at the end of the row, but Tola starts to pull ahead on the way back.

"No way is this young buck going to beat me." Boaz tells himself, but it takes everything that he has, and even then he barely passes Tola before they get back to the edge of the field.

Tola stands up and shakes his head. "Tired already? Let's go another row."

Boaz tries to quit gasping for breath, takes his hands off of his knees, and straightens up slowly. "I'd better leave some for the rest of you." He bows to the watching threshers. "Hope you were paying attention to my method."

Aram joins the men in the pavilion, and father and son watch the men and women settle back into their work. As Boaz drinks another dipperful of water, Aram asks wryly, "Don't you think it's about time to drop the yearly spectacle, Father?"

Boaz laughs even though the same thought had occurred to him, but Aram doesn't even crack a smile. "Then I'd have to come up with another way to keep that young man in line." Boaz rotates his shoulders and changes the subject. "Look at the grain! Yahweh be praised for ending the drought with His gentle rains."

Ignoring the pangs of jealousy—not even sure if they stem from his father's ease with Tola or the admiration of the men—Aram nods and shows Boaz some charcoal scratches on a piece of bark. "Look, we are bringing in almost double the amount of sheaves that we harvested in this field last year." Aram has compared the yearly harvests from each of the fields since he was old enough to work in them.

"He studies these records so much, I bet he has them memorized," Boaz thinks as he looks at the lines scratched in groups of five and nods before handing the tally back to his son. While he appreciates Aram's attention to detail, Boaz has never understood what use these records will be, except they are important to his son.

Boaz looks at the workers—in addition to those who work on their estate year round, Aram has been able to provide work for many who depend on it to feed their families. "I am glad to see that you have hired so many this year."

Aram holds up the tally sheet with a smile. "And this shows me that we will be able to hire some of these same men after the harvest is completed to build some tiers into the hillside and expand our vineyard."

Boaz doesn't reply, because something about the women stacking sheaves has grabbed his attention, and he can't quite figure out what...A young woman—someone he hasn't seen before—is methodically gathering up dropped stalks into a carrying sack instead of stacking them. "Who is that?" he asks Aram. "Did you hire her?"

Aram shakes his head. "I wondered how long it would take you to notice. She's the widow of Naomi's son Mahlon. Her name is Ruth."

"Why isn't she stacking?...Oh, she's gleaning! Right in the middle of our women!" Boaz looks at Aram with a questioning look.

"I gave her permission to glean among the workers." Aram looks the other way as he replies, and Boaz is intrigued.

"Very unusual; Aram rarely goes against tradition," Boaz thinks as he follows his son's gaze to the field just as Ruth straightens up to take a drink of water. "I can see that it could be hard to say no to this young lady."

As if she feels the men's gaze, Ruth bends back to her work, using sheaves and other workers to shield herself from their sight. "There's grace and strength in the way she moves." Boaz thinks and nods his head knowingly as he tells Aram, "I see...She is an attractive woman."

Startled, Aram protests quickly. "You know that's not...I hadn't really noticed."

"So, if that's not it, what is she doing gleaning in the field right alongside the women?" Boaz can seldom resist teasing his ever-so-serious son.

Aram clears his throat. "She asked why Yahweh would make a law that allowed gleaning for the poor if we don't allow them to gather enough grain to keep them alive for more than a day."

"But we do. We're generous, more than most..."

"I mentioned that." Aram shook his head ruefully. "But she was persistent and quite convincing. Ruth said generosity doesn't seem to make that much of a difference for those who have no other means to gather food. 'Just look at them,' she told me. 'Do they look like they've been getting enough to eat?'" Aram shrugged his shoulders. "Look at the gleaners yourself. What would you have said?"

Boaz continues to watch Ruth as he tries to sort out his reactions to her challenging question. "She makes a good point—are we doing enough? Have we ever done enough? We always leave larger corners of standing grain than any others in Bethlehem do—just look at all the gleaners in our fields. And we instruct the women stacking the sheaves to leave some grain on the ground for the gleaners to pick up." Turning his gaze to those who are waiting for the opportunity to glean, Boaz realizes he hasn't looked at them closely since the drought ended. "There are so many, and our leavings won't feed them for long. Are we doing what Yahweh desires us to do?"

Boaz finally turns to his son with a response. "Your decision was made with your heart—one that seeks to follow Yahweh—and I commend you for that. But now that you've had some time to think, it sounds as if you may be having second thoughts?"

RUTH & BOAZ : BETHLEHEM

Aram hesitates and frowns and replies with hesitation. "I don't know—it will make trouble if the other gleaners want the same thing. It will eat into our profits, and we still haven't recovered fully since the drought. I don't see how giving this same permission to others could be a good thing." Boaz remembers then that Aram already has plans for the profits.

"The other field owners won't like this either, you know." Aram is unhappy as he lists the repercussions from his impulsive decision, but Boaz doesn't seem to be concerned. "Grandfather's generosity spread our finances so thin, we almost had to sell much of our land," Aram thinks as he waits for his father's response. "Father's cut out of the same cloth—he doesn't look beyond the people and their supposed needs to what our success brings to them." Aram discusses this subject at length with his wife, but hasn't found a way to broach it with his father.

Boaz starts speaking, and Aram isn't surprised that he skipped all the details and went straight to the people issue. "Nobody wants to hear that what we've always thought is the right thing to do really isn't right enough—especially when it's brought to our attention by a Moabite. Maybe I should bring this question of gleaning practices up with the city elders. So many people suffered during the drought—especially the poor, and if we could persuade others to join us in this change, our generosity would go a long way to bring health and recovery back to Bethlehem. Perhaps this young woman's question is an important one that all of us should be asking ourselves: are we following Yahweh's laws in the manner that He intended us to?" Boaz's mind races as he plans the best way to present the idea. "I don't have to mention that she was the one who sparked the conversation—there are some that would take offense—but perhaps a suggestion that our humble town can set an example for others..."

"While you are thinking about the poor, it would be good to remember how close we are to once again becoming one of them!" Aram hears the resentment in his tone and stops to draw a deep breath. His next words, although calmly stated, reveal his intense emotions. "We are still rebuilding what we lost, and there is a lot yet to be done."

Boaz looks at his son, trying to understand what he is saying. "Have you changed your mind, then? Will you tell her not to come back?"

Aram raises his fists, opens them, and shrugs in exasperation.

"I thought Aram would be relieved to let me take the responsibility for this, but he seems almost angry with my suggestion," Boaz thinks. "There's no way he wants to be the one responsible for the upset this is going to cause among wealthy landowners—he hates departing from tradition—and it's costly. But he made the decision from his heart this time—in response to Yahweh—and for that, I will gladly be held accountable. Perhaps when the lands become fully his, he will continue to be generous instead of holding on so tightly to

LESS THAN A WIDOW

every penny." Boaz says none of this out loud, but instead asks another joking question.

"And your young woman Ruth, how has she done today?"

Aram scowls, but he evidently can't help but be impressed. "She's *not* my young woman, Father, but she is a hard worker. Ruth hasn't stopped all morning except to take sips of water. And she gave some of the stalks she collected to Rebekkah."

"Bold, hard-working, and generous. No wonder Naomi returned to Bethlehem safely," Boaz states aloud as his mind complains, "So much for leaving the tough questions on the judge's bench—we face a difficult issue in our own fields."

"So Yahweh sends a Moabite to challenge our charity—and I am pleased that Yahweh placed a good heart in you, Harvest Master." Boaz puts his hand on Aram's shoulder. "But you are in charge here. What do you propose we do about this whole situation?"

He shakes his head, but Aram knows what he must decide. "Ruth may continue to glean," he answers with a sigh.

"And do you wish me to bring this matter to the city council?"

Aram appreciates what it took for his father to ask that question, and his earlier anger fades. "Talk to the elders, and we'll see what happens. I will see if I can still find a way to pay for the improvements to the vineyard."

Boaz throws his robe over his shoulder and crosses the field to talk to this audacious young Moabite woman. When Ruth notices his approach, she casually moves off in the other direction, still gleaning. Even sweaty and covered with dust and chaff, there is something about Ruth that draws the eye, and Boaz tries to determine what it is. Her skin is darker than most of the others; her hair is covered in a scarf, but curls have pulled out of the braids and stick to her damp forehead. She must be tired, but she still moves with the grace of a gazelle. Surprised by how much he has noticed about her, Boaz laughs at himself. "Guess I'm not such an old man after all. But, she's a Moabite, a relative of my cousin, and someone in need...that's all I need to think about."

As he picks his way over the stubble, Boaz hears Yahweh's voice in his heart: "This is just the beginning."

TWENTY-ONE

It's not hard for Ruth to guess what Boaz and Aram are talking about, but still she wishes she could overhear what they are saying.

"This could be the last time I get to glean in Boaz's fields," she worries and tries to hurry in case Boaz decides she needs to take her place with the other gleaners, but that just makes her clumsy, so she settles back into the rhythm of the morning: stoop, pick up dropped stalks, and push them into her shawl. When Boaz starts to cross the field, Ruth changes direction to stay out of his path.

"You are welcome in my field, my daughter."

"He's talking to me!" Ruth wills her lungs to take a breath and straightens up. Boaz's gaze is on her hand, and Ruth is embarrassed to feel her fingers wrapped around the handle of the knife hanging from her belt and quickly drops her hand to her side. "Say something, you fool!" she thinks, but her mind's a blank. Instead Ruth bows awkwardly around her shawl full of grain stalks, so she finally takes it from her shoulder and turns towards Boaz.

"Thank you for your kindness, sir." Ruth keeps her eyes lowered and waits for him to leave, but he has more to say.

"Don't glean in any other fields but mine—it's not safe." The tone of Boaz's welcome was friendly, but this is the voice of a man used to being obeyed. "Watch where my men are harvesting and stay with my women—follow along with them. I will give orders to my men that no one is to harass you."

"Former slaves know how to obey orders," Ruth thinks and keeps her head down to not betray any emotion.

"You cannot carry enough water in your small flask for these hot days, so when you are thirsty, go and get a drink from the water jars under the pavilion," Boaz continues. "My men keep the jars full."

"I expected to be sent away, and instead he is giving me more than I asked for." Confused, Ruth sneaks a glance at Boaz's face, and finds the he is watching her closely. "What does he want from me in return?" she thinks, and this time she bends her knees and presses her face to the ground as warning bells toll in her head. Her mouth asks a question before her brain can stop it. "Why have I found such favor in your eyes that you notice me—a foreigner?"

"I know all about you."

LESS THAN A WIDOW

Ruth's hand involuntarily returns to her knife hilt as she stands up. Boaz notices her distress and spreads his hands wide, palms up.

"Don't be afraid. I only mean that others have told me how much you have done for your mother-in-law Naomi since the death of both of her sons and how you left your homeland to come live with her here among a people you did not know before."

He begins a formal blessing that reminds Ruth of Elimelech, and her eyes fill with tears.

"May the Lord repay you for what you have done.

May you be richly rewarded by Yahweh, the God of Israel,

under whose wings you have come to take refuge."

"Zebidah is right—this is a good man," Ruth thinks, feeling shame for her suspicions.

"Again, I must thank you, sir," Ruth responds. "You've spoken kindly to me, your lowly servant—even though I don't have the standing of one of your maidservants."

Ruth bows low again, and when she looks up, he is walking away. The women had been watching their exchange, and everyone returns to work as if they had never stopped, but it's different now—Ruth is not just a day's anomoly any more. Boaz invited the foreigner to have a place with them for the whole harvest, and their glances range from curiosity to malice.

When the sun reaches its zenith—during the hottest time of the day—the workers stop to eat, drink, and rest in the shade of the shelters that Boaz and Aram have provided.

Ruth's flask is already empty. "Boaz is right," Ruth admits to herself. "I won't make it through the afternoon if I don't drink some water." When all the workers finish their hand-washing and dig into the meal that is provided for them, Ruth timidly skirts the edges of the pavilion, trying to be invisible, as she makes her way to the water jars.

"Come and eat with us." Boaz calls out as he holds out some bread toward her. "You can dip this in the wine vinegar."

Tola sits next to Boaz, as do many others—both men and women. They make space for Ruth, and she can't think of a way to politely refuse. When she sits down, Boaz offers Ruth a pile of roasted grain on a piece of flatbread—a very large handful—so she eats as nonchalantly as she can, eyes on her bowl as conversation flows around her.

When Ruth sneaks a quick glance around, Tola catches her eye. With a grin he offers her another piece of bread. She smiles a thank you and reaches to dip it in a bowl of seasoned oil when someone else's hand beats her to it.

After a long soak, the hand raises dripping bread to the smiling lips of a stunning young girl—a smile which is not echoed in her eyes. Ruth wraps the bread with the leftover grain in a cloth to take home and excuses herself.

Rather than carrying all the extra weight of the stalks on the long walk home, gleaners do their threshing at the field as much as possible.

"I don't know who that girl is, but she sure doesn't want me here—or is she mad that Tola smiled at me?" Ruth tries to make sense out of the interactions during the meal as she beats the stalks over a carrying cloth, and the kernels of grain make a small mound. "Unfortunately, people don't need a reason to hate each other—that's the same here as it is in Moab."

As Ruth heads back toward the field to join the others for the afternoon's work, she hears Boaz's voice as he speaks to the drovers who transport the bundled grain to the barn. "…Even if she gathers among the sheaves, don't embarrass her. In fact, pull out some stalks from the bundle and leave them for her to pick up, and don't rebuke her…"

"Boaz not only asked Yahweh to bless me, but he is helping to make it happen," Ruth realizes in amazement. "I don't need to worry what others think."

Gleaning is hard, but it's the kind of tedious work that only requires your body stay in motion while your mind travels wherever it wants. As she works Ruth digests what she has learned about Boaz from every angle—he is not what she expected. "He's not as old as I thought he would be—at least he can still take on Tola. And he said he knew all about me—and it wasn't all bad. I wonder who could have told him—I don't really know anyone here."

Boaz's face wasn't the only one making an appearance in Ruth's thoughts. She replayed Tola's smile as he offered her the bread. And then there was the contest—she'd watched him as much as she had watched Boaz. "His arms and shoulders are muscular, like Mahlon's. I remember rubbing balm into tired muscles…Stop! That part of my life is over, remember? Think about something else."

Ruth loses herself in the thoughtless rhythm of work until someone sticks out a foot and trips her as she bends to pick up a dropped stalk. She tries to move out of the way, but is surrounded by a group of young women. Ruth's not surprised to see the striking face attached to the body, attached to the leg, attached to the foot that tripped her.

"Boaz goes too far this time." The young lady's hissed words are full of venom, and her friends follow her lead.

"What is he thinking?"

"It's obvious, isn't it? What do men always think about?"

Ruth tries to walk away, but the beautiful girl with hate-filled eyes steps in front of her. "We don't want you here, selling yourself to our men."

An older woman calls out, "Maacah, come help me tie up this stack."

LESS THAN A WIDOW

"I'll be right there." But before Maacah leaves, she hisses at Ruth, "Go back to Moab with your own kind!"

Ruth's daydreaming takes a much darker turn for the rest of the afternoon, so much that she doesn't notice how much more quickly she fills her carry sack than she had in the morning. As the workers pack up for the day, Ruth beats the stalks with a wooden flail so the stubborn kernels fall into her shawl.

"I can't believe how much is here," she murmurs to herself. Her cramping back muscles believe it—the carry sack weighs as much as a well-fed child!

"It's enough to feed us for a month!" That thought gives Ruth the energy to carry the heavy load home, alone in a crowd of Hebrews.

יְהוָה

Ruth hides her full carrying shawl when she gets home and makes a big show of dumping the threshed grain that she carried home in her apron into the storage basket.

Naomi watches and runs her hand through the barley. "Who was so good to you?"

Instead of answering, Ruth pulls her full carrying shawl from its hiding place and adds its contents to the basket. Naomi covers her mouth with cupped hands and her eyes glisten with tears. She takes a deep raggedy breath before asking again, "Whose fields were you in?"

"They belong to Boaz. But it was his son Aram who first gave me permission to glean in the field alongside the women tying sheaves."

"With the women? Oh, Ruth, what did you do?"

"I can't believe you asked me that!" Still smarting from her altercation with Maacah, all Ruth's stored-up anger comes out in a flood of words. "You know me, and the first thing you think is, 'Oh, she is a Moabite, so she must have offered her body...'

Ruth jerks away from Naomi's fingers pressed softly on her mouth to stop her angry words. "Get away from me."

Naomi holds her hands out in regret. "I am so sorry! Please forgive me. I know you would never...I spoke before I thought. I would rip those words away from between us if I could. May we begin again?"

The leak of emotion becomes a gush, and Ruth can hardly contain her rage. She turns her back on her mother-in-law and gives way to her angry thoughts. "I have given up everything for her. I practically carried her on my back to get here, to clean this place up, to find food. She says almost nothing for months, and now that she's talking again she accuses me of being a whore?!"

Ruth can't even stand to look at her mother-in-law, so she pours dippers of water into a bowl, strips down to her shift, and tries to wash her anger away. "She said she was sorry," Ruth tells herself. "And the one I should really be mad at is that shrew Maacah—I'll have to watch out for her. She heard everything Boaz said and still spreads lies. Besides, Naomi didn't ask me to come here—she told me not to."

Ruth sits down to wash her feet, but Naomi kneels before her and gently takes the cloth from her hands. Naomi bathes Ruth's feet one at a time and then dries them softly, never once looking up at her daughter-in-law's face.

Her anger fading, Ruth relaxes under Naomi's gentle hands. "How can I stay angry at this precious woman who raised me, who married me to her son, who taught me about Yahweh?"

"Thank you, Mother."

Naomi smiles, "Let's begin again," and sits next to Ruth. "Please, tell me all about your day."

So she does. Ruth tells her about her request to Aram and his response. About the tedious work in the hot sun, about running out of water before noon, and about being invited to eat a meal with the workers. Naomi enjoys the story of Boaz and Tola's contest so much that Ruth gets a little carried away with her descriptions of the two men. But when she repeats Boaz's blessing and his command—"well, that's what it was really," Ruth states—Naomi claps her hands.

"May Yahweh bless Boaz for showing kindness to us as well as to our dead husbands."

Ruth's stomach responds with a loud growl, and she remembers the roasted grain left over from lunch. Naomi adds it to the meager fare she had prepared, there's plenty for both of them. They concentrate on eating.

Ruth is exhausted, but Naomi isn't ready for sleep. Even after the two women settle onto their sleeping mats, her voice comes softly out of the darkness. "I believe that perhaps Yahweh has not deserted me after all."

Ruth's tired response is a soft grunt as she squirms around trying to find a comfortable position for her aching muscles. The smile on her face surprises her, and she thinks, "It's amazing how our attitudes improve when we know we have enough food for the next week."

"Boaz is one of our go'els, you know." Naomi isn't finished talking yet.

That's a new word for Ruth, and her curiosity pulls her back from sleep's invitation. "I knew he was related to you somehow, but what's a go'el?"

"It's another Hebrew law from Moses' time about taking care of others in need, like the law about gleaning. If a man falls on hard times and is forced to sell his land, a close relative—a go'el—is responsible to buy the land to keep the property in the family."

"Like this house?"

"Well, yes, if Elimelech had sold it, but he didn't because we thought we would be back in a year or so."

In the darkness Ruth hears Naomi adjust her blankets and pillow before she adds, "It didn't work out quite like we thought it would."

Ruth likes to understand things thoroughly, and that impulse is strong enough to keep her awake in spite of her body's desire for sleep. "So if Elimelech had sold this house, Boaz would have had to buy it back for you when we came back?"

Naomi coughs. "If he is our nearest kinsman—I've been gone too long to know for sure—and if, as go'el, he would choose to do so. Not every man can or will do this."

"Why not?"

"It takes a lot of money—how many people do you know who are willing to give their own money away without any hope of ever getting any of it back?"

"But I thought you said it was a law."

Naomi's smile—although not visible in the darkness—is obvious in her voice. "There are a lot of ways to obey the law. But you don't need me to explain that to you—I believe that was the point you made to Aram just this morning."

Ruth's snort of laughter sounds like a snore—it might be one—but she needs to understand one more thing before she can sleep. "So, is this the same law you were talking about before we came here, the one you told Orpah and me about, that you were too old to marry someone else so you could have a son who would have to marry one of us?"

"No, they are totally different laws: a go'el redeems property. This other law from the Torah—the law of yibum—is to make sure that there is a son to carry on the family name if a man dies without an heir."

"That happened to us—well, sort of. Elimelech died first, and his heirs died later—still there is no one to carry on the family name. So isn't someone from Elimelech's family supposed to marry you?"

"No, and that's exactly why I tried to convince you not to come. I'm too old to have a child, and you are…well…"

"A Moabite who hasn't been able to bear children."

"You're my devoted daughter-in-law, and I love you very much, but our circumstances are unusual."

Ruth doesn't know if Naomi slept that night, but her exhausted body demanded—and received—deep, unmoving sleep.

TWENTY-TWO

Even though she is grateful for Boaz's invitation to eat with the hired workers, Ruth uses her flail to thresh the morning's grain before she goes to the pavilion—and then she tries to be invisible, unnoticed. She refills her water flask, piles roasted grain on a piece of flatbread, and sits off to the side, as far as she can from Maacah and her friends with their gossip, insinuations, and slurs. Today Maacah has Tola cornered again, and it's plain to see that he enjoys the attention.

"I'd like to wipe that flirty smile from her face," Ruth thinks. As if triggered by her anger, Ruth hears Elimelech's voice speaking half-remembered lessons in her mind, the same lessons that have filled her dreams every night for the last week. "Do not seek revenge or bear a grudge against anyone, but love your neighbor as yourself. I am Yahweh."

Ruth forces herself to stop devising ways to pay back Maacah for her continued spitefulness. "Yes, I heard your reminder, Yahweh," she thinks and unclenches her fingers from around a rock.

"Let it go. Let it go." Elimelech's voice echoes in her head again. He began quoting this commandment from the Torah the day after he'd found her hiding in drying flax on a rooftop shortly after she came to their home as a slave. He'd seen the pile of throwing stones next to her, but pretended not to notice them. The next day his Torah lesson was about revenge and how it belonged to Yahweh, not his people. It was a lesson he went back to time and again for months—until Ruth got the message and stopped throwing stones at the priests.

"I guess I'd better apply the revenge lesson to Maacah, too." Grumbling under her breath at the realization, Ruth scatters her pile of well-balanced throwing stones.

Ruth stopped gleaning to thresh the grain before the workers quit—as she does every day—to make sure she is ready to walk home in the safety of the group. Today, the last of the women are gathering their possessions as Ruth starts to heave her heavy carrying shawl to her back, and she doesn't notice Maacah approaching from behind.

"Watch where you're going!" Maacah gives her a shove. When Ruth lunges back at her, a corner of her carrying shawl comes loose and grain spills all over the ground.

"Oh, you poor dear. Looks like today's grain will be full of stones." Maacah laughs and runs to catch up with her friends.

Anyone who's ever been hungry, with a stomach so empty that when you rub it you can feel your backbone, will never leave food behind. Even though she knows that staying to pick up all the grain will make her easy prey for any famished people or depraved men hungry for something else, Ruth refuses to leave a single grain behind. Flaming with anger, she doesn't care—until the sounds of their voices fade, and she's alone in the slowly gathering darkness.

Zebidah's dire warnings run through Ruth's head as she looks around nervously. "Everyone warned me to not be out here alone, but what was I supposed to do—leave everything I worked so hard for? But if anyone comes after me, all this grain is gone anyway—there's no way I can fight or run carrying this load."

Ruth has always preferred anger to fear, so it's not too hard for her to fan those flames into a roar again. Fuming, she turns off the road at a shortcut—a questionable name for a path that climbs and descends in zigzags designed to slow you down. "I bet I can beat you home," she says out loud.

Fueled by anger, Ruth walks quickly even with her heavy load. When she finally is close enough to spy the top of the watchtower near Bethlehem's gate, Ruth quits peeking carefully around corners and slows her pace. She's so busy congratulating herself on making it home, Ruth never sees the man standing in the path.

"We meet again, habibi, just as I promised."

Backing up, Ruth smells the aroma of unwashed bodies behind her. "I'm surrounded," and her heart sinks.

"Allow us to assist you with your burden." The man blocking her way mocks her with a bow.

Someone lifts her carrying sack from her back—Ruth doesn't dare to look away from the evil face in front of her. He looks at her carrying sack and back to her with lifted eyebrows. "It appears that you have managed to gather a very large amount of grain in just one day."

One of the men behind her pretends it's too heavy to lift from the ground. "I wonder how one woman could ever glean so much grain?"

"It's probably because Boaz told them to drop extra grain for her." Ruth turns toward the familiar-sounding voice and recognizes Simon—the man Tola hired to be one of the water carriers. Ruth edges up against the cliffside behind her, trying to get as far away from the men as possible and looking for a way to escape.

The leader of the gang runs his fingers up her arm. "The real question, my lovely lady, is: what is he getting in return for all this grain?"

Ruth jerks her arm away and spits at him. He slaps her face, splitting her lip. Ruth wipes the blood with her left hand, looks at it to draw their attention, and slashes at the leader with the knife in her right. Stepping quickly to the side, the man grabs her wrist, and cruelly bends it until she drops the knife. Twisting her arm behind her back, he pulls her to him, and Ruth smells his sour breath as he nuzzles her neck.

"You can have the grain." Ruth hates the tremble in her voice.

"A generous offer." He pulls Ruth's scarf from her head and tosses it to his henchmen. "What do you think, men? Shall we invite her to stay for supper?"

"I don't know. Can she cook?" The two men roar with laughter at their wit.

Ruth's hair muffles his voice but does nothing to filter his breath as the leader whispers in her ear. "I thought I'd have to wait until the threshing parties for a chance at you, but here you are in my arms already."

"What's going on here?"

Ruth's foul-breathed captor pulls her tighter and puts her between him and danger. Silhouetted by the setting sun behind him, a muscular man stands with feet apart, a sickle in one hand and a short staff in the other.

Ruth recognizes Tola's voice, but so does Simon who steps toward him with a friendly wave. "Hey, Tola. Um, we saw Ruth here had a heavy load, so we offered to carry it for her."

"What do you want, boy?" There is a warning in her captor's voice, and Ruth winces as he tightens his grip on her arm.

"Ruth is one of my workers. It is *my* responsibility to see that she makes it home safely." Tola's brusque tone answers the challenge.

"She's got all the help she needs already." Her captor strokes Ruth's hair and tightens his other hand on her neck.

"That may be, but I will take over from here." Tola looks at each one of them, club and scythe at the ready.

"You're not in charge here, boy. Walk away while you still can." Ruth's captor jerks his head, and his two henchmen move to each side of him facing Tola, knives in hand.

Tola rolls his shoulders and adapts his stance, ready to fight. "If it were up to me, I'd do that, but, you see, Boaz asked us," he raises his staff as if signaling others, "to keep an eye on Ruth and offer our assistance. He's concerned for her safety."

As the three thieves nervously look around to see if Tola has really brought reinforcements with him, the hands pinning Ruth's arms to her side loosen slightly. Stamping her sandal-clad foot onto his instep, she twists from his grasp, and backs toward Tola.

Ruth surprises everyone—herself included—with a curtsy to the leader of this wretched gang.

"If it comes to a fight, we're going to lose. There's got to be another way out of this," she thinks desperately.

"I want to thank you for your assistance." Ruth opens her arms to include both henchmen in her recognition. "And both of you as well. I am sure my cousin Boaz will be happy to hear how helpful you all have been."

Ruth turns to Tola, hoping he will follow her lead. "Why, they may even receive some kind of payment for their help, don't you think, Tola?"

With only a moment's hesitation, Tola plays along. "Now that you mention it, I think you're right. Boaz always says that a man should get exactly what he deserves." Tola beams a sarcastic smile at the three men.

My captor glares disgustedly at his cronies who have been slowly backing up. Ignoring Tola, he speaks only to Ruth. "Another time then, habibi. I'll be waiting." He whirls and strides away, his two followers scurrying behind him.

יהוה

Tola puts his hand on Ruth's arm, but she jerks away and leans back against the hillside—legs shaking and stomach heaving.

"Those filthy swine." Ruth grabs a handful of sand and pebbles and throws them in the direction the men went. Then she picks up a rock and throws that, too. "Ahhh." Ruth's voice doesn't sound human, even to herself.

Tola picks up Ruth's scarf, holds it out to her, and blurts out the first thing that comes to his mind. "What were you thinking—going off on your own? You were told to walk with the women."

"You are so wise—that's just what I needed to hear right now!" A lifetime of hard experience keeps those words from coming out of her mouth, but Tola can see them written all over Ruth's face anyway. She grabs her scarf and turns her back to him, checking the knots on the carrying sack before heaving it to her back.

Tola steps forward and reaches for the sack. "That's heavy. Let me help…"

"Get away from me." Tola reels away from the venom in Ruth's voice as if she had stung him.

"Whoa. I'm the good guy, remember?" Tola puts his hands up and backs away.

"If you'd keep your mouth shut, maybe it would be easier to keep that in mind." Ruth doesn't say that out loud either; instead she answers, "I can carry it."

Ruth turns and stamps away. Tola hesitates before following, making a big show of scanning the hills around them looking for threats.

Ruth's legs wobble, and her stomach still threatens to empty its contents. Her angry thoughts do little to help her calm down. "Maybe I should have let Tola carry the grain—but who is he to scold me when it was his sweet little girlfriend Maacah who made sure I was left alone? Men are so stupid sometimes…but he did come looking for me."

Ruth glances at Tola and almost feels guilty for the dejected look on his face. She tries to think of something nice to say to him for coming to her rescue, but she was still angry. "I thought Hebrews were supposed to be such good men."

Tola's face brightens at her attempt at a conversational tone. "Well, those guys aren't from Bethlehem."

"As if that makes it acceptable!" is what Ruth thinks as she snorts her disgust.

Tola defends himself. "Well, they're not. There's so much grain to bring in this year, Aram had to hire some extra men…"

"Pigs!" That was the only insult Ruth could think of that she was willing to say out loud.

"They couldn't be khahzeer—they're Hebrews." Tola laughs at his own wittiness. When Ruth looks at him blankly, he explains. "Pigs, get it? It's a joke. Khahzeer—pigs—are unclean—Hebrews don't even touch them."

"They're still pigs—smelly, unwashed, filthy pigs."

"You win. If you say they're khahzeer, that's what they are."

Their path meets the main road about a half mile from Bethlehem's city gates. Ruth's mind keeps jumping to the pictures of what could have happened if Tola hadn't arrived. Desperate for something else to think about, Ruth imagines the gossip that will erupt when she—disheveled as she is—and Tola enter the gates of Bethlehem together, a long time after all the rest of the workers came back from their day's work. She stops walking and she realizes the truth of her thoughts. "I can't let that happen! I know what they think about me already, and they will imagine that… That would be a disaster for both of us!"

Ruth moves to the side of the road and shrugs the heavy grain sack from her shoulders.

Tola looks at her with concern. "I would be happy to carry that for you."

"Here I am picking a fight with you when I should be saying thank you," Ruth said. "You did a brave thing back there coming to my rescue."

"I'm glad I got there in time…um, that you are still…You're welcome."

His embarrassment almost makes Ruth laugh. "It's good of you to think of my 'reputation.' By the way, why did you come that way? Were you following me?"

"No! Well, yes, I guess I was. I like to keep an eye on things, you know, making sure everyone gets home safely. I saw Maacah and her friends hurrying to catch up with the group, but then I looked around and noticed that you weren't with them. I thought I'd go back to help you out, but then you weren't on the road." Tola looked at Ruth waiting for an explanation.

"I dropped my sack and it took me a while to gather up all the spilled grain." Ruth didn't meet his gaze. "I was tired, annoyed, and eager to get home, so I thought I'd take the shortcut and try to catch up with everyone."

"That's not good. You shouldn't…"

LESS THAN A WIDOW

Ruth interrupts heatedly. "I know! I know! And you can be sure I won't do it again, but..." Ruth shakes her head, pushes her anger deep inside, and speaks calmly. "There's something else we have to talk about. I know that you will understand why we shouldn't arrive in town together, the two of us by ourselves, without anyone else with us."

"What are you talking about?" Tola looks at her with a frown. "You can't think I'm going to leave you alone out here again."

"That would be foolish, and believe me, I'm trying to avoid more trouble." Ruth finds it hard to explain without causing more embarrassment to both of them. "People will get the wrong impression, you know, if the two of us are alone after dark together, and we come in the gate looking like this."

Ruth holds out her arms and twirls around. Her head scarf hangs from her shoulders, bits of straw and chaff are stuck in her hair, and her overdress is ripped.

Eager to convince him, Ruth touches his arm and speaks earnestly. "If someone saw us together, if the two of us entered Bethlehem and someone saw us, they'd tell their friends, who'd tell their friends—and you know how stories grow."

Understanding breaks out on his face like the sun rising and is immediately covered by storm clouds. "But we didn't...I did nothing to...I rescued you!"

"I know that, Tola, and I'll always be grateful, but wouldn't it be better—for both of us—if we didn't give the gossips anything to talk about?" Ruths puts her hand on his arm. "Please, grant me this favor. Would you wait here a bit while I go into Bethlehem alone? You will be able to watch over me until I enter the gates to make sure there's no more danger."

Tola's grumbling assent is more full of bravado than dissent. This time Ruth lets him help her pick up the grain sack and settle it on her shoulders.

Ruth drags herself home on leaden legs, dumps the sack in the courtyard, gropes in the dark to find her mat, and falls into exhausted sleep.

TWENTY-THREE

Boaz is surprised to see Aram waiting for him in the morning. "Good morning, Son. You're usually halfway to the fields by now."

"I wanted to talk with you," Aram said. "I thought we might have time to talk alone while we eat our morning morsel."

Boaz settles onto the mat and helps himself to a honey cake. Leaning forward, he dips it into a relish of oils blended with herbs and takes his time chewing a large bite. "Your wife makes the best honey cakes I've ever tasted." He finishes his first one in two large bites, then leans back and looks at Aram. "It must be something serious for you to take time away from the fields during harvest."

Even though he has rehearsed this conversation with his father over and over in his mind, Aram squirms uncomfortably, unsure of the best approach. "It's the whole gleaning thing. It's causing some problems."

Boaz smiles. "There's been quite an uproar—people are coming to the city elders both for and against any change. I assume we are both hearing the same things."

Aram nods. "It's hard to make it work. Chava tells me that some of the women are very unhappy that Ruth is not only working with them, but has been invited to eat in the pavilion. But there are bigger issues with gleaning—I've had to divide the gleaners up and only let a few in the fields at a time as we're harvesting or there are fights. Yesterday, two men tried to get away with stealing one of the sheaves the women had already stacked and tied."

"If you put someone in charge of watching…" Boaz began.

Aram interrupts with irritation, "You don't have to tell me what to do. I've already taken care of it."

Surprised at his son's vehement reply, Boaz leans forward for another sweet cake, dips it, and chews slowly. "Of course you have." Focusing his attention on eating, Boaz waits for Aram to go on.

"Besides, all our barley is in, and it will be a week or two before the wheat is ready. I thought it might be a good idea to talk about gleaning before we start harvesting again."

"I'm listening."

"It's just that I'm not sure…Are we doing the right thing? It seems like the more help we give certain people, the more they depend on us for help. We're working hard all the time—planting, irrigating, weeding, harvesting, threshing—and we are supposed to just give it all away?"

"That's the debate," Boaz waits for Aram to continue.

"And everybody has such a sad story. If I listened to them all and gave everybody what they asked for, I wouldn't have anything left to feed our household much less help anyone else. It seems to me that giving Ruth permission to glean with the harvesters has brought a plague of locusts to our fields."

"It can feel that way." Boaz remembers his own unwillingness to face hard issues after the death of his father. "It's often easier to stick with tradition rather than examining whether or not what we are doing is the right thing."

"Who's to say our traditions are wrong?"

"I believe the question isn't about right or wrong, but does our traditional practice of gleaning do enough? Does it fulfill the intent Yahweh had when he gave us his laws?"

"Well, whatever answers we come up with eventually, I couldn't see any way to undo the changes during the barley harvest—but maybe we should go back to the traditional way of doing things during the wheat harvest." Aram adds emphatically, "If I had known what a big problem this one little decision was going to bring…"

"Would you have decided differently?"

Aram slammed his hand down on the mat. "I don't know. I might have. It's taking so much time, energy, and attention. Besides, it's hurting us."

"In what way?"

"Everything is all tied in knots—and we actually have to hire people to help us give our crops away. It's crazy. Plus, it's taking away money for improvements to our vineyards that will give us bigger harvests and more ways we can help the poor. I'm not sure we are doing the best thing in the long run."

Boaz struggles to keep his strong opinions on the subject to himself. He'd had to find his way through the maze of decisions that men in their position have to make, and now he needs to let his son discover his own path. "Well, it looks like you have a tough decision to make. If you go back to the traditional method, will you take away the permission from Ruth as well?"

"Ruth is another problem," Aram looks quickly at his father and then looks away.

"Oh? In what way?"

"There's talk all over town." Aram looks to Boaz for a response, but his father waits calmly for him to continue. "You can't tell me you don't know about it."

Boaz just shrugs. "There's always talk. Anything special you feel we have to recognize?"

"You know what people say about Moabites, about what they do in their temple, about their spring rites and all that." Aram looks at his father, hoping he will not make him have to give all the particulars, but Boaz passively waits for him to go on. "Well, Ruth is a Moabite, so people just assume she, um, is the same way."

"The same way?"

"You know what I mean. I gave her special gleaning privileges. Then you added water, food, and protection. You even told all the workers not to bother her and to drop extra grain for her to pick up."

"Yes, we have publicly shown our concern for Ruth and her mother-in-law. They are our near relatives, I might add." Boaz remains unabashed.

"Father, you know what I'm talking about. There are rumors going around that Ruth is granting you extraordinary favors—physical favors—in return for all the special attention she is getting." Just saying it out loud makes Aram feel dirty. "Some stories even include me in this same way!"

"The 'stories' have no basis in fact," Boaz replies.

"You know that, and I know that, but it's gone too far." Aram talks louder as his agitation rises. "People say you haven't gotten married again since Mother died because of your association with Ruth and others like her. One of my wife's friends stopped her in the marketplace yesterday and expressed sympathy for how hard things must be at home now."

"Surely she doesn't believe everything she hears," Boaz replies. "Your wife is far too intelligent and well-loved to take these rumors seriously."

"That's not the point, and you know it," Aram insisted. "We have to do something, change something, to prove these rumors are all lies."

Boaz frowned. "People will believe whatever they want to believe and will be more than happy to share their warped stories with any who will listen. This is an impossible battle to fight, and frankly, not worth the effort."

"So we do nothing."

"For now. Before long people will find something more interesting to talk about," Boaz assured his son.

Tola clears his throat. He'd been standing in the doorway for a few minutes, unwilling to interrupt the discussion.

Aram looks at him sharply. "Is there a problem already? The day's hardly begun."

"Not really. I mean, it's already taken care of, but I thought you should know." Tola blushes as he adds, "It's about Ruth the Moabitess."

He has the complete attention of both father and son as he gives a brief explanation of Ruth's brush with danger the evening before, about how he happened along in time to stop any real harm from coming to her...

"Ruth again. That woman is a plague," Aram growled.

"They didn't accost her in any way?" Boaz asked at the same time as Aram's complaint.

"She seems to be fine." Tola answered Boaz's question, then asked, "What should we do about Simon?"

Boaz points to Aram. "Talk to your boss," he said. Standing up, he heads toward the door. "I don't want to keep the other city elders waiting." With a wave, he was out the door.

יהוה

Ruth wakes to the smell of fresh bread wafting in from the courtyard and realizes she is famished. She rubs her face—grainy with dried sweat and dust—still filthy from yesterday's gleaning. Ruth holds her hands in front of her face and grimaces at the dirt caked under her nails and streaking up her arms.

Water is already poured into a wash bowl for her, and clean clothes lay neatly folded beside it. Ruth washes and dresses carefully, adjusting her tunic to cover the bruises on her upper arm from the lecher's tight grip.

Naomi stands to greet her as she enters the courtyard, and Ruth kisses her on both cheeks. "Thank you, hamot. I was so exhausted last night, I fell to sleep without eating."

Naomi hands her a round flatbread. "Careful, it's still hot." She places some roasted grain and figs in front of her. "Eat, eat, before your growling stomach scares the neighbors."

Ruth is glad to obey, and Naomi waits for her to finish shoving food into her mouth before she starts asking questions about last night's late return. Keeping her eyes on the food, Ruth chews every bite longer than necessary while she wrestles with her conscience. "She will only worry more if I tell her what happened."

When the last morsel is eaten, Ruth licks her fingers. "Mmmm."

"You brought home quite a load of grain last night."

Ruth stretches her back and groans a little. "It was heavy! I had to stop and rest a few times on the way home. Sorry I was late—hope you didn't worry too much."

Ruth doesn't meet her mother-in-law's gaze, and Naomi doesn't push her. Instead, she stands and busily cleans up after the meal. "It's good then that you have a few days off before wheat harvest begins—I assume you are determined to glean then as well."

At Ruth's silent nod, Naomi grabs two baskets and hands one to Ruth. "It's market day. Let's go trade some of your hard-earned grain for olives."

"Olives!" Ruth's mouth waters—they haven't had any olives since they left Moab. She puts her arms around Naomi and hugs her close. Naomi pats her cheek before she pushes Ruth away, and sets off for the market square. Ruth finds a corner to stand in and lets Naomi negotiate for the olives on her own, thinking, "She will get a better deal without a foreigner in tow."

Crowds of people mill around the merchants' wares. People barter, argue, laugh, and bump into friends. If Ruth closes her eyes she can pretend to be back in Moab. A smile flits across her face, "And today—thank Yahweh for his blessings—we actually have something to offer in trade."

Two servants push through the crowd, clearing the way for a stout man who struts through the path they make. His finely-woven robes and flashing rings signal wealth and prestige. A young man follows in his wake, mimicking his father's stride, pouty lips pursed as he looks down his nose at anyone who doesn't get out of the way fast enough. Merchants bow deeply as the duo parades through the marketplace turning up their noses at the poor offerings the lower classes have on display.

Naomi returns to find Ruth watching the men as they parade around the busy square. Ruth says with mocking wonder, "They put on quite a show. Do you know who they are?"

Naomi's face looks like she is sucking on bitter herbs. "Balak is a sly, greedy man and his son has learned his father's lessons well. Balak comes to the marketplace every week to collect interest on his loans—many people had no choice but to borrow from him during the drought if they wanted to live." With a sniff, Naomi hands her a bulky cloth sack, and Ruth breathes in the delightful aroma of olives. "Don't eat all of these before I come back. I have enough grain left to get a little jar of honey." And Naomi disappears into the teeming crowd.

Ruth pops an olive into her mouth. After chewing all the meat from the pit, she sucks on it to savor the flavor as long as she can. Closing her eyes Ruth lets the taste unlock memories that she's been pushing away: sitting on the roof on a summer evening to catch the breeze blowing down from the hills, feeding each other olives, Mahlon's hand caressing her cheek and playing with her hair...

"Ruth!...Ruth?"

The insistent voice doesn't match the scene in her mind.

"Are you well?"

Ruth just stands there blinking foolishly, trying to drag herself back to reality. Boaz hands grip her shoulders, and he repeats his question with a worried frown.

"Are you well? Did they hurt you?"

"No." Ruth takes a startled half-step back and bumps into the wall. "I mean...No, sir, I'm fine."

"This is the truth?"

Touched by the concern written across his face, Ruth starts to babble. "They didn't...it was just words...then Tola came...how did you know?"

A thought struck her, "Shouldn't it be noisier than this?" A quick glance shows that those closest to them are watching and listening intently.

Boaz notices her gaze, drops his hands to his sides, and takes a step back. He bows slightly, and speaks in a formal voice loud enough for the listeners to hear. "I was concerned for your welfare."

"You are too kind, sir."

Naomi returns and places her basket on the ground next to Ruth's. "Shalom."

Boaz greets her warmly, glad for an interruption. "My dear cousin, shalom. I apologize for taking so long to welcome you home. I can only plead the call of my duties."

"Your generosity to two widows has been all the welcome we have needed. May Yahweh bless you and keep you."

"And may He comfort you among all the mourners in Zion."

Naomi bows her head to accept this traditional phrase of comfort. "Surely your kindness knows no bounds, sir. Bethlehem's poor have more food to eat because of your kindness."

Ruth looks at her mother-in-law in astonishment, thinking, "How does she know about that? I thought she was still moping around the house all day while I was gleaning, but she must have been talking to someone in the village." Ruth almost misses Boaz's reply which is also meant for the onlookers to hear.

"When my son Aram brought the needs of the poor to my attention, we discussed whether or not our traditional efforts really fulfilled Yahweh's command to care for those in need. At his request, I was happy to bring this question to Bethlehem's Council of Elders who gave it serious consideration and made recommendations in light of the Torah." Boaz acknowledged the listening crowd with a wave and continued in his public speaking voice: "The elders are awaiting my arrival at the city gates, so I must be off."

Turning his back to the crowd, Boaz speaks softly so only Naomi and Ruth can hear. "Aram told me that you were the source of the gleaning question, and I am grateful for your insight and boldness in bringing it to our attention."

He's looking Ruth straight in the eye, and she just stands there mute. "How could I stand up to those pigs last night, lash into Tola, and not be able to come up with one word to say to this man?" Ruth is mystified by her inability to come up with a reply.

"You will continue gleaning with us during the wheat harvest?" Boaz asks.

Ruth manages a nod, and he continues. "Then I am sure you will also ensure your safety by walking with our women to and from the fields." Boaz bows to Naomi. "Cousin, if you will excuse me, I must attend to my duties at the city gates."

Boaz exchanges greetings, listens to complaints, and offers blessings as he makes his way through the marketplace, including Balak whose sharp eyes never miss any intrigue. He exchanges a few words with Tola before continu-

RUTH & BOAZ : BETHLEHEM

ing on his way. Tola watches Ruth and Naomi until Maacah steps out of the shade of a merchant's stall, places her hand on his arm, and draws him into the booth.

Ruth shakes her head and picks up both of their baskets. "Shall we go home, hamot?"

Naomi's sharp eyes also don't miss a thing. She pulls one of the baskets out of Ruth's hand. "Give it to me," she snaps. "I'm perfectly capable of carrying a small jar of honey."

Naomi doesn't say another word until they step into their courtyard. She sets her basket down with a sigh, straightens up, and looks Ruth straight in the face.

"I thought you walked to the fields and back with Boaz's women."

"Usually."

"But not yesterday."

"This is the Naomi I thought we'd left behind in Moab. I'd forgotten how hard it is to keep things from her," Ruth thinks, but she answers simply, "No."

Naomi stands looking at Ruth, waiting for more. To her own surprise, Ruth doesn't spill the whole story.

"You're not going to tell me what happened yesterday."

Ruth shrugs her shoulders. "There's nothing to talk about. I'm fine."

"Boaz and Tola were very concerned…"

Ruth interrupts. "And now they're not." Taking Naomi's hands in her own, Ruth brings them to her lips, and kisses her fingers. "I promise I will walk with the women to the wheat fields. You don't need to worry."

"Ech!" Naomi pulls her hands away and clasps them together. "I've worried about you since the afternoon Elimelech brought you home. Don't think you can make me stop now."

Naomi turns away and looks around the courtyard. "Look at this place. You have lots of projects that are only half-way done." She points at the crumbling dome oven. "Now that we have grain, I'd like to have a proper oven to bake in."

Ruth grins and bows. "Yes, hamot. Anything you say, hamot."

"You get to work." Naomi gives Ruth a mischievous smile. "It's time for my nap."

יהוה

This year there are two weeks between barley and wheat harvest. Landowners use the time to repair and sharpen equipment and organize for the next push. Gleaning practices fuel heated debates wherever people meet, and Boaz is hounded constantly to explain his point of view. His answer is simple, "Every man must satisfy his own conscience." Inevitably, the next question is, "What will be the practice in your fields during the wheat harvest?"

LESS THAN A WIDOW

Boaz has a straightforward answer for that as well. "You will have to ask my son Aram. He is the harvest master."

For Aram, the answer is more difficult, which he complains about to Boaz in another early morning meeting. "The whole time I've been running things, you've just stepped in whenever you wanted to and changed things," Aram's complaint reveals more than he intended. "Now, you tell everyone to ask me because I'm in charge. Why change now?"

"It can be just as hard to lay things down as it is to pick them up," Boaz smiles a little to hear another of his mother's saying come out of his mouth. "Harvesting and threshing—these are the times I have looked forward to year after year. And if I have stepped in and weakened your authority, I want to assure you that it was done unintentionally."

Aram is quiet for a long time struggling with his thoughts. "If I tell him how hard it is when people look to him for answers when I'm standing right there or that I'm jealous of the respect people show him, it'll sound like I'm whining. It would just be easier if he would stay away from the fields—but I can't tell him that."

Finally Aram settles on a question he feels comfortable asking his father. "Why won't you tell people what you think about the way we let people glean during the barley harvest?"

"It's not my opinion that matters," Boaz replies. "Everyone has to choose for themselves and will have to answer to Yahweh for those choices. The fields are your concern now, so the choice is yours."

"But you brought it up for discussion by the City Elders," Aram protested.

"The question was asked. In my opinion, it was valid and deserved to be brought before the Council," Boaz said. "At the time, you agreed, but since then you have found that putting your resolve into practice is often more difficult than agreeing in principle."

"So, you will not step in if I decide to return to traditional gleaning?" Aram challenges.

"Son, I trust your heart, and I trust your desire to live rightly in Yahweh's eyes," Boaz replies. "Therefore, I will trust your decision."

Aram laughs, but his amusement holds an edge. "I don't think I'll say thank you for this one."

"No, I didn't think you would," Boaz smiles.

Aram gets up to leave, but turns back with one more question. "Does this mean that you won't be guarding the grain piles this year after threshing? I've already talked to Tola, and he's willing to take over the guard duty any time."

This time it is Boaz who laughs. "Sorry, Aram. This is one of the few traditions I will not pass on to anyone else until I'm too feeble to make it up the hill for the threshing."

"No, I didn't think you would," Aram replies with a smirk as he leaves the courtyard.

Boaz daydreams about the upcoming threshing festivities—a favorite of his since he was a boy. As harvesting ends, grandmothers direct the boys who are too young to work in the fields to sweep circles on the hard earth on a hillside to get rid of stones and debris. All grain growers in Bethlehem take turns using the threshing floors and help each other with the hard work of separating the grain from the stalks by driving an ox team pulling a sledge or beating the year's harvest with flails. Winnowing comes next—tossing the resulting mounds into the air so the heavier grain falls to the ground and chaff floats away in the wind that blows in the hills.

"I can remember Father explaining to me that we all work together this way because it's safer—raiders wishing to steal our grain would look for easier pickings," Boaz laughs aloud at this thought. "For me it was as exciting as a festival."

Boaz brushes the crumbs from his lap and gets slowly to his feet.

"It still is."

TWENTY-FOUR

The barley fields are empty of crops, and it will be more than a week before the wheat is ready to be harvested. Even though Ruth doesn't have to go out searching for food every day, there isn't much of a chance to rest her weary body. Now that Naomi has left her depression behind, she's back to her old self—telling Ruth what to do and how to do it.

"If I weren't so happy to see her feeling better, she could drive me crazy," Ruth thinks with a shake of her head.

Nahshon shows up by midmorning of the first day.

"Did Zebidah send you?"

"I don't have to listen to women any more. I am a man with a job." Ruth manages to hide a grin even though he sounds more like a boy who has just escaped his mother and grandmother's instructions. Ruth is happy for help and even for his constant chatter as they clean out the only other room with walls mostly intact. They use salvaged material from the rubble pile to make this room serviceable as a storage area.

Then the wheat harvest begins.

Ruth thought she knew what it's like to sweat, but gleaning in the wheat fields under a blazing summer sun gives perspiring a whole new definition. Without the plentiful supply of water and shade that Boaz and Aram provide their workers, many of them would have collapsed. The exceptional heat of this harvest season brings with it one blessing—it takes all the strength the workers have to get through the day's work and back home again. No one has the energy to make mischief, not even Maacah.

Naomi and Ruth sleep on the roof to take advantage of any breeze—warm though it is—wafting its way from the Mediterranean Sea. The nights are never long or cool enough.

Ruth's days blur together in a rhythm of stooping, gathering, and carrying punctuated with periods of rest that resemble a nearly unconscious stupor. Dry stalks scratch the workers' skin, and the excessive heat produces rashes that burn with their trickling sweat.

Aram is delighted with the large harvest. He adds more slash marks on his bark ledger and shows it off during Boaz's frequent excursions to the fields. "It's a great year for wheat," he tells everyone with a broad smile.

LESS THAN A WIDOW

Finally there are no more fields with standing wheat. The sheaves are stored in barns waiting for final processing. Boys prepare the threshing ground on a flat hill above Bethlehem, but the afternoon and evening breezes leave for other realms. For some, the gleaners who worked on the thresh-as-you-go plan, threshing took place at the end of each day to get the grain from the stalks in order to carry it home. For the landowners and their workers, threshing time is an opportunity for celebrating a job well done, and the city is growing impatient. This year's yield is good, the grain is safely gathered, and there will be plenty to eat. Now everyone eagerly waits for the winds to blow in so they can pitch their tents around the threshing floor. The hard work of threshing the grain is a small price to pay for the festivities of feasting, dancing, and making merry, often to the extreme.

For Naomi, the lack of wind gives her time to harvest a seed planted in her mind the day the women met Boaz in the marketplace. She has secretly prayed over and nurtured this seed as it sent shoots twining around the trellis of her idea, coaxing its growth until the seed became a well-thought-out secret plan.

Ruth is oblivious, at least for the first few days of her special treatment. She enjoys having her mother-in-law fuss over her with balms for her rashes and oils to soften her skin, but as Ruth's body recovers from its exhaustion, so does her curiosity.

On the third day of the threshing party in the hills, Ruth steps into the courtyard after an early-morning trip to the well.

Naomi slides the barrier across the entrance to the street behind her. "Grab the water pitchers I've had warming in the sun and join me." She heads into their main room without a backward glance.

The lamps burning inside arouse Ruth's curiosity. "What's going on? We haven't used precious oil for lamps since we came to Bethlehem."

The best of their clothing is spread on a mat, and Ruth's wedding jewelry lies polished and shiny next to it. Naomi points at another mat spread out with a bowl, sponges, drying cloths, and oil, and Ruth puts the pitchers of warm water on the floor.

"What's all this?"

"You should see the look on your face." Naomi laughs. "I'll help you wash your hair. Then I will tell you."

"Why don't you just tell me now?" Trying to get Naomi to alter her plan of attack is wasted effort, so Ruth strips down to her tunic and sits on the mat. They work together to unravel the numerous braids that keep her unruly hair in place. Naomi doesn't say anything more until she pours water over Ruth's hair and rubs in the soap.

"When Elimelech and my sons died, I wanted to die, too. But not in Moab."

"This is going to be one of those search-for-the-answer-inside-of-the-story games." Ruth sighs inwardly and tries to push aside her impatience.

"I wanted you to stay in Moab, to get married again, to be happy and safe—like Orpah. But you are so stubborn, you refused to accept that there is no hope without a man to provide for us and protect us. That doesn't change the fact that there is no good life for a woman without a man, and I was sure you would never find a husband in Bethlehem."

Ruth starts to respond, but Naomi says softly, "Wait; let me finish."

She rinses Ruth's hair and wraps it with a dry cloth.

"I told everyone that I came back empty and alone—with nothing to live for—but I was wrong. I am sorry that I hurt you that way." Naomi has to clear her throat to continue. "Yahweh was with me. You were with me. And your love."

Now they're both crying, and Ruth gives Naomi a big hug. After a minute, Naomi releases her daughter-in-law and starts picking through the tangled mess of her hair. Naomi splashes some sweet-smelling oil on her hands and rubs it into Ruth's scalp and down to the tips of her hair.

"Ruth, it's time for you to leave your widow's clothes behind and dress like a bride."

"That explains the dress and the jewelry," Ruth thinks, but she has no idea what Naomi is talking about. "Sure, I've been thinking about…but those are only daydreams."

"Ouch!" A tight knot of tangled hair dangles from Naomi's comb. "Hamot, I don't understand," Ruth tells her.

"You've been working so hard, and we have enough food for months to come. But then what will we do?" Naomi intensely attacks another stubborn tangle, and Ruth yelps. "I'm an old woman, and it doesn't matter what you think or how hard you work, I will die one day. Then what will become of you here in Bethlehem? The only thing I can do to prepare for your future, to give you a chance to have any kind of a life, is to find a husband for you."

Ruth pulls her hair from Naomi's hands and glares at her thinking, "Is this some kind of cruel joke?"

Turning to face Naomi, Ruth asks, "A husband, here in Bethlehem? You said yourself no one will marry a foreigner, especially one who can't have children."

"I know I did, but…"

"But, nothing! We talked about this before we ever left Moab."

Ruth stares at Naomi. "How dare she utter that word—husband—when we both know that nothing good can come of wishing for something that cannot be," and she is surprised at the bitterness in her thought.

"Don't even say that word—husband—to me. I knew that I would never marry again if we came to Bethlehem, but I came anyway to be with you and to worship Yahweh. I've accepted that, and I don't need…"

"Boaz."

"...What?"

"Boaz will be your husband."

Ruth laughs—at least that's what she intends to do—but tears, hiccups, and coughs make it hard to tell exactly what sound she is making.

Naomi continues persuasively. "He is a godly man, a man of character and integrity. He knows you and has gone out of his way to take care of you already."

Ruth tries to get control of her crazy emotions that are spinning through anger, doubt, fear, pain, and hope so quickly that she can't settle on any one of them.

"He thinks about you," Naomi repeated.

Ruth shakes her head in disbelief. "What makes you think that could be in any way a true statement?"

"I knew it the minute he approached you in the marketplace that day," Naomi's voice is smug with certainty. "Why else would such a man—a judge, an elder who sits at the city gates, a man of position and power—react as strongly as he did, especially in a place so public as the marketplace. You are obviously a woman with the heart of Yahweh in her breast. He is not an infatuated youth, but a widower and a man of reason. Still, he is a man, and you are a woman—a beautiful woman of interest to him."

"I might as well ask or this conversation will never end," Ruth closes her eyes and takes a deep breath. "How is this marriage supposed to happen?"

"You will ask him."

"Good idea." Ruth's emotions have run full circle, and she's back to anger. "No breaking of tradition here: a woman propositions a man, a young person approaches an elder with a plan of matrimony, a destitute field worker—a Moabite no less—propositions Bethlehem's largest land owner. Next time I see him at the marketplace, I'll just prance right up to him and ask him to marry me."

"When you are ready to listen, I'll tell you my plan." Naomi takes the bowl of dirty water to the courtyard and leaves Ruth alone in her confusion.

"Why am I so angry?" Ruth asks herself. "Laughing would make sense—it's a absurd idea."

Ruth catches the glint of her wedding jewelry and puts a bracelet on her arm, remembering what it was like to be married and loved.

"Sad—I could understand feeling sad," she thinks, but introspection is not her forté, so Ruth prays. "Yahweh, should I even listen to Naomi's crazy idea?" She doesn't really expect an answer, but a voice in her heart responds, "Take my hand."

Ruth reaches out and feels Yahweh's fingers close around hers.

יהוה

"Are you ready for me yet?" Naomi stands at the doorway. Ruth shrugs her shoulders and sits on the mat, and Naomi talks while braiding her hair.

"Tell me what you saw yesterday when you went to watch the threshing." At Ruth's start of surprise Naomi gives a little tug on the hair she's twisting. "Of course I know you went to watch."

"You warned me about the men and what they…so I took the path that winds up the back of the hill above the threshing place and watched from up there. I was pretty far away, so I couldn't see everything."

As Naomi continued her intricate pattern of braids, Ruth tells her what she'd seen. "…Oxen pulled a sledge over the stalks. The men throw everything in the air with forks—sure glad I wasn't downwind. The women sieve the heavy grain that doesn't blow away and make large piles of grain around the edges of the hill."

Naomi winds colorful threads into her daughter-in-law's braids.

"It looks like the whole city is there. There are canopies set up for people to eat and drink. The rich people have their own tents off to the side, and there are a few tents set up away from all the others—ouch! Yes, hamot, when I saw the stream of men coming and going I figured it out and didn't go anywhere close."

"Did you see Boaz?"

"Yes, he was there with Aram waiting for their turn to thresh."

"They always save threshing their grain for last, and Nahshon informs me they have so much grain that it will take all afternoon and evening to finish the job. After all the lean years, there will be lots of singing, dancing, and flowing wine tonight."

Naomi wraps string around the end of a braid and continues. "Zebidah tells me that Boaz still sleeps alone on the desert side of his grain pile at night to guard it—something he started doing when his father was still alive. That is where you will go to him tonight."

"I can't do that! Everyone will think I am there to sell myself…"

"Not if they don't see you." Naomi tugs on the braid as she bends down and whispers in her ear for emphasis. "Just be quiet and listen to my plan—I've thought this through very carefully."

"Here's what you do," Naomi tells her. "Make sure you know which grain piles belong to Boaz. Wait until he's eaten and drank his fill. Watch for him to leave the party—he'll be feeling generous—the harvest is good and his barns will be full. When he settles down on the far side of the grain pile away from all the noise, you creep up to where he's sleeping, crawl into bed with him, and lay at his feet."

"He'll think I just want to…why would he think I want marriage?"

"You will no longer be dressed in your widow's garments, but will wear your finest clothes and jewelry. Your perfume will be in the air, you will uncover him, and lie down by his feet. He will know what it means."

LESS THAN A WIDOW

Ruth doesn't know why she's still listening to this plan. "Naomi, you are only thinking about what you want to happen, not about all the awful things that probably will. What if he just pleasures himself for the night and throws me out in the morning? What if…?"

"Ruth, I have known Boaz since he was a little boy," Naomi interrupts. "I knew his father and mother. He's an honorable man, our kinsman, and he is kind. Remember, when he wakes up and finds you there, you must do whatever he tells you to do, do you understand? Do everything he tells you to do—you can trust him. By tomorrow morning you will be a married woman again."

"And if he throws me from his bed?"

"He will do it quietly to protect his honor and yours, and you will be no worse off than if you had not tried."

"I don't think I can do this."

Naomi gives Ruth *the* look—the one she used to give her when as a child she balked at some of the changes required of her in order to live in a Hebrew household, to be a worshipper of Yahweh, a people set apart. Her voice is gentle when she speaks again.

"Elimelech always believed that Yahweh brought you to our family for a reason. Yahweh has a plan for you, and I believe this is it."

"But I am nothing, a Moabite. There would be no benefit for Boaz in such a marriage—only trouble."

"And yet, Yahweh brought you here, to this place. He won't leave you alone now." Naomi throws Ruth a challenge—all softness gone. "Where is that brave young woman who vowed to leave everything, bring me here, and take up a new life?"

"I'd rather fight a lion."

Ruth wants to run screaming from the room, but instead she finds herself going along with this craziness.

יהוה

Ruth leaves home late afternoon and makes her way on the round-about path she'd discovered a few days ago, taking care that no one sees her. Arriving at a hillside on the far side of the threshing grounds just as the sun sets, Ruth wraps her dark robe around her and settles down to wait in the deepening twilight.

The flattened hilltop below is crowded with tents and most of Bethlehem's population is there celebrating the bountiful harvest. Ruth's perch is right above the private tents of the wealthy, and she shifts position until she has a clear view of the bonfire blazing in one of the empty threshing circles at a safe distance from the piles of grain that surround it. Musicians play while people dance, eat, drink, and laugh.

RUTH & BOAZ : BETHLEHEM

The path to a small group of tents is visited by men and soon-to-be men who furtively travel to their doors. Ruth knows that the women working in these tents will earn enough to feed themselves for months, and that they have no other alternatives. A violent shiver shakes Ruth's body as she watches a man step through the door-flap and make his way uphill toward the threshing floor.

"If our plan doesn't work, I will have to join them." She pulls her mind back to the present. "This is not the time to lose courage."

Ruth spots Tola right away, and it's hard to tear her eyes away even though Maacah is hanging on his arm.

"What if Naomi had dreamt up a plan about Tola instead of Boaz?" Ruth mused.

She had asked her mother-in-law that very question, and her answer was simple, "Tola is Boaz's ward and has no chance to inherit any property. His livelihood depends on the good will of those who employ him. He's a man—*a very good-looking man*— without influence or property. Marriage to a foreigner could easily put an end to all that he has worked for."

Yet Ruth fixes her eyes on Tola again and tries to sort out her feelings for him. "He's very handsome, but marriage takes more than good looks, and Tola's young, full of pride, and impulsive—more like Killion than Mahlon ever was, even as a boy."

"Where is Boaz?" she thinks as she scans the hilltop below. "Maybe Naomi got it all wrong, and he's not even here tonight." Ruth rubs the gooseflesh on her arms wondering if she's relieved or disappointed until she spots him in the middle of a large group of men. Now all that's left is to observe and wait until all those singing, dancing, eating, laughing, drinking, and merrymaking exhaust themselves.

Watching from her hiding place, Ruth hugs her knees to her chest and lays her cheek on the smooth surface of her overdress, so silky compared to the widow's garb she has worn for the last year. Wrapping a shawl around her shoulders, she rubs her fingers over the embroidered section that Naomi added to disguise a mended rip. Ruth is wearing the best of both of their wardrobes and all their remaining jewelry.

"I'm dressed as a bride—surely Boaz will respond in the way that Naomi is so positive he will," Ruth worries.

Rubbing oil into her legs and feet, Ruth runs through Naomi's scheme in her mind again as she has done incessantly since Naomi shared it with her.

"I've thought it out step by step—it might work out just as Naomi said it would—but somehow it doesn't feel like enough—enough! I have nothing, I am nothing, and now I'm unhappy because Naomi's plan isn't enough?" Ruth shakes her head, frustrated at herself.

Ruth spots Boaz and a few friends as they leave the crowd and make their way to a pavilion to sit, drink wine, and talk. Boaz invites his son Aram to join them, and as they hug each other in greeting they seem to be mirror images. Not tall, but their wiry muscles and erect carriage demand respect. Hawk nose, brown hair, bushy beards—with Boaz's showing some gray.

"Naomi's is still preparing to die—that's what this plan is all about. She just wants to be sure I will be safe when that happens. She must still believe that Yahweh has cursed her family, that Elimelech's name and lands will disappear into history without heirs, that she is being punished for going to Moab." Ruth shakes her head in denial at Naomi's hopelessness, but continues with the mental argument. "If Yahweh is not blessing us, then why did He bring us safely through the desert to Bethlehem, move Aram's heart to allow me to glean with the women, and move Boaz's heart so that he would influence others to do more to feed so many hungry people?"

Too tense to sit still, Ruth rocks back and forth. "Even if Boaz takes me for his wife tonight, what about Naomi? Nothing will have changed for her—her family line died out when Mahlon and Killion died without sons."

A shiver runs down her spine as she looks to the sky and speaks softly to Yahweh. "Elimelech believed that you brought me to this family for a reason—I can't believe it would be only to take care of myself even if that is what Naomi is asking for. Please, Yahweh, open my eyes. Show me what you want me to do."

Ruth's mind fills with pictures of Elimelech bent over his wheel forming a pot out of a lump of clay, of Mahlon and Killion taking over the work after their father died, and of the black pit of despair as deep as the pile of rocks and debris that buried their bodies. She returns her gaze to the stars just as she had the night before they left Moab.

"I still don't know what I think I will see in the stars," she thinks, but as she scans the sky for an answer, Ruth remembers Naomi's voice telling her favorite story:

"Yahweh spoke: "Lights! Appear and shine

in Heaven's sky!

You will separate day from night and,

mark seasons and days and years.

Let there be lights in Heaven's sky to give light to Earth.

And there it was."

"Yahweh. Everything we do revolves around Yahweh—what we eat, what we do, how we think...So why is Naomi so convinced that her family is supposed to be erased from history? In her mind, all that is left for her—after making sure I am safe—is to die, too."

Suddenly, Ruth sits up straight. "The family—that's what's missing!" She covers her mouth to stop a shout of excitement. "Elimelech believed Yahweh brought me to their family. Naomi is convinced that their family line will disappear because Elimelech, Mahlon, and Killion died. But does that have to be true?"

Ruth racks her brain trying to remember the Hebrew laws that govern family issues. Naomi called Boaz a go'el—a near relative who steps in to help someone in financial trouble who is forced to sell the family land. A go'el uses his own money to come to the aid of his needy relative.

"But Naomi isn't trying to keep Elimelech's land because women don't own land and she has no sons left to inherit it," Ruth realizes. "All she's trying to do is make sure that I will be protected when she dies."

"What's that other law that Naomi told me about—the Torah law of yibum? A dead man's brother is supposed to marry his widow to produce an heir to carry on the family name. Their son will be considered the dead man's heir and inherit all of his property," Ruth thinks with a surge of hope. "I remember asking Naomi why anyone would do this because he would not only miss out on a larger inheritance, but take on the additional costs of a wife and a child—a child not of his making that he would raise, mentor, and even manage the child's estate—one that his own children would never own. The financial strain could endanger his own assets and decrease what his own children inherit. Naomi had just shrugged and said, 'It's Yahweh's law.'"

Ruth begins rocking and praying again—for guidance, for words, and for Naomi's belief to be true—that Boaz is a righteous and generous man.

TWENTY-FIVE

The night is half over before quiet engulfs the plain below. The last of the revelers have at last returned to Bethlehem or fallen asleep where the week's hard work and the night's drink caught up with them. Even the trail to the prostitutes' tents is empty.

Ruth stands slowly and picks out the best path to the encampment. She feels fear churn in her stomach and spread through her body. Hands covering her face, she takes one last deep breath, telling herself, "Don't rush. Is there anyone still awake and watching? Where are the guards?"

Ruth stretches her arms and legs to ease their stiffness after hours of cramped waiting. Tucking the edges of the over-dress into her belt, she begins to descend toward the flat plain below. The slight crunch of her sandals and the echo of dislodged pebbles rolling downhill shout out her progress, but no one appears to be listening—at least there is no sound of stirring in the sleeping tents of the upper classes as she weaves her way through them toward the threshing floor and the mounds of grain on its opposite side.

Pausing in the shadows at the edge of the open ground of the threshing floor, Ruth sits on her heels and scans its open flat area faintly illuminated by the crescent moon and stars. Going directly across the open circle would make her visible to anyone still awake, but the shadows along the edges with its low walls hide sleeping bodies which are practically invisible in the dim glow of the banked embers in the fire pits.

Naomi warned her about the guards, but she said they would be stationed on the far side of the grain piles to watch the surrounding desert for thieves.

"It's so late—please let them be asleep, too," Ruth prays silently before going over Naomi's assured description of where she will find Boaz: "He never hires a guard for his grain, but takes pride in doing the job himself."

Ruth locates the food merchant's booth, counts the mounds of grain, and notes the direction of the valley where Bethlehem lays sleeping. "Those must be his."

Mentally replaying Naomi's confident instructions, Ruth creeps across the open ground bathed in the faint moon glow: "Boaz will be on the edge of the plain between his piles of barley and wheat. Be very quiet, and don't let anyone see you. He might not be asleep, but if he is…"

Ruth holds up her hand as if her mother-in-law were actually beside her instead of in her head. "Enough. I'll take it from here, hamot."

Ruth tiptoes around a pile of wheat, straining to see any signs of danger, but the shadows are dark at the base of the grain piles. She is almost upon a guard before she knows he is there—the sound of liquid gurgling down his throat and a loud belch alerts her just in time. Hoping that drink has dulled his senses, she backs up the way she came and makes her way around the inner edge of the mound, and around another.

"Just one more...This should be it."

Worried that the night is passing too quickly, Ruth extends her hands and feels with her toes before each step, groping for something besides sand and gravel. Her breathing comes in shallow gasps.

"Could Naomi have been wrong? Where is Boaz?"

As she reaches the desert's edge and follows the grain pile curving back toward the threshing floor, Ruth almost sobs in tension. "Did I make a mistake? Am I in the wrong place?"

A sound freezes her in place—until it repeats itself—the slight whistle of exhaled breath. Again it sounds and again, and Ruth allows her lungs to suck in some much-needed air.

On hands and knees now, Ruth follows the sound until her fingers touch the edge of a rug. Her heart thumps so hard it rattles her ribs. "Surely, he can hear it!" she thinks as she tries to see the face of the man snoring in the gloom. He stirs and turns toward her, and she freezes in place until his breathing settles back into the pattern of a man deep in sleep. Only then does Ruth slowly stand, remove her outer garment, fold her shawl, and finger brush her freshly washed and perfumed hair.

Clad only in her shift and wedding jewelry, Ruth carefully lowers herself to the rug, carefully lifts the edges of the cloak spread over Boaz, and slips underneath it to lie at Boaz's feet.

Naomi's positive voice chants its instructions in Ruth's mind: "Boaz will be in good spirits having feasted and drank his fill, content and satisfied over the work accomplished—the harvest was a good one this year. He will understand why you are there—a beautiful young widow who is done with mourning, and lies—perfumed—at his feet in petition. Listen to him, and do what he tells you..."

But Ruth doesn't share Naomi's confidence as she tries to keep herself still as she waits, and waits, for him to wake up.

One second he is asleep, and the next Boaz is crouched above her, knife in hand.

"Who are you?!" It sounds more like a threat than a question.

Ruth opens her mouth to speak, but nothing comes out.

Boaz moves astride her, pinning her arms at her sides with his knees, and puts his knife to her throat.

RUTH & BOAZ : BETHLEHEM

"Who are you?" he growls again as he strains to make out her features in the gloom.

"Ruth. It's Ruth, Naomi's daughter-in-law."

The knife no longer pricks Ruth's throat. Boaz rises to his feet, but maintains his grip on her arm as he pulls her up beside him. Drawing her with him out of the shadows into the faint light of the moon and stars, he puts his hand under Ruth's chin, tips her face up, and looks at her closely. "It is you, but what are you doing here?"

Ruth lowers herself to her knees in supplication. "I am your maidservant, and I have come to ask for the blessing you gave me the first day I gleaned in your barley fields. You said, 'May you be richly rewarded by Yahweh, the God of Israel, under whose wings I have taken refuge.'"

Boaz nods. "I remember the blessing."

"This isn't what Naomi told me to do, but it has to be about more than just taking care of me when she dies. And maybe I won't have to tell her..." Uncertainty fills her mind again until she refuses to submit to it, takes a big breath, and launches her adaptation of Naomi's plan.

Ruth's words come out in a rush. "As Yahweh has spread his wings of protection over me, I beg you to also cover me with your cloak. Will you be my go'el and the father of Elimelech's children?"

Boaz doesn't reply.

Ruth sits back on her feet, head down, and struggles to continue breathing until she hears the sound of his knife sliding into its sheath and his feet moving away.

Finally, Boaz clears his throat and speaks hoarsely. "My daughter, do you know what you are asking?"

"I've gone too far, and he's angry. I should have done this exactly as Naomi told me to do it, but it's too late now," her fear screams in her head.

Raising her head, Ruth sits on her feet looking up at Boaz. "Yes, I do. I have come to you, as Elimelech's go'el, to ask for marriage."

"His go'el and marriage? Do I understand you correctly? You are not only asking me for marriage, but you want me to buy his lands and father his sons to inherit his estate—the one I will have purchased?"

"It sounds greedy when he says it that way—that's not what I meant! It's not all about me," Ruth thinks and hurries to explain. "It's for Naomi—she and I are the only ones left of the family. Elimelech is dead, as are his sons. There is no one left alive to carry on his name or to claim his inheritance. But Naomi told me you are his go'el, and I thought...I thought, couldn't a go'el also marry a widow to have children to carry on Elimelech's name? Go'el and yibum are both Hebrew laws, are they not?"

Boaz laughs, and a shiver passes through Ruth's entire body, though it's no longer from anxiety, but from anger.

LESS THAN A WIDOW

"He's laughing at me." Of all the things she had imagined, this was *not* one of them. She stands up, ready to make her escape.

"Forgive me." Boaz raises his palms signaling peace. "Once again you not only demonstrate your knowledge of Hebrew law, but you suggest an interpretation that I have not encountered before—a combining of the laws of go'el and yibum." He shakes his head, and asks with a half-smile, "Are you sure you're a Moabite?"

"Is he offended?" Ruth thinks, straining to see his features clearly. "He knows who and what I am, so surely he doesn't expect an answer." She clamps her mouth shut to keep any scalding words from escaping. What he says next unnerves Ruth further.

"Ruth, you are a woman of noble character—of hayil. You have won many hearts in Bethlehem by your dedication to Naomi, and there are younger and more handsome men who would gladly take you as wife. Yet you come to me."

"No, there aren't. Tola, maybe, but surely no others." It's Ruth's turn to shake her head as confused thoughts run through her mind. "Even if there were any other interested men, no one else would listen, consider my words seriously, and be willing or able to act on them the way Boaz does." Ruth blushes as she begins to let herself imagine how wonderful it would be to be married to this man.

Boaz is silent for a long time, and Ruth wonders if she missed something. "Did he ask me a question? Is he trying to think of a way to turn me down gently?"

Boaz repeats, "Yet you come to me."

"Oh...He wants to know why I came to him with this proposal! He wants to know if it's his power and money—am I selling myself for that?" Ruth thinks and has to admit to herself that she would do even that for Naomi, for Elimelech, for Mahlon.

Her blush deepens, and Ruth is glad that the darkness masks it. "The truth is, I am attracted to Boaz, to his character, to his strength, to his wisdom, and yes—to him as a man—I can't say that!" she thinks. "But that's what he wants to know."

"You, Boaz, are the only man to whom I would make this request," she says quietly.

Boaz starts to pace, mumbling and pulling at his beard. "A go'el isn't required to marry...but yibum could apply here...Aram will not be happy...but perhaps Yahweh has brought her here..."

Boaz eventually comes to a stop in front of Ruth. She stands with her head bowed until he once again lifts her face with a finger under her chin. At the same time he moves closer, and Ruth can feel the heat of his body.

"You are a beautiful and courageous young woman, even if you do turn our laws upside down."

RUTH & BOAZ : BETHLEHEM

"Is he complimenting me or scolding me?" Although she doesn't ask the question out loud, Ruth's confusion shows on her face.

"I will do everything you ask."

Boaz bends down and gently kisses her on the lips, taking Ruth totally by surprise.

"He kisses me, and I just stand here like a stick," she berates herself silently.

"I will marry you, and may Yahweh bless us with a son to carry on Elimelech's name," Boaz continues.

Ruth is ready for his next kiss and returns it until he tenderly pulls away.

"There's something I need to tell you—I am sorry, but there is a legal issue I will need to deal with before any of this can take place. I am not your nearest kinsman, and there is another go'el who has the first rights to claim or renounce your proposal. If for some reason he refuses, I am yours."

Yes. No. Yes. No. Ruth's body rebels at the rapid movement from hope to rejection and back again—she begins to shiver uncontrollably. Boaz half-carries Ruth to his mat, helps her lie down, and covers her with his robe.

"You're shivering. Are you cold?" At her nod, Boaz covers her with a blanket, and lightly tucks her in. "Stay here tonight; in the morning I will talk with this kinsman. If he chooses to fulfill your request as the closest go'el, it is his right to do so; but if he isn't interested, as Yahweh lives, I will redeem you myself."

So Ruth lies alone in Boaz's bed watching him pace.

יהוה

When the first glint of sunlight shows in the sky Boaz dons a prayer shawl, raises his hands to the heavens, and quietly chants:

"Baruch atah Adonai, Eloheinu Melech Haolam;

Ana Adonia hoshia na; Ana Adonia hotzlichah na."

Ruth gets up to stand beside him, and they pray together to greet the new day.

"Blessed are you, Yahweh, our God, King of the Universe;

Please, Yahweh, save us; Please, Yahweh, make us successful."

Boaz bows his head and silently removes his prayer shawl before he turns to Ruth. This morning his demeanor is all business, and he speaks authoritatively.

"Bring your shawl. You can't go home to your mother-in-law with empty hands." Ruth spreads it out, and Boaz pours six scoops of wheat into the center. "Now hurry home before it gets light enough for anyone to recognize you—it is important that no one knows you were here."

Ruth doesn't encounter anyone as she creeps down the path to Bethlehem and home on wobbly legs. Naomi is baking bread over hot embers in the courtyard, and she shrugs at Ruth's surprised expression. "It helped me pass the time. Did you expect me to sit here with folded hands while I waited?"

Ruth shows her Boaz's gift of grain, and the two women sit together as Ruth relates every detail of her long night. In response to Naomi's pointed questions, Ruth admits her expansion of Naomi's script. Naomi shakes her head and exclaims, "Ech! Why does this not surprise me?"

Boaz's information about another go'el having first rights of denial is also not a surprise to Naomi, even though she refuses to say who it is. Her only response to Ruth's anxious question is, "Just be patient, my dear daughter, until we see how things turn out. Mark my words, Boaz won't delay, but will settle everything promptly."

"It's going to be a long day," Ruth thinks and hangs her head.

TWENTY-SIX

"I didn't see this coming," Boaz smiles to himself in amusement as Ruth kneels at his feet in the dark night. There is very little that goes on in Bethlehem and the surrounding areas that Boaz doesn't predict, know about, or instigate. "How did this young woman take me by surprise like this?"

"Her argument has some merit, but combining the laws in the way she proposes hasn't ever been done. Would it hold together in court?" Boaz goes over Ruth's idea, testing it for weaknesses. "It's unusual, but I can think of no way in which this breaks any rules…and why should not our laws be applied for such a cause—the continuation of a good man's family heritage? We have had to uphold the laws for other reasons that had no such merit."

Boaz feels admiration welling up in him for the courage and clear thinking of this beautiful Moabite woman. "She's doing it again—speaking Yahweh's heart into a situation," he thinks. "This must be how Aram felt when she approached him with her request to glean in the fields with the women. How does she think of these things?"

Boaz glances at Ruth who is quietly waiting for him to speak and marvels that she dared to come to him tonight. In the field covered with sweat and grime she was attractive, but seeing her dressed in wedding clothes with her hair braided and oiled, looking demurely at the ground, Boaz's body is waking up to desire.

"It's not only her beauty that draws me to this Moabite woman. She has spirit. Even afraid I will answer 'no,' she's still ready to challenge me if that is my answer." Boaz thinks and stifles the urge to laugh again. "I don't want her to get angry and leave."

Aware of the desire that is growing so quickly in him, Boaz turns his mind to logic and thinks this situation through carefully. "She is so much younger than me—no man in his right mind would turn down the opportunity to have her in his bed every night, unless—unless she'd rather be in bed with someone else. That would be hell on earth."

Boaz stops his pacing right in front of Ruth, but she doesn't look up even while he quietly watches her for a few minutes. "Is it fear?" he wonders. "Maybe, but if so, it's well controlled. Weakness? Meekness? Somehow I doubt that! It's more likely that she has another law expansion in mind."

It's that thought that keeps Boaz standing here admiring her. "She said she wants to be a part of my life, to be in my home where she will have the opportunity to bring her perspective to Yahwah's laws every day...and I'm looking forward to that and more, but I have to know her heart."

"Ruth, you are a woman of noble character—of hayil. You have won many hearts in Bethlehem by your dedication to Naomi, and there are younger and more handsome men who would gladly take you to wife. Yet you come to me." Boaz's measured tones give no hint of his thoughts as he watches her dark skin flush.

Ruth peeks at him through her lashes as she finally responds, "You, Boaz, are the only man to whom I would make this request."

It takes Boaz a few seconds to think through Ruth's reply. "The only man! But that could still mean I'm the only one with enough money and position to give her what she wants. Standing here watching her is making it impossible to think clearly!"

Boaz starts pacing in the space between the mounds of barley and wheat and all the way out to the ledge above the valley, trying to make a decision. "Do I really want to turn my life—the lives of my whole family—upside down? Aram will not like it—and he's not the only one! Gossips will say it sets a dangerous precedent for an elder and a judge to marry a Moabite, even if she has left her people and their heathen gods and joined her heart to Yahweh and his people. And when Ruth speaks, I hear Yahweh's voice in my heart of hearts. They said the same thing about my father when he married my mother." Boaz smiles as he realizes that he could follow in his father's footsteps in his marriage also.

"When Ruth speaks, I hear Yahweh's voice," Boaz thinks and suddenly realized at that moment that he has chosen to say yes to her request—and not out of a sense of duty or filial laws. "She would be as much a gift to me as I can be to her. Thank you, Yahweh."

So Boaz does what his body has wanted to do since her perfume tickled his nose and he woke up to find her at the foot of his bed—Boaz agrees to her request and kisses her, not once but twice.

"I must make sure there are no questions about the legalities—both for my sake and for Aram's." At that thought, Boaz steps away from their embrace and holds Ruth at arm's length—something that makes neither one of them very happy.

"I am sorry to say that there is a legal issue I will need to deal with first. I am not your nearest kinsman, and there is another who has the first rights to claim or renounce your proposal. If for some reason he refuses, I am yours."

Ruth's body begins to shake so hard that her legs threaten to give way, and Boaz manages to catch her before she falls. He lays her on his mat, tucks the blanket around her, and allows himself a chaste kiss on her forehead before standing up.

Boaz moves away and sits looking over the desert night, letting the beauty of Yahweh's creation and cool night breezes clear his head.

יהוה

The eastern sky lightens with the hint of approaching morning, and Boaz dons his prayer shawl to begin the day with Yahweh, as is his custom. Ruth joins him, and they pray together: Yahweh, Ruth, and Boaz beginning this day together.

Boaz has a mental list of the things he must accomplish, and he is anxious for the day to begin. First, he sends Ruth home to Naomi with a gift of wheat—conveying a message to Naomi that she can trust him. For this plan to work, no one else must suspect that Ruth was here.

"I will find Balak later and bring my case before him in the presence of the elders, but first I must talk to Aram. This news will not make him happy." Boaz thinks as he goes to Aram's tent.

He asks his son to walk with him to Bethlehem so they can have a private conversation. Aram accedes without question, but his stride reeks of tension as the rising sun peeks over the horizon and begins its daily arc through the sky.

"He's expecting bad news, and, for him, I suppose that's just what this is," Boaz thinks regretfully.

When his father tells him that he desires to use the funds that Aram had set aside for expanding the north vineyard to purchase Naomi's lands, Aram erupts with anger.

"What are you talking about? Women don't own land," Aram bites off his word.

The argument continues as Boaz explains that in order for Elimelech's family to continue to be a part of the tribe of Judah, Naomi needs to be able to hold the property for his sons. When Aram points out that Naomi has no sons and is too old to bear more children, Boaz tells him the rest of the news—that he intends to marry Ruth and father a son for Elimelech.

"Why are you doing this to me?" The words are full of venom, and Boaz wonders if he has poured salt into a wound he didn't even know Aram had.

"How long have you been planning this?" Aram asks.

"I didn't plan this—at least not until late last night." Boaz's voice comes out hard, responding to Aram's anger with a touch of his own. "If I had, I would have talked with you about it long ago."

"Or not." Aram clenches his fists. "You don't talk, you tell."

"Your opinions are important to me..."

Aram throws up his hands in disgust. "You say that I am in charge of the estate, but you are always promising things to others without even consulting me. A loan for this man, a job for another, justice for another—all gifts from

LESS THAN A WIDOW

Boaz the merciful, from Boaz the man with Yahweh's own heart. And meanwhile, his lackey son has to try to hold everything together and rebuild the estate, even when the assets he was counting on are given away by his overly-generous father."

"Yahweh has given us much so that we may care for others in need."

"So you would have us beggar ourselves to help others who sit around waiting for handouts?"

"Aram, my son, when have you ever experienced hunger or had no clothes to cover yourself? When have you had to wonder if there was any future for you or your children?"

"So, what are you saying? That I am selfish?"

"I'm not sure what you are angry about—the land, the money, or my decision to marry Ruth?"

"I haven't even begun to be angry about Ruth yet. Have you grown so lustful that you would marry a Moabite?" Realizing he had gone too far, Aram hesitates before changing his tone to one of pleading. "Forgive me, Father, for I spoke in anger. But Ruth is a Moabite—her people are our enemies.

"As were your grandmother Rahab's people, yet both women gave their hearts and lives to Yahweh and came to live among us."

"It's useless to argue with you. You have spoken."

Boaz watches Aram storm back up the path toward the threshing floor and chides himself. "He has worked very hard to rebuild the estate since the famine, and I just undermined his efforts—again—by claiming this year's profits, something I have obviously done before. Does he think I should ask for his permission first? Does he have a point?"

Boaz unclenches his fists and slows his pace, releasing the physical symptoms of his anger and waiting for his feelings to follow his body's example.

"Of course it would have been better to have talked this over with Aram first. He has a generous heart, and his response may have been different if I'd asked for his input," Boaz sorts his thoughts and finally shrugs. "But that's not how it happened, and I gave my word to Ruth—I won't back out now..."

Boaz pauses and turns his face skyward as he prays silently. "Yahweh, help me to heal this wound between us. Help my son to believe that I love and trust him and guide us both as we adapt to the changes that are coming. Open the eyes of his heart to see your hand in my decision in the same way you grabbed his heart at Ruth's request to glean among the women."

"No time to brood," Boaz sternly tells himself and begins to review his stratagem as he makes his way down the steep path toward Bethlehem and the elders' council at the city gates.

יהוה

RUTH & BOAZ : BETHLEHEM

As a result of the bountiful harvest, Bethlehem is overflowing with people buying and selling. Boaz mingles with those entering the city—threshing time brings all in the surrounding area to town. The influx of people and the threshing festivities always mean more work for the elders who function as justices of the peace, settle property disputes, and pass judgment on crimes in an alcove carved into the wall located in the middle of this chaos.

Before long Boaz spots the man he's been looking for! As always, Balak makes a grand entrance, fine robes billowing around his corpulent figure as his burly servants push villagers aside to clear a path through the crowds. Balak's son minces in his wake, arms close to his sides to avoid any contact with common rabble.

"Cousin Balak, shalom. Blessed be Yahweh, King of the universe, who has given his people a bountiful harvest."

"Shalom, Cousin Boaz." Balak's overloud reply turns heads. Rings flash in the sunlight as he places his hands on Boaz's shoulders and kisses him on both cheeks. "May Yahweh continue to pour blessings on his chosen people."

Boaz answers just as loudly—drawing a curious crowd is part of his plan. "I am delighted our paths have crossed this morning. I hope I am not keeping you from any important business."

Balak preens and continues to include the onlookers in his reply. "You know how it is for men of our station. There is always something that requires our personal attention."

"When the mighty speak, common people tremble." Boaz doesn't let his face show his amused thought at Balak's delight in this dance-of-importance-and-wealth as he replies, "Your words ring true this morning, Balak. A possible land acquisition has only recently been brought to my attention, and I'd like to discuss it with you."

Boaz ushers the two men into the alcove where the elders are seated. As Balak, with his son at his right shoulder, and Boaz position themselves to address Bethlehem's legal counselors, a curious crowd starts to gather around the alcove.

Boaz bows to the elders and presents his case. "Our cousin Elimelech was greatly affected by the famine as were so many of us. He wanted to sell his lands, but as all of us were coping with dried-up fields, crop failure, and efforts to feed our families, no one was in a position to help him. To care for his family, he journeyed to Moab to wait out the famine. Meanwhile, his fields lay fallow, and so they remain until this day. Tragically, neither Elimelech nor his sons returned home to us."

"May they rest in peace." Elders and crowd members murmur the traditional response. Balak's voice rises piously above the others.

Boaz acknowledges their condolences with a solemn bow. "We rejoice that our late cousin's wife, Naomi, has been able to return and is living among us here in Bethlehem. I have come before you to represent Naomi in the sale of Elimelech's abandoned lands."

"What nonsense is this? Women don't own land." Balak's son steps forward in protest, but is silenced by his father's glare. Feigning indifference, Balak clasps his hands and narrows his eyes as he watches Boaz.

The elders put their heads together and speak quietly as they try to untangle the knotty tangle that Boaz has placed before them. "Can a woman sell her husband's land?" "Is that even allowed by law?" "It's unusual, but not expressly forbidden." "Let's see what Boaz has in mind."

Waiting for their response, Boaz casually—he hopes—searches the faces in the crowd until he spots Aram leaning against a wall with his head scarf shadowing his face. The elders signal for Boaz to continue.

"Balak, I sought you out because you are Elimelech's closest relative, his kinsman-redeemer, his go'el. As such, you have the first right to purchase Naomi's property." Boaz seeks confirmation from the elders. "Is this not so?"

An elder stands up and quotes the law. "If a relative falls into financial difficulty and needs to sell a piece of property, then the closest kinsman is responsible to purchase it."

Boaz turns back to Balak and bows respectfully. "Because you are Elimelech's closest kinsman, I have asked you here to discuss the sale with me in the presence of the elders. Do you know the fields of which we speak?"

Balak yawns disinterestedly. "I know the fields you refer to—I offered to purchase them from Elimelech before his ill-fated pilgrimage to the evil country of Moab—but as neither Elimelech nor his sons are here, I can see no purpose for this meeting."

Ignoring his rebuttal of Naomi's rights to own land, Boaz continues. "If Naomi were to sell the fields outright, it would ease her poverty. Sadly, we have all suffered from the long years of drought, so it's possible that the purchase of these lands is not feasible for you at this time. However, Cousin Balak, I offer you this opportunity because, under the law, you have the first rights of purchase. Do you wish to redeem this land?"

Although his son is clearly agitated, Balak shakes his head and sighs with studied patience. He appeals to the elders, "This request is a clear departure from the practices of our ancestors in this matter, and I am sorry that Boaz has chosen to take up your valuable time with such foolishness. However, I too am moved by Naomi's plight. Therefore, I would like to request a few minutes to confer privately with my son and heir about Boaz's unmerited proposal."

Balak and his son move farther into the alcove and turn their backs to everyone.

The son speaks first. "Why should we buy anything? All we have to do is wait for Naomi to die, and the fields will be mine."

"Nothing is yours."

"Forgive me, Father. I only meant..."

"The fields are mine unless Naomi gives birth to a son."

"Surely the hag is far too old."

Balak gives his son's arm a cruel squeeze. "Keep your voice down, you fool. Has it escaped your feeble brain that Boaz is up to something?"

"But we want those fields and they will double ours! The estate should be ours soon anyway, without any money changing hands."

"Keep quiet. I will deal with this. Watch, and if you are capable, learn."

Balak addresses the elders and the crowd. "I have only the highest regard for our venerated judge Boaz. Therefore, even though he is twisting the law with his unusual request to purchase fields from a mere woman, and despite my misgivings that we will all regret giving in to his whims, my son and I are generous men." Balak lays his hand on his heart, and his son apes his actions. "For that reason alone, I am willing to think about purchasing the land if the price is agreeable. We must consider the damage that years of drought and neglect have rendered—the fields are no longer worth what they were when Elimelech approached me before his fateful journey so many years ago."

"I thank you for your courtesy." Boaz addresses Balak, but his clearly spoken words are intended for the villagers, many of whom had to sell much of what they owned to stay alive during the famine. "As generous men, I know you understand the importance of a family's inheritance—it cannot be sold cheaply. I also understand the financial strains that we have all recently endured—some here have had to sell everything to feed their families. I am sure no one in Bethlehem would think any less of you if you are unable to pay the asking price." It is Boaz's turn to put his hand over his heart. "It is not my desire to cause any distress, so if purchasing the land is not possible for you at this time, I offer to pay the full price myself."

The crowd's approving hum does not escape Balak. "There's no need to be hasty. I am sure we can come to an agreement."

With a serious face, Boaz acknowledges Balak's reply. "I am pleased to hear it, because there is also one other issue that we need to consider."

Aram pushes away from the wall and takes a step nearer to the proceedings. His face gives nothing away, but his crossed arms speak volumes. Boaz turns to the elders.

"When Naomi returned home to Bethlehem, Mahlon's widow Ruth accompanied her. For many years, Ruth has put aside her pagan gods to worship Yahweh. A woman of noble character—hayil—she also chose to brave the perils of life in an unknown land for the love of her mother-in-law Naomi and the God of her people." Boaz turns again to Balak. "On the day that you purchase Naomi's fields, you will also acquire Ruth the Moabitess as your wife to preserve the line of Elimelech."

"Have you lost your mind?" Spittle sprays from Balak's mouth as he confronts Boaz.

"This is the reaction I had hoped for." Boaz thinks, struggling to keep his relief from showing on his face.

"My family's bloodline is pure and will remain so." Balak yells this to the crowd and struggles to rein in his anger as he turns back to face Boaz. "For you, who have no such claim to purity, to suggest such an arrangement—this is an insult I will not endure."

Boaz reassures the elders and the crowd. "I mean no slander to Balak's character or that of his family. I seek only to look for clarification of the law passed down to us from our forefathers. Was it not Yahweh who commanded the division of the lands and gave us laws to insure each family's inheritance? And if Yahweh's laws were given to us for the good of the family, should it not follow that a go'el may also follow the law of yibim and take on the responsibility to produce an heir for Elimelech?"

"An heir for Elimelech! You must think me a fool." Balak growls quietly in Boaz's ear as he sweeps by him to continue his rant. "Would you have me buy these fields only to father a half-breed who would steal from me?" He, too, addresses the crowd as well as the judges. "I have toiled for many years to build up my estate so that I am able to give more to Yahweh. This self-proclaimed wise man—a judge, no less—would see me ruined, impoverish my estate, and take away from my own son's inheritance. To do so would be to steal not only from me, but from Yahweh also."

Boaz schools himself to wait quietly, head bowed, for the decision of the elders. He offers a silent plea, "Yahweh, guide their hearts." He steals a glance at Aram, but the young man still refuses to acknowledge his father.

The crowd takes advantage of the lull to voice their opinions: "Balak is so 'generous,' he gave me less than half of what my land was worth." "Boaz has always been openhanded to a fault." "Surely the Moabitess has bewitched him." "Hush. Aram's standing right next to you."

An elder stands and raises his hands beckoning for quiet, and the voices from the crowd fade away.

"Our law states that a kinsman-redeemer—a go'el—will purchase lands from a needy kinsman with the purchase being binding until the year of Jubilee, at which time all debts are forgiven. During Jubilee, all property will revert to the original owner without any further exchange of funds. Therefore, the sale of the land is valid."

"We know what the law says." Balak's son blurts out, until a fierce look from his father forces him to step back.

The elder continues. "We have made the following ruling: Marriage to Ruth will be considered part of the contract. If, as a result of said union, Ruth gives birth to a son, that son will be considered Elimelech's heir, and, as his heir, will inherit Elimelech's land when he grows into manhood."

"This is nothing more than a wicked plot to sully my family's lineage and bring me to ruin. I refuse to have any part of Boaz's twisted scheme." Balak turns defiantly to the elders. "I claim my right of first refusal or will that be taken from me as well?"

"Your right of refusal is within the law."

Boaz speaks quietly, but his voice carries through the hushed crowd. "Then you are not interested in purchasing the fields?"

Balak puffs as he pulls a sandal from his foot and slams it on the bench. "Buy them yourself!" Balak glares at his son until he finally removes his own sandal and fits it on his father's foot. Servants clear a path for them, and Balak sweeps out of the city gates, his son limping behind him.

Boaz lifts Balak's sandal high in the air to signal to the onlookers that a legal transfer of land has just occurred and holds up his own next to it. They feel strangely heavy.

"My life will never be the same again," Boaz thinks as he holds up the sandals for all to see. "But I'm not done yet."

Boaz bows first to the councilors and then to the watching villagers. "Elders and good people of Bethlehem, today you are witnesses that I pledge to purchase the property of Elimelech and his sons. As a part of this covenant, I will also acquire Ruth the Moabitess, Mahlon's widow and Elimelech's daughter-in-law, as my wife in order to preserve this family's inheritance. Elimelech's name will not disappear from his tribe nor from the town records. Today, you are witnesses to this agreement."

Boaz places the sandals on the elders' bench. "Will you accept these for Naomi?"

The elders all stand and say together, "We are witnesses." The crowd echoes, "We are witnesses."

The elders then pronounce formal blessings—some include subtle warnings and disguised disapproval.

"May God make you a pillar of the community."

"May the Lord make the woman who is coming into your home like Rachel and Leah, who together built up the House of Israel."

"Rachel and Leah may have been loving sisters, but their home was not a happy one when they married the same man." Boaz's face doesn't change expression at his thoughts, but he glances at his son, and Aram shakes his head, knowing the turmoil that will take place in their home when his father marries Ruth.

"May the Lord give you children with this young woman, and may your family rival the family of Perez, the son Tamar bore to Judah." One more elder offers a double-edged blessing.

"Another unhappy story full of trickery and pain, even though it ended in obedience," Boaz thought as he acknowledged the blessings. "Obviously, the elders think this marriage is as good of an idea as my son Aram does."

LESS THAN A WIDOW

Sadly, Boaz watches as Aram pushes his way out of the crowd and strides out of the city gates without looking back. "Oh, my son, I'd hoped you would understand."

The crowd parts to let Boaz through as he follows his son out of the gates and down the dusty trail.

יהוה

Boaz finds Aram standing in the shade of a large olive tree. Boaz offers him a drink from his waterskin and waits for his son to speak. Aram takes a long gulp before handing it back to Boaz.

"That woman turns everything upside down."

"Exactly what I told her," Boaz nods and takes a long drink of water himself, waiting for Aram to continue.

Picking up a stick, Aram breaks it in two. "Doesn't it matter to you that we will be scorned and laughed at because you are married to a Moabitess?"

"As have others in our family tree, as the elders so recently reminded us. But I am not concerned about what others say. Yahweh knows Ruth's heart."

Aram breaks the stick into smaller and smaller pieces and throws them at Boaz's feet. "You've made an enemy of Balak, you know. He will not let this matter rest."

Boaz shrugs. "Balak and I have always disagreed."

Annoyed, Aram throws his arms up in the air. "You would do this for her?"

"He does not see Yahweh's hand in this. How can I make him understand?" Boaz thinks as he struggles to explain his feelings to Aram.

"Is it any more than what you have already done for her?" Boaz asked. "And you declared that desire for her had nothing to do with your decision."

"Yes, but I only let her glean among the workers. I didn't marry her." Aram is yelling now.

Boaz keeps his voice level. "You allowed Ruth to glean in the fields with the women because she asked you what Yahweh intended for the poor when he gave us the law."

"It's not the same thing at all! I only made sure she would not die of starvation. I didn't take her into my home and into my bed!"

"Because she only asked you if our traditions of gleaning really fed the poor—and your answer followed Yahweh's leading. She asked me different questions—about acting as her go'el as well as providing an heir for Elimelech. I also considered Yahweh's intention for his laws."

"And where in those laws does it say it is proper to steal from your children and heirs to satisfy your cravings?"

"And here we reach the root of the issue, my son," Boaz thinks as he turns away from Aram without answering his rage-induced accusation. Although neither of the men leave the shade of the olive tree, the distance between them seems insurmountable.

"Yahweh, breathe your spirit on our hearts and reunite this family with your love," Boaz prays silently.

Finally Boaz clears his throat and turns back to face his son.

"Aram, I understand that I have acted in ways that have hurt you. What is worse, before today I didn't even recognize that I had done so. For that I apologize, ask your forgiveness, and will seek your counsel on such decisions in the future."

Aram nods an acknowledgement of Boaz's words, but remains silent.

"On this occasion, however, circumstances were such that I didn't have the opportunity to talk with you before making a decision, but that doesn't mean that you—your wife and children, my grandchildren—weren't foremost in my mind as I prayed for Yahweh's leading."

Aram opens his mouth, but Boaz continues speaking before he can interrupt.

"To make this easier for all of us, I came up with an idea—the beginnings of a plan—for how to work out all of the difficulties that my marriage to Ruth will cause."

"Of course you did." Aram is no longer lost in rage, but his voice drips bitterness.

"I ask forgiveness for that as well. Instead, I would like to propose that we each take a day and night to think and pray before we meet together to resolve the issues in a way that will satisfy both of us."

"You mean, before you tell me your plan?"

Boaz shakes his head. "No, not this time. Not any more. I would like to discuss all the issues and come up with a solution between us—working together."

Aram's inner struggle is evident on his face.

"He needs more assurances than a vague promise," Boaz thinks and attempts to be more specific without pushing a solution on Aram that he had no part in deciding.

"We can talk all of this through later, but I want to assure you that the management of our estate will remain in your capable hands. In the future, as I said, I will consult with you before making promises, something that I am beginning to realize I have not done before."

Boaz takes a step toward Aram and holds his arms out to his sides. "Aram, my son, I believe that this is the issue between us—not money. But whatever our differences are, I make this promise to you: Any loss you experience because of this marriage will be temporary. Everything that is mine will still belong to you and your children—except for the cost of the fields. If Yahweh chooses to bless Ruth and me with a son, that money will return to me as Ruth's husband and be used to give Elimelech's family the opportunity to continue and grow strong again."

"There's no arguing with you." Aram shakes his head, but doesn't flinch away from the hand Boaz places on his shoulder.

"Then let's not argue, but reason together. Surely you know that my love for you will remain as strong as it has always been."

Aram nods his agreement and starts to walk away, but can't resist having the last word. "I'm willing to go along with this marriage, but I don't have to like it."

TWENTY-SEVEN

Voices wake her. Ruth's hand still clutches the shuttle, but she has made little progress on the weaving—the only task Naomi would let her do.

"Boaz will take care of this today. You want to be ready when he sends for you," she had said.

Ruth hadn't thought sitting still would be possible. "I can't believe I fell asleep," she thinks as she rubs her eyes.

"Shalom, Zebidah." Naomi's voice carries from the courtyard. "Sit down; catch your breath."

Ruth slides over until she can see the two old women in the courtyard. Zebidah fans herself and sips at a cup of tea while Naomi fills a bowl with dried figs and places it between them.

"I have some news…" Zebidah chooses a fig, takes a bite, and chews slowly.

Knowing her friend's inclination for spinning out a tale, Naomi smiles and nods. "Let me guess. Rachel's had her baby?"

"No, she's still waiting and growing—all out in front. I tell you, this will be another girl. Wait and see."

"Well, what is it then?"

Zebidah fans herself and pretends to be confused by the question.

"Your news. Tell me your news."

Zebidah leans forward and speaks quietly as if sharing a secret, but loud enough for Ruth to hear. "I was at the city gates this morning. There was quite a commotion, let me tell you."

"She knows I'm listening," Ruth thinks, ducking down to remain out of sight.

Naomi nods encouragingly as she pours more tea into Zebidah's cup.

"There he was, his fancy rings and full belly, looking down his nose at everyone."

"Who are you talking about?"

"Balak, of course. Boaz asked him to buy your fields. Oh, Balak has been coveting your fields all right—he just doesn't want to pay for them."

"*My* fields? You mean Elimelech's fields."

LESS THAN A WIDOW

"Oh, no. Boaz specifically said Naomi's fields, clear as day. Everybody heard him."

Naomi shook her head. "But women can't own fields. What did Balak say?"

"You can be sure he didn't want any of his precious money to leave his purse."

"But did he buy the fields?"

"He was all set to, complaining about the sorry state they were in, trying to get the price lower, until Boaz told him he would have to marry Ruth, too." Zebidah slaps her knee and rocks with laughter. "You should have seen his face."

Naomi looks toward the open door and sees Ruth standing in the shadows watching and listening. "I wonder if my face is as white as hers?" Naomi thinks.

Naomi clears her throat before asking, "Boaz told Balak to marry Ruth?"

"He sure did." Zebidah nods her head. "I thought his son would jump right out of his skin." She rocks back and forth laughing. Wiping the tears from her eyes, she continues. "That's when all the yelling started."

Ruth feels a sharp pain in her hand and looks down to see a little trickle of blood oozing from her palm. She had been clutching the shuttle so hard, she poked the end right through her skin. Tossing it aside, Ruth presses on the cut with her other hand to stop the bleeding, thinking, "She's enjoying dragging this out, but I can't take it much longer. Get on with it."

"Who was yelling?"

"Not Aram. He didn't say a word, just stood there watching and stormed out of town when it was all over."

Zebidah leans forward and takes her time choosing just the right fig, pops it into her mouth, and chews slowly. Naomi looks at Ruth and raises her eyebrows in exasperation, and Ruth mimes choking it out of her. Zebidah sneaks a peek in Ruth's direction, and a smug smile appears on her face.

"You're loving this, you old goat!" Ruth thinks as she moves out of the shadowed doorway.

Naomi stands up and refills their tea cups, although she hasn't taken a sip of hers. "Aram was there, too?"

"With a face like he was drinking sour wine."

"Ech!" Naomi suddenly loses patience. "Zebidah, stop teasing, and tell me what happened. Did Balak agree to marry Ruth?"

"One of the elders stood up and quoted the law. They agreed that the go'el who buys the fields should also father an heir for Elimelech."

"An heir for Elimelech..." Naomi looks at Ruth, who avoids her gaze.

Zebidah nods and leans back, fanning herself as if her story were done.

Ruth, standing in full view in the doorway, takes a step forward, thinking, "I'll wring her neck if she doesn't get on with it."

Naomi leans forward and puts her hand on Zebidah's knee. "Zebidah, please! No more games. Just tell me."

Zebidah smiles in satisfaction and turns to include Ruth in the conversation. "I'm not one to gossip, but that man thinks he is Yahweh's gift to the world."

Naomi throws Ruth a warning glance, but relief floods her voice. "Balak refused to marry a Moabitess."

"Not his exact words, but close enough." She's close to the point of the whole story now, but she still enjoys playing with her audience. "When the elders brought up Jubilee and told him he'd have to give it all back, he couldn't get out of there fast enough."

Naomi clasps her hands together in her lap, waiting for Zebidah to finish cackling. "So, Balak didn't buy the fields or agree to marry Ruth?"

"Made quite a commotion, let me tell you. I was right there, saw the whole thing."

"What did Boaz do?"

"Why, he took off his sandal—all formal and businesslike—and gave it to the elders. He asked us all to be witnesses that he was buying your fields."

"And Ruth? What did he say about Ruth?"

Zebidah claps her hands in delight. "I thought you'd never ask. Boaz claimed Ruth as his wife. He wants to give you an heir."

Naomi throws her apron over her head, and Ruth can hear her sobs. Suddenly dizzy, Ruth sinks to the ground, her head on her knees.

Zebidah beams as if she is the source of all happiness. She's not done with the story, but neither Naomi or Ruth is listening any more.

"And you should have heard the elders' blessings! Some people think that Boaz has lost his mind. Not me, mind you, but it was obvious. Adah was telling everybody that she knew this was going to happen all along—she thinks she knows everything. Benjamin called Ruth some names I won't repeat. Tola wasn't there, but he'll hear about it soon enough. He'll be unhappy, but Maacah will find a way to console him, you can be sure of that…"

TWENTY-EIGHT

TWO YEARS LATER

Boaz's uncle, Elon, is blind now and very frail, but Boaz still visits him every week. They sit together in the shade sipping wine and remembering the past. Elon, his mother's brother, served as the family's retainer since before Boaz was born—no one knows more about the running of their estate than Elon does.

Boaz watches the old man's eyes close and head nod as they sit by the fountain. Boaz leans forward and dips his hand in the water. Running his fingers back and forth, Boaz thinks about how this faithful man has been a part of his life through all the good and tough times—when he and Sarai lost their baby, when his father and mother died, when he didn't know the best way to manage a crisis, this stalwart man was always quietly available.

"You never were one to sit still too long," Elon said in the reedy voice of the very old. "At least you're not pacing—must be an old man now."

Boaz laughs. "I turned that job over to Aram."

"We have made peace—Aram and I—and this old man had his hand in that, too," Boaz thinks as he looks at his uncle. "He insisted that I learn to rely on Aram to make the decisions, without interference from me—at least most of the time."

Elon helped them to draw clear lines of responsibility. Aram has become a very astute estate manager with a great attention to detail and a strong grasp of the big picture, and his heart is opening to people little by little. During last year's harvest he had to resolve an issue between workers.

As he told Boaz about it afterwards, he remarked, "I tried to look at everything upside down, the way Ruth does."

The quiet time with his uncle—a man of few words who has become quieter with age—allows Boaz to think without interruption, and that makes it doubly precious. "My wife and my son are not exactly friends and may never be, but their respect for each other is growing."

It was also Elon's suggestion that Tola act as the manager of Elimelech's lands. Naomi gave him her house to live in, and Ruth asked that their workers repair the roof as a wedding present. Maacah and Ruth are also not yet friends, but they manage to work together with a degree of civility.

LESS THAN A WIDOW

"Ruth—my wife—is a gift from Yahweh. She warms my bed, challenges my thinking, listens and responds to all my ideas, and asks "why" more times than I care to answer," Boaz thinks as he pours more wine into his goblet, leans back against the pillows, and sips it. "Yahweh's hand of blessing is on our house."

Boaz looks at Elon and wonders if the old man will stay alive long enough to bless their child—his seed but Elimelech's and Naomi's child—who will be born in a few months.

יהוה

THREE YEARS LATER

Ruth's favorite spot is under a little bower where vines twine and bloom up the trellised walls. Seated on pillows in the fragrant shade, listening to the music of the courtyard fountain, Ruth weaves on her upright loom.

Boaz originally built this space years ago as his quiet sanctuary from an increasingly chaotic family home as Aram and his wife had children...and more children. Boaz had added additional rooms when Naomi and Ruth came to live with him four years ago. The serene retreat in a little nook off the courtyard was Boaz's wedding present to Ruth.

Evening meals are frequently communal affairs in the main house where Aram's large and active family lives, and there are often visitors at the table as well. Even though it's been years since Ruth and Naomi joined Boaz in his family's compound, Ruth almost feels as if she, too, is a guest with no responsibilities or duties when they eat in Aram's wife's house. Everyone is polite, even courteous, but Ruth knows that they still regard her as that strange woman from Moab who turns everything upside down. So Ruth disrupts their home as little as possible and only at Boaz's side.

The marketplace is a different story—not everyone is courteous there. Balak isn't the only one who believes Moabites should be banned from Bethlehem. Others—including many of the women that were working in the fields when Ruth gleaned—are friendly, but not really friends.

"Does that even make sense?" Ruth wonders as she moves to find a comfortable position on the pillows. "I can't really blame them, though. So many are worried about being shunned themselves if they show kindness to me."

Naomi's old friends, on the other hand, are Ruth's staunchest allies. When Obed was born, and Ruth asked Naomi to raise him as Elimelech's son, they told everyone, "Naomi's daughter-in-law—who loves her—is better to her than seven sons."

Ruth smiles as she remembers. "I love them, too."

"Praise Yahweh, I have nothing to complain about," Ruth smiles to herself. "It's amazing how attitudes change over time—even Maacah and I are civil to each other now."

RUTH & BOAZ : BETHLEHEM

Thinking about their last feisty encounter makes Ruth laugh, which wakes up the baby who begins his hourly exercise routine—kicking her ribs.

Ruth's home—her sanctuary—is this courtyard and the rooms that surround it. It is in this inner sanctum they say their prayers, prepare their meals, and entertain their friends. It is here that Naomi delights in raising a son again—a son born from Ruth's once-barren womb—to carry on Elimelech's family name. This home is the place where Boaz teaches Obed the scriptures, and Naomi tells him stories.

Glancing at her hands working the shuttle on the loom brings a picture of her mother to her mind. "These could be my mother's hands weaving intricate designs—the only picture I wish to remember of my early childhood—the different colored threads hanging down and my mother's hands drawing them into subtle patterns of light and dark."

Ruth can't sit very long now, even with soft cushions supporting her. She lays back to ease the crowding of the child growing so quickly inside her, and her daydreams ease her into sleep.

A soft chuckle wakes her, and Ruth peeps one eye open as Boaz sits down beside her, laying his hand on her swollen belly. "How can you sleep with all that kicking going on?"

"I'm so tired from carrying this baby around all day and night, I can sleep through almost everything." Ruth sits up and stretches. "But I'm not really complaining—every kick reminds me of Yahweh's blessings."

The crash of breaking pottery and Naomi's startled exclamation announce Obed's entrance into the courtyard. He runs up to Boaz and hugs him around the neck. "Father! Is it time to go yet?"

"We'll go after you help Baba clean up the mess you just made."

"Aww, it was an accident." Obed tugs on his father. "I want to go to the fields."

"Clean up first, then we'll leave and let your mother finish her nap."

"Maybe Obed will give me some of his energy." Ruth clumsily sits up and Boaz helps her to stand.

"He'll come home tired tonight; I'm training him to challenge Tola for me." Boaz pantomimes cutting grain with a scythe.

"I'm sure Tola is worried." Boaz puts his arm around Ruth, and she leans into his embrace.

"Obed can actually cut some wheat now." Boaz kisses his wife on the top of her head. "And we met the gleaners yesterday. I told him any grain that he cuts today, he can give to them."

Obed is back, dancing with excitement. "Let's go!" He grabs Boaz's hand and drags him out of the courtyard.

יהוה

Ruth paces slowly back and forth across the roof enjoying the cool evening breeze. The baby will be here any day now, and walking eases the cramping. The voices drifting up to her make her smile.

Naomi tells a story to Obed before he goes to bed—their nightly ritual. As a girl Ruth had always loved Naomi's stories, and she still listens in whenever she can. Her all-time favorite narrative is about how Yahweh made the world.

"I can still remember it word for word." And Ruth whispers part of it to herself:

> "And God spoke: "Earth, bring forth life
>
> of every sort and kind:
>
> cattle and reptiles and wild animals—all kinds."
>
> And so it did. God saw that it was good."

Obed's favorite stories are about Moab and the fearsome journey to Bethlehem. Obed wants to hear one of those stories tonight, so Naomi obliges.

"I had always thought that Naomi had no idea of what was going on around her at that time, but her stories are full of vivid details," Ruth thinks as she moves closer to listen.

"When we prayed, those mean men always made fun of us—until the night your mother raised her hands to the heavens and howled like a wild animal. The men grabbed their weapons and looked around, but they couldn't find anything to fight—just your mother muttering and moaning. She sank to the ground for a few seconds, then leaped up again waving her knife.

"They had no idea what she was saying—I hardly recognized the words myself. 'Ana Adonia hashia na.' She ran around the fire, slashing her knife to the sky and thrusting it toward them. They thought she'd gone mad so they made the ward sign with their fingers to protect them from the evil eye and your mother's curses.

"Still muttering and swaying, your mother pressed the knife into her thumb and wiped a bloody line across her neck as if cutting her throat. Then she pointed her knife toward the men by the fire and licked the blood dripping from her thumb."

"Was she crazy like they said?"

Naomi's voice breaks as she answers. "No. No, she wasn't crazy."

"Then why did she do that? That's not how we pray."

"Tonight's questions are new ones," Ruth thinks as she stops herself from leaning over the edge of the roof, quietly straining to hear Naomi's soft answer.

"That's what I said to her that night—'that's not how we pray.' But she had remembered something that I'd forgotten, and she showed it to the men and to me. I didn't understand then." Naomi clears her throat. "But I do now."

"Then why did she do that? Did it sound like this?" Obed lets out a loud yowl.

"That's close—I can tell you've been practicing." Naomi covers her ears, and they—an old woman and her grandson—laugh together.

"Baba, what did you forget?"

"I was afraid because I forgot that Yahweh was taking care of us. Your mother remembered, and that's what she showed those mean men—and me: 'We worship Yahweh, the God of all the earth, and He will take care of us.'"

"She wasn't afraid?"

"No, because she knew Yahweh was with us."

"But...*you* were afraid."

"Because I forgot then. I remember now."

"Can I see her knife?"

Naomi laughs. "You'll have to ask her. Go give your mother a kiss goodnight."

יהוה

The neighborhood women called him "Naomi's boy!" His real name was Obed.

Obed was the father of Jesse, and Jesse was the father of David, who became king.

יהוה

LESS THAN A WIDOW

This is the family tree of Perez [son of Tamar and Judah]:

Perez was the father of Hezron,

Hezron's son was Ram,

Ram's son was Amminadab,

Amminadab was the father of Nahshon,

Nahshon's son was Salma,

Salma [and his wife Rahab of Jericho] had Boaz,

Boaz was the father of Obed,

Obed's eldest was Jesse,

and Jesse's son was David.

ADDENDA